Eric

Wilder

Oyster Bay Two Step

Edmond, Oklahoma

Other books by Eric Wilder

French Quarter Mystery Series
Big Easy, Book 1
City of Spirits, Book 2
Primal Creatures, Book 3
Black Magic Woman, Book 4
River Road, Book 5
Sisters of the Mist, Book 6
Garden of Forbidden Secrets, Book 7
New Orleans Dangerous, Book 8
Cycles of the Moon, Book 9
Half Past Midnight, Book 10
Thief of Souls, Book 11

Paranormal Cowboy Series
Ghost of a Chance, Book 1
Bones of Skeleton Creek, Book 2
Blink of an Eye, Book 3

Oyster Bay Mystery Series
Oyster Bay Boogie, Book 1
Oyster Bay Tango, Book 2

Standalone Novels
Of Love and Magic
Diamonds in the Rough

Anthologies and Cookbooks
Murder Etouffee
Over the Rainbow
Lily's Little Cajun Cookbook

This book is a work of fiction. Names, characters, places, and incidents either are products of the author's imagination or are used fictitiously. Any resemblance to actual events or locales or persons, living or dead, is entirely coincidental.

Gondwana Press
1802 Canyon Park Cir. Ste C
Edmond, OK 73013

Front Cover by Gondwana Graphics

ISBN: 978-1-946576-17-0

Acknowledgments

I wish to thank Donald Yaw and Linda Hartle Bergeron for beta reading, editing, and providing valuable input involving timeline and character development.

for Marilyn

"It's better to be slapped by the truth than kissed with a lie."

–Russian Proverb

Oyster Bay Two Step

A novel by
Eric Wilder

Chapter 1

Jack Wiesenski cranked his old truck's air conditioning as he and Chief La Tortue headed north on St. Claude toward New Orleans.

"You're the last Atakapa Indian on the face of the earth," Jack said. "How does that make you feel?"

"I'm not," Chief said. "I have a daughter and three granddaughters."

"Why don't you ever invite them to the island?" Jack asked.

"Never going to happen," Chief said.

"Why not?" Jack asked.

"An ex-wife problem," Chief said. "She poisoned whatever relationship I might have had with my daughter. I've never spoken with my granddaughters, and not even sure they know I exist."

Jack was five-eight or nine and weighed less than one-hundred-forty pounds soaking wet. Chief stood at least a foot taller and weighed a hundred pounds more.

"Maybe you should reach out to your granddaughters," Jack said. "What can it hurt?"

"I'm not into rejection," Chief said.

"Except for a first cousin in Boston, I have no family," Jack said. "If I did, I'd be reaching out."

"Maybe one of these days," Chief said. "Right now, I'm looking forward to some raw oysters in the French Quarter and then watching naked women dance at our favorite Bourbon Street strip joint."

"Right on," Jack said. "I love cooking, though now and then I enjoy eating something I didn't cook."

"How much money did you bring?" Chief asked.

"Plenty," Jack said. "I wasn't expecting to sell Venus so soon or to get as much as we did for her. What about you?"

"Two grand," Chief said.

Jack and Chief were part owners of a service dog training facility on Oyster Island. Jack was also the lighthouse keeper on the island off the Louisiana coast in the Gulf of Mexico. Chief was the last male Atakapa Indian. His ancestors had owned the island though his ownership was in dispute.

They'd had an unexpected windfall when Josie, the daughter of Frankie Castellano, the man claiming ownership of the island, had purchased Venus for her son Jojo for fifty thousand dollars.

"Two grand won't last long for a person who goes through rum, oysters, and table dances as fast as you do," Jack said.

"You think? Maybe we should stop at an ATM," Chief said.

"Good idea," Jack said. "Been a while since we celebrated."

"Too long," Chief said.

The median lights of Canal Street illuminated palm trees and foot traffic on the sidewalks, an old streetcar rumbling toward the intersection with St. Charles Avenue.

"There's a parking garage not far from here," Jack said.

"Why not find a spot that doesn't cost anything?"

"We'll enjoy ourselves more if we don't have to worry about the truck getting towed."

"Your money," Chief said.

"You buying dinner if I pay for parking?"

"Only if you let me choose where we eat," Chief said.

"Why not?" Jack said. "There are no bad restaurants in the French Quarter. I can't lose."

"Then maybe you should pay half," Chief said.

"No way," Jack said. "You eat at my house practically every day. You need to do some catching up."

Though Chief rarely smiled, Jack would have seen one on his face if he had glanced around.

"Fine," Chief said. "Park this heap, and I'll decide where we eat."

The inside of the Acme Oyster House on Iberville was all old wood, neon beer lights, checkerboard tablecloths, and French Quarter atmosphere. If you weren't hungry when you walked in the door, the aroma of fresh fried seafood wafting from the kitchen would quickly change that.

"I'm Josh," the waiter with long sideburns and handlebar mustache said. "What can I get you to drink?"

"Oyster shooter," Jack said.

"Make it two," Chief said. "And a couple of dozen raw oysters."

Barely dark outside, the restaurant had begun to fill with hungry diners.

"Cheers," Jack said, clicking his shot glass against Chief's.

The shot glass filled with vodka, cocktail sauce, and a freshly shucked oyster went down quickly.

"Tasty," Chief said. "I could drink these all night."

"Not and make it to Rockie's, you won't," Jack said. "Let's eat here and do our drinking at Rockie's."

"Yessir, boss," Chief said.

"I'm not your boss," Jack said. "If I were, I'd have you bend over so I could kick your big ass."

Jack and Chief continued bantering as they waited for their oysters. Bourbon Street wasn't far away, the dissonance ramping up whenever someone opened the door.

"Anything else?" Josh asked when they'd finished their oysters.

"Bowl of gumbo and the fried oyster platter," Chief said.

"Oyster po'boy for me," Jack said.

"Good choices," Josh said.

Sometime later, their appetites sated, Jack and Chief tabbed out and joined the revelers on Bourbon Street. COVID-19 had almost put the French Quarter out of business. Like malaria, yellow fever, and all the past plagues that had engulfed New Orleans, infections finally began to wane, the crowds returning.

"I love the smell of Bourbon Street," Jack said.

Chief shook his head. "Piss, sweat, and raging endorphins. Pretty damn heady!"

"Got that right," Jack said. "How long since we've been to Rockie's?"

"Almost a year," Chief said. "We won't recognize anyone."

"Right about that," Jack said. "Stripping at Rockie's isn't what you'd call a 'forever' job."

"No, it isn't," Chief said.

They took their time, people-watching as they hiked to Rockie's on the far end of Bourbon Street. Music wafted from the open door, a red neon scorpion in the front window inviting them to enter. A half-naked waitress with a pitcher of beer smiled as she took Chief's hand.

"Vacant seats at the pussy bar," she said.

"Don't mind if we do," Chief said.

Jack and Chief grabbed the last two chairs surrounding the elevated stage as a naked young woman gyrated to an old 70s rock anthem.

"What'll you have?"

"Pitcher and two cold mugs," Jack said.

The room was dark, only the supernatural glow of rotating spotlights illuminating the room. A fog machine beneath the dance floor shot periodic clouds of mist to the ceiling. The song the naked young woman danced to blasted out of giant speakers.

Chief nodded when Jack said, "Can't remember the last time we managed to grab a seat at the pussy bar."

"Let's enjoy it," Chief said.

Their waitress returned with a pitcher of beer and two chilled mugs.

"I'm Angela," she said. "I remember you two."

Angela's bouffant blond hair highlighted her great smile and toned body clad only in the skimpiest blue bikini.

"Jack and Chief. Finish your degree yet?"

"One more year," Angela said.

"I can't remember what subject you're majoring in," Chief said.

"Political science," Angela said.

"Is there a law degree in your future?" Jack asked.

"If I can pass the bar," she said.

Chief handed her a hundred dollars. "You will," he said. "Keep the change."

"Thanks," Angela said. "I'll check on you in a bit."

The rotating strobe lights, cool mist blowing up through holes in the floor of the elevated stage, many pitchers of beer, and one naked female after another intoxicated Jack and Chief. Chief was all but unconscious when Angela tapped his shoulder.

"There's an open table in the corner," she said. "Vixen can give you a table dance if you change locations."

"Why not?" he said.

Chief grabbed the beer pitcher and followed Angela and Jack through the crowd of noisy voyeurs. Once situated in the dark corner, Angela brought them more beer. Another young woman soon approached the table.

"I'm Vixen," the woman said. "Want a table dance?"

Vixen was tall, every inch of five-ten, her short hair naturally blond and her green eyes sultry. Chief handed her a hundred dollars.

"You have a strange accent. Where you from?"

The woman named Vixen had yet to smile.

"No idea," she said.

When a slow rock anthem began blaring from the speakers, Vixen removed her sequined bra and g-string and began to dance. Despite her height, she was so slender her ribs protruded from her torso.

Vixen's every movement synched with the music, quickly becoming an erotic adventure for Chief. She picked her blue outfit off the floor and disappeared into the darkness when the song finished.

"Damn!" Jack said. "That woman's drop-dead gorgeous."

"Tell me about it," Chief said.

"Is that the best table dance you've ever had?" Jack asked.

"The strangest," Chief said.

"What do you mean?"

Chief wriggled his nose. "That girl hasn't had a bath in a month."

"You're kidding me," Jack said.

"It wasn't horrible," Chief said. "I've never been so turned on in my life."

"She's up next at the pussy bar."

Vixen wasn't simply attractive; she was startlingly beautiful. Everyone's eyes focused on the young woman as she climbed onto the stage. When the music fired up, she began gyrating slowly, her facial expression as impassive as if she were mopping a dirty floor.

Vixen's gloriously green eyes rolled to the back of her head when the song crescendoed. The mouths of many drunk patrons dropped open as Vixen began to levitate, rising almost to the ceiling and falling in a dull thud to the stage floor when the song ended.

Vixen smashed several pitchers of beer, drenching everyone sitting at the pussy bar as she rolled off the stage. An angry bouncer with neck tattoos hurried from a door behind Rockie's.

The massive man was probably no taller than six-two though he weighed three hundred pounds. Except for his protruding stomach, his arms and upper chest appeared the work of a dedicated weight lifter. After hoisting Vixen like a sack of potatoes, he carried her off the stage. Chief followed them through the crowd.

Jack handed Angela a handful of hundreds as the gigantic bouncer kicked open the backdoor and dropped Vixen unceremoniously on the cement.

"I've had it with you, you stinking bitch!" he said. "Don't ever come in here again."

Chief blocked the bouncer's path, "Wait just a minute," he said. "You need your ass kicked."

The bouncer produced a billy club from his belt and slammed it into Chief's temple. Chief crumbled to the ground beside Vixen as Jack burst through the back door.

"Get that big motherfucker out of here before I call the cops," he said.

The door slammed shut as Jack dribbled rum from his flask into Chief's mouth and then Vixen's. Their eyes finally opened.

Chief was rubbing his temple as Jack patted Vixen's cheek.

"You okay, baby?" he asked. "Chief and I will take you home."

"I am home," she said.

Jack followed her when she walked behind the trash dumpster. A duffel bag sat beside the remains of a fire someone had started. Vixen pulled out a ragged pair of jeans, a blue work shirt, and flip-flops and began putting them on.

"You're homeless?" Jack asked.

"This is my home," she said.

As Chief joined them, the thought crossed Jack's mind the young woman was mentally ill.

"We'll take you to the emergency room."

"No hospitals," Vixen said.

"You may have broken bones," Jack said. "You fell from ten feet, and the bouncer dropped you directly on the cement."

Vixen's accent became more pronounced when she said, "No broken bones. Leave me alone."

"We just want to help," Jack said.

"If you try to rape me, I swear I'll scratch your eyes out."

"Jack and I wouldn't rape anyone," Chief said. "We only want to help you."

"I do not need your help," she said.

"We live on Oyster Island," Chief said. "He's the lighthouse keeper, and I'm Chief, an Atakapa Indian. Come with us to the island. We'll feed you and give you a room for the night. We won't lay a finger on you."

When they reached the parking garage, Vixen said, "You sit in the middle. If either of you touches me, I'll jump out."

Chief scooted to the middle of Jack's bench seat, remaining silent as they headed south toward Chalmette beneath the full moon's light. Clouds had begun rolling in from the Gulf of Mexico, Jack's headlights illuminating a late model Chevrolet in front of them. The vehicle pulled to the side of the road.

As they watched, someone opened the front door, a dog bouncing in the ditch after tumbling out. The door slammed, and the car sped away. Quickly recovering from its roll in the dirt, the dog ran after the car.

"Son of a bitch!" Jack said.

When the dog dropped from exhaustion, Jack stopped on the side of the road. Vixen ran to the animal, sobbing when Jack and Chief reached them.

Chapter 2

The hour was late, and the cars passing on the rural highway sparse. When Vixen's tears finally dried, she tried to lift the dog into her arms. The blond cocker spaniel squirmed away, shaking as she backed against Chief's legs.

"Why is she afraid of me?" Vixen asked.

She frowned when he said, "Not all abusers are males."

Chief lifted the frightened dog and carried her to Jack's truck. When he slid to the center, Vixen climbed in beside them. The cocker was covered with burrs and mud, cowering in Chief's lap as Jack rubbed her head.

"What's your name, little girl?"

The cocker had a choker chain around her neck with a nametag attached to the collar.

"Mollie," Chief said. "Now, we have two females needing a bath."

The cocker's tail wagged when Jack petted the dog's head and said, "Good girl, Mollie."

Still distraught, Vixen rested her head against the passenger-side window and closed her eyes. Cradled in Chief's lap, Mollie relaxed.

Oyster Island was about twenty miles from Chalmette on narrow parish dirt roads. Bar ditches filled with crawfish and other creatures bordered their path. Their only illumination was Jack's headlights and a full moon, mostly covered with dark rain clouds. He slowed when he crossed the wooden bridge to the island.

"What is this place?" Vixen asked.

"Oyster Island," Jack said. "Not much south of us except the rolling waves of the Gulf of Mexico."

"Mollie's bleeding," Chief said. "Better stop at the clinic and check her out."

The Oyster Bay Canine Training Facility, several buildings with various functions, was finally taking shape. Chief sat Mollie atop a stainless steel examination table and switched on the overhead light. Vixen peered over Jack's shoulder as he and Chief examined the dog.

"Bring me a pan of warm water," she said. "Her wounds need cleaning."

Jack and Chief got out of the way as Vixen trimmed the burrs from Mollie's fur, cleaned the mud with a wet rag, and disinfected the lacerations.

When Jack said, "You seem to know what you're doing," Vixen didn't respond."

"She has a deep cut on her back leg. Do you have a medical kit?"

"We have everything you need," Jack said.

Chief and Jack assisted as Vixen deadened the wound, stitched and bandaged it.

"Your vet can look at her tomorrow," Vixen said.

"We don't have a vet," Chief said.

Dark clouds had covered the moon, and rain was falling as they followed the covered walkway to Jack's house directly below the Oyster Bay lighthouse. When Jack pushed open the door and turned on the lights, his English bulldog Oscar and Chief's Chihuahua Coco, and German

Shepherd Ol' Joe came running to greet them. Vixen backed against the wall and eyed the open door.

"Ol' Joe won't hurt you," Chief said.

Their tails wagging, Coco, Oscar, and Ol' Joe gathered around Vixen. Seeing her distress, Jack took her hand and led her to his old recliner. He covered her with his orange Afghan. Within minutes, her closed eyes and soft breathing told him she'd fallen asleep.

Chief had placed Mollie in a doggie bed near the fireplace. Her tail was wagging as the three other dogs checked her out. Chief was sitting at the plank table when Jack brought him a mug of rum.

"Thought you'd never ask," he said.

"You got one hell of a bump on your head," Jack said.

"Tell me about it."

Jack gave him a bag of ice and two aspirins.

"When you're my size, you learn not to pick fights you can't win," he said.

"You're giving me a headache," Chief said.

"Don't blame me. Want something to eat?"

"Now you're talking," Chief said. "Need help?"

"When it comes to cooking, you're about as helpless as tits on a boar hog. Sit and relax. I don't know how you survived until I moved here."

"My head is throbbing like a bass drum," Chief said.

"You probably have a concussion."

A storm had picked up outside the house, the curtains whipping in the wind. Jack slammed the window shut and returned to his food preparation in the galley.

"Damn!" Chief said. "Glad Vixen took your recliner. Looks like I'm sleeping on your couch tonight."

"Why bother?" Jack said. "It'll be dawn in a

few hours."

"I can barely keep my eyes open," Chief said.

Jack handed him a blanket. Chief was soon snoring on the couch, Coco sleeping on his chest. Ol' Joe curled up beside the recliner.

"Damn!" Jack said. "Come on, Oscar. If no one's eating, we may as well catch a few zees."

Though the sky was lighter, the rain continued as Odette Mouton and her two dogs, Mudbug and Bruiser, ducked out of the storm and burst through the door. Mudbug and Bruiser were puppies; Mudbug was small, and Bruiser was already bigger than most adult dogs.

Odette was a former stripper who'd worked in the same club on Bourbon Street as Vixen. While Odette and Vixen were attractive, their size difference was as dramatic as the two puppies.

Odette was short, barely five feet tall, with wind-swept blond hair contrasting her dark Cajun eyes. She'd hitchhiked to Oyster Island after meeting Jack and Chief at Rockie's and was now part owner of the dog training facility.

"Can't believe you and Jack are still asleep," she said. "Late night?"

Chief grumbled as he hoisted himself off the couch and entered Jack's bathroom. When he returned, he started a fresh pot of coffee, not speaking until he'd microwaved a cup and downed half of it.

"We decided to celebrate last night. Eat at a French Quarter restaurant and watch the naked ladies at Rockie's."

"What happened?" Odette said.

"We were planning to stay out all night," Chief said. "Plans change."

"Who's sleeping on the recliner?" Odette asked.

"Vixen," Chief said.

Hearing her name, Vixen opened her eyes. "Where am I?" she said.

"Oyster Island," Chief said. "Remember?"

Vixen didn't answer as she lowered the footrest and struggled out of the recliner. Chief pointed her to the bathroom. When she returned, he gave her a cup of freshly-brewed coffee.

"I'm Odette. Who are you?"

Vixen didn't respond.

"Her name is Vixen," Chief said. "She was dancing at Rockie's. Jack and I rescued her and Mollie, the cocker in the bed beside the fireplace. Vixen isn't much into talking."

Odette wrinkled her nose when she got a whiff of Vixen's body odor and grabbed her by the hand.

"You need a shower," she said.

Jack was coming out of the bathroom when Odette and Vixen entered it. After pouring coffee, he joined Chief at the plank table.

"What's that all about?" he asked.

"Vixen's body odor offended Odette. She took it on herself to do something about it," Chief said.

"I can't believe Vixen went with her," Jack said.

"Maybe she doesn't like men," Chief said.

"I'm guessing some man did something to piss her off," Jack said.

"Or men," Chief said.

"Why do you say that?"

"We Atakapas have an extra sense," Chief said.

"An extra stomach, I'd believe," Jack said. "I don't need to ask if you're hungry."

J.P. Saucier and his chocolate Lab Lucky hurried through the door as Chief said, "I stay hungry."

"Come see," J.P. said. "You're not going to

believe this."

Chief and Jack joined him and peered out the open door.

J.P. was six feet tall with dark hair and eyes. He had the good looks of a movie star and the self-confidence to go with it. He'd spent over twenty years as a deputy with the police department and had wanted to retire for years and start a dog training academy. When his captain fired him, he had no further reasons to procrastinate.

A steady sheet of rain almost masked the procession of trucks, vans, semis, and R.V.s crossing the short bridge from mainland Louisiana to the sandy beaches of Oyster Island.

"What the hell!" Jack said.

"Looks like they're headed for the Majestic," J.P. said.

The Majestic Hotel & Casino was the giant, multistoried Prohibition Era resort once owned by rum-running gangsters. Though mostly forgotten, the magnificent over-water structure was once the destination spot for people worldwide who liked to drink and gamble. It had lain abandoned for decades, the home of ghosts and forgotten memories.

"Looks like a traveling circus," Chief said. "Wonder why they're here."

"We'll find out soon enough," J.P. said. "I missed you boys last night. Where were you?"

"Went to New Orleans to eat and watch the naked ladies," Jack said.

"You went to town and didn't invite me?" J.P. said.

"We decided to head up to the French Quarter on a whim," Chief said. "We waited till almost dark for you. When you didn't show, we went without you."

"I have a cell phone. You could have called

me," J.P. said.

"Sorry," Jack said. "It was on a whim, just like Chief said. We didn't think you were coming back to the island last night, and we were right."

"No problem," J.P. said. "Next time I visit Pauline's, I'll go alone."

Pauline ran a house of prostitution at a large truck stop on the highway to Chalmette. Jack and Chief stared at the floor when Odette and Vixen came out of the bathroom clad only in bath towels. Their hair was still wet, and they were giggling.

"You boys have something else to tell me?" J.P. said.

"Long story," Jack said. "We'll explain later."

"Uh-huh!" J.P. said. "What else is happening around here I don't know about?"

"Nothing," Chief said. "Don't get your panties in a wad."

Jack poured coffee into a mug leaving enough room for a healthy slug of Dominican rum.

"Have some coffee and calm your nerves. The only thing we got out of the ordinary last night was a billy club to Chief's head. You can still see the bump. Vixen was dancing at Rockie's."

"She went into a trance and levitated ten feet above the stage. When she fell, she dumped over beer glasses and half a dozen pitchers of beer," Chief said. "She soaked everyone at the pussy bar."

"A big ugly bouncer carted her to the backdoor and dropped her on the cement. When Chief intervened, the bouncer cold-cocked him."

"Vixen is homeless and lived behind the dumpster," Chief said. "We brought her here because she had nowhere to go."

"Uh-huh!" J.P. said. "Where does Odette come into this story?"

"Vixen smelled like she hadn't bathed in a

month," Chief said. "When Odette showed up before you did, she took her into the bathroom to clean her up."

Hearing her name, Odette said, "Come see."

J.P., Chief, and Jack gawked when Odette removed Vixen's towel. She was used to being naked around men, so she didn't try to cover up.

"Damn, girl!" J.P. said. "Jack and Chief weren't lying. With all those bruises, I can't believe you have no broken bones. I can count your ribs. When was the last time you had something to eat?"

"Her bruises are turning yellow, and I nicked her when I shaved her legs," Odette said.

Odette picked the towel off the floor and used it to wipe away the trickle of blood on Vixen's leg. Jack, Chief, and J.P. were gawking at Vixen's bruised and emaciated body when two women hurried out of the rain into the house. One of the women was blond; the other had dark hair.

When the attractive blond saw Odette and three men gawking at a naked woman, her hand went to her mouth, and she said, "What the hell!"

Chapter 3

Vixen grabbed the towel, covering herself as everyone wheeled around to see who had entered the house. They stared into the intense blue eyes of an angry woman. She wasn't alone. Another woman was looking at J.P., her grin indicating she knew him. She did.

"Is that you, Lilly Bliss?" J.P. said.

Lilly's open jean jacket displayed her zebra-print tee shirt and exposed belly button, her khaki shorts showing off her tanned legs. She could barely suppress a smile.

"I might have known if I ever encountered a scene like this in Louisiana, John Pierre Saucier would somehow be involved."

J.P. broke away from the others and hugged the dark-haired woman.

"Miss Lilly, you never fail to catch me with my pants down."

"Just the way I like it," she said.

"It's a long way from L.A. What are you doing on Oyster Island?"

"This lovely woman is Avory Dorean. I've written a screenplay for her, and we're here to film it."

"Pleased to meet you," J.P. said.

J.P. grabbed Avory's reluctant hand and shook it."

"Avory is directing *Monsters and Angels.* We intend to shoot as much of the movie as possible here on location," Lilly said.

Avory's flowing azure gown and Gucci pumps seemed more suitable for a power luncheon at L.A.'s Polo Lounge than Jack Wiesinski's little house on a Louisiana barrier island. Her long blond hair draped her shoulders, the blue dress framing her impressive cleavage. J.P. noticed. She had yet to smile.

Avory glanced at Lilly and said, "How do you know Mr. Saucier?"

"We survived a Cat 4 hurricane together on an island not far from here," Lilly said. "It doesn't get much more intimate than that."

"Take your word for it," Avory said. "Which one of you is Jack Wiesinski?"

Jack stepped forward and said, "How can I help you?"

"I need the keys to the Majestic," she said.

"Something I no longer have," Jack said.

"You work for Mr. Castellano, don't you?"

"No, ma'am, I don't. Mr. Castellano fired me with a text message. I gave the keys to the new owner."

"Mr. Castellano is the owner of the Majestic," Avory said.

"Maybe yes and maybe no," Jack said. "I believe Grogan La Tortue owns the Majestic."

Chief stepped forward when Avory asked, "How can I find Mr. La Tortue?"

"Call me Chief," he said.

"We're here to film a movie and couldn't care less who owns the Majestic. Do you have the keys, Mr. La Tortue?" Avory asked.

"Ownership of this island, including the Majestic, is being litigated. My lawyer, Mr. Eddie

Toledo, has the keys."

"Where can I find Mr. Toledo?" Avory asked.

"He just drove up outside," J.P. said.

Eddie slammed the door to his Porsche 911 and hurried through the rain into Jack's house. Dressed in a pink seersucker suit, blue tie, and pink socks, he looked like anything except a conservative Louisiana lawyer. His roving eyes quickly focused on Avory's cleavage.

"Am I missing something?" he said.

"I'm Avory Dorean. We're here to make a movie with most scenes filmed in and around the Majestic. We're on the clock, and I need the keys."

"The ownership of Oyster Island and the Majestic Hotel & Casino is in question," Eddie said. "The case is presently in District Court in Chalmette."

"Then we have a problem," Avory said.

"What's your problem?" Eddie said.

"We paid Mr. Castellano a hundred thousand dollars for the right to film on Oyster Island."

Eddie grinned. "You can kiss your money goodbye," he said.

"Unacceptable," Avory said.

"Maybe we can work something out," Eddie said.

"Like what?" Avory said.

"You paid Mr. Castellano for the right to film a movie on Oyster Island. Pay Mr. La Tortue a hundred grand, and we'll grant you the rights to begin filming."

"Highway robbery," Avory said. "You don't even own the island. How can you pimp the rights to it?"

Eddie grinned at Avory Dorean's allusion that the island was a lady of the night.

"You're a writer, aren't you?" he said.

"Right now, I'm furious," she said.

"Take it or leave it," Eddie said.

After huddling with Lilly in the corner of Jack's house, Avory called someone on her cell phone. When the conversation ended, she and Lilly approached Eddie.

"You have a deal," she said.

"Not until you wire good funds into Mr. La Tortue's account, we don't," Eddie said.

"We can do that," Avory said.

Avory made another call and finally smiled when she handed the phone to Chief.

"Give the person on the line your bank's routing and account numbers. The money will reach your bank shortly." Avory turned to Lilly and said, "Call Josh. Have him start unloading the trucks and setting up the living quarters."

"Anybody hungry?" Jack asked.

"Starved," Lilly Bliss said.

"You can eat later," Avory said. "We have a job to do."

"Suit yourself," Jack said.

"Lilly and I will be staying at the Majestic. Everyone else in the crew has trailers and portable accommodations," Avory said. "Someone needs to get us situated."

"I'll check you in," Eddie said.

"Can't someone else do it?" Avory asked. "I've had about enough of your arrogance for one day."

"Sorry if I insulted you," Eddie said.

"You're rude," Avory said. "And your cheap suit suggests you're a total loser."

Eddie grinned. "You don't like seersucker?"

"Maybe on a used car salesman," Avory said.

Before Eddie could reply, Odette grabbed his wrist.

"I'll take them to the Majestic and get them situated," she said. "It's raining cats and dogs outside, and the top is up on the ATV."

"The Majestic is undergoing renovation," Eddie said. "We don't have house cleaning and room service yet," Eddie said.

"Yes, you do," Odette said. "This is Vixen. She needs a job and a place to stay."

Vixen was almost as tall as Eddie. Odette had found her a pair of clean shorts and a tee shirt.

"You're hired," Eddie said. "We'll discuss salary and benefits later."

"I have a dog," Vixen said.

"No problem," Eddie said. "I love dogs."

"Come with me, ladies," Odette said.

Vixen scooped up Mollie and followed Avory and Lilly out the door. Mollie whined and jumped out of her arms, quickly returning to the doggy bed by the fire. The storm had intensified, rain pouring from the overhang of the covered walkway. Odette tugged Vixen's arm.

"She'll be waiting for you when we return," Odette said.

"Damn it!" Avory said. "I was planning to start filming today."

"Have the cameramen film the storm," Lilly said. "We can use the footage. Relax."

"Hope you like the Majestic," Odette said. "Eddie is the only human who has lived there in decades."

"As opposed to?" Avory asked.

"Ghosts, vampires, you name it," Odette said.

"I've never known an attorney who wears pink seersucker," Avory said.

"He is one good-looking man," Lilly said. "I could tell he had eyes for you."

"He wasn't looking at my eyes," Avory said. "What kind of lawyer is he if he's living on a practically uninhabited island in the middle of nowhere?"

"A great one. Eddie has never lost a case," Odette said.

"Probably because no one has ever hired him," Avory said.

"He's one sexy hunk of a man," Lilly said. "I'd sleep with him."

"Hell, Lilly, you'd sleep with any man with a pulse," Avory said.

"He had my pulse pounding," Lilly said.

Thunder shook the little vehicle as Odette headed down the sandy hill from the lighthouse. Lightning flashed across the sky as Odette parked beside the wooden walkway leading over the water to the Majestic. Odette handed them sheets of plastic.

"Drape these over your heads," she said. "Eddie hasn't installed a covered walkway as yet."

The pontoon walkway sounded hollow as the four women hurried through the rain to the old hotel and casino entrance. Odette fumbled with the cranky old lock for a moment before it opened with a swoosh of stale air.

"Kind of creepy if you ask me," Lilly said.

"Wait'll tonight," Odette said.

"Maybe we should stay in the R.V.," Lilly said.

"If you like," Avory said. "This place is a perfect inspiration. I'm staying here."

Odette led them through the casino and restaurant. Even in the muted light, the surroundings were regal.

"The hotel hasn't changed since Prohibition," Odette said. "There are no elevators or modern conveniences."

"Perfect," Avory said. "I like it just the way it is."

"Hell, girl," Lilly said. We may as well send our set crew home. We don't need to change a thing."

"It's like we've entered a time capsule," Avory said.

"The place hasn't changed much since the owners abandoned it," Odette said. "It has three floors. The ones with the best views are on the third floor, though there's no elevator."

"Great," Lilly said. "I need the exercise."

"Rooms on the top floor have access to the deck on the roof."

"I'm in," Avory said. "Lead the way."

Vixen had yet to speak as she followed Avory and Lilly up the narrow staircase. They were out of breath when they reached the third floor of the Majestic.

"Only the richest customers stayed in these rooms. They are large and have magnificent views of the Gulf of Mexico."

"What's the deal with the little room?" Lilly asked.

"A rape gang kidnapped the daughter of the lighthouse keepers and kept her there to service their most perverted clientele," Odette said. "She was barely fifteen."

Avory's hand went to her mouth. "Oh, my God! What happened to her?"

"She was never allowed to leave the room. Sort of like a breeding cage at a puppy mill."

"I hate that analogy," Avory said.

"A vampire infected her. A young man took care of her, and they were in love," Odette said.

"And?" Lilly asked.

"If you're afraid of ghosts, you might not want to hear," Odette said.

"Don't you dare keep us in suspense," Lilly said.

Stale air met them when Odette opened the door to the fourth room on the third floor. The covers on the little bed dominating the space were unmade.

"Laurel and Christopher were murdered by the mob who enslaved Laurel."

"Please explain," Lilly said.

"Christopher was an escaped convict hired by the hotel owners to feed and care for Laurel when she wasn't working. He killed a man who was abusing her."

"What about Laurel?" Avory asked.

"She and Christopher were vampires," Odette said. "They were asleep when they died. Paula and I found their skeletons locked in an embrace with stakes pounded through their chests. Vampires can't cross over, so they were confined to this room forever."

Though Vixen hadn't spoken, she'd begun to cry.

"Where are the bones?" Lilly asked.

"My friend, Paula, is a traiteur, a Cajun witch. We gathered the bones in a pillowcase and took them to the beach, where we performed a consecrating ceremony. It purged the Majestic of evil spirits and sent Christopher to heaven."

"Why didn't Laurel cross over?" Avory asked.

"She chose to remain at the Majestic. She roams the halls and rooms at night. You'll see her," Odette said.

"And Christopher?" Lilly said.

"He's a guardian angel and has saved Paula and me more than once," Odette said.

"You're making this shit up," Avory said.

Odette's hair moved in the muted light when she shook her head.

"Want a room on the first or second floor?" she asked.

"Third floor," Avory said.

"Then you'll see Laurel before you leave. Protect your neck when she's around."

Avory was grinning. "You're so full of shit! I don't believe a word you're saying."

"You'll believe before you leave here," Odette said.

"This place is a bit too morbid," Avory said. "Maybe you should show us our rooms."

"Follow me, ladies," Odette said.

Odette opened the first door and handed the key to Avory. Vixen ducked into the hall, returning with a mop and broom she'd found in a storage closet. Dust cloths covered the furniture, and the curtains to the windows overlooking the Gulf of Mexico were closed.

"I will clean the room," she said.

"Here's the key to the room next door," Odette said. "After I take these two ladies downstairs and fix them something to eat, I'll help you."

"No need," Vixen said. "Both rooms will be spotless when you return."

"You sure?" Odette said.

Vixen was already removing the dust covers, a head nod Odette's only answer.

Chapter 4

Odette seated Avory and Lilly at a cozy table in a small dining area adjacent to the kitchen. The rain continued outside. Only lightning flashing through the windows illuminated the room until Odette lit a candle and placed it on the table.

"There's no permanent electricity yet. Temporary generators power parts of the hotel. We do have a full bar. What can I get you to drink?"

Like the rest of the old hotel and casino, the mahogany bar featuring carved cherubs was one-of-a-kind, colorful bottles on the wall giving it the look and feel of an antique store.

"Can you make a martini?" Avory asked.

Odette nodded. "Anything your heart desires. What'll you have, Ms. Bliss?"

"Vodka with a twist of lime. No ice. And please, my name is Lilly."

"You got it, Lilly. Mr. Castellano bought the Majestic after seeing this bar. He said it would have cost a fortune in today's dollars."

"The ambiance is palpable," Lilly said. "Wish I could go back in time and experience what it was like amid all the gangsters and assorted wealthy characters."

Odette scooted under the bar and said, "Maybe we can find you a time portal."

When Odette returned with the drinks, Avory said, "What caused the rift between Eddie and Mr. Castellano?"

"My girlfriend Paula and I are to blame. I'll tell you about it after I duck into the kitchen and fix you something to eat."

Avory grabbed Odette's arm. "No way! Get something to drink and join us. I'm too curious about how you and your girlfriend upset the Oyster Island applecart to eat."

Grabbing a tumbler and a bottle of Dominican rum from behind the bar, Odette sat beside Avory and Lilly. After filling her tumbler with straight rum, she began to explain.

"Eddie is a brilliant lawyer who worked for the Feds. He was engaged to Mr. Castellano's daughter, Josie. She ditched him when he jilted her."

"What a prick," Avory said.

"He's so good-looking," Lilly said. "I wouldn't mind snuggling with him."

"And he knows it," Odette said. "He thinks he can have any woman he wants."

Lilly raised her hand. "I volunteer," she said.

"There's no way he's ever touching my tits," Avory said.

"Wouldn't it be wonderful to have him as your sex object?"

"Lilly, you are so full of shit," Avory said. "You're thinking like a man."

"We're all victims of our desires," Lilly said. "Mine get pretty wild sometimes."

"I hear that," Odette said.

Avory had finished her martini and was eyeing Odette's rum.

"What's that you're drinking?" she asked.

"Dominican rum," Odette said.

"Must be pretty good," Lilly said.

Odette handed her glass to Lilly. "Taste it," she said.

After a sip, Lilly pushed the horn rims to the top of her head and grinned.

"Damn!"

"Good?" Avory asked.

Lilly passed the glass to her. "This is the smoothest alcohol I've ever tasted," Avory said. "You say it is rum?"

"Dominican rum," Odette said. "Jack and Chief found a case washed up in the shallow water beneath the bridge. Turned out it was almost a century old."

"Where did it come from?" Avory asked.

"Bootleg alcohol brought to the island during Prohibition," Odette said. "A government gunboat probably sank the rumrunner. I believe there's a wealth of liquor somewhere beyond the barrier islands.

"Sunken treasure," Lilly said. "Love it."

"I can drink martinis anytime," Avory said. "Pour me a shot of your rum."

"Me too, please," Lilly said.

Odette grabbed two more tumblers from behind the bar and filled them for Avory and Lilly.

"Wonderful," Lilly said. "This could be my new favorite drink."

"Watch it! It creeps up on you," Odette said.

"Tell us how you and your girlfriend managed to fuck up things on Oyster Island," Avory said.

The candle flickered when lightning flashed across the open windows, and thunder shook the old wooden building, rattling the crystal chandeliers.

"I'm sure you know Frankie Castellano is the Don of the biggest crime family in the south. He was devastated when Eddie jilted Josie."

"Because?" Avory said.

"As I said, Eddie is a brilliant lawyer. Frankie had visions of Eddie becoming his consigliere. He decided to give him a second chance in hopes Josie, in time, would forgive him."

"Something to do with Oyster Island?" Avory said.

"Frankie dreamed of restoring the Majestic to its former glory. He offered Eddie half interest in the venture if he would steer the project. When Eddie accepted his offer, Frankie decided to celebrate."

"And?" Avory said.

"Frankie has a world-class resort on an abandoned jack-up drilling platform in the Gulf of Mexico. He invited us to celebrate with him, all expenses paid."

"Sweet," Lilly said.

"My best friend, Paula, and I got a little messed up and were lucky to make it to our rooms. Neither of us was ready to stop the party."

"Go on," Avory said.

"Our suite was on the level Frankie reserved for family and friends. It featured a deck with an infinity pool and hot tub overlooking the Gulf. Paula and I thought we were alone on the deck."

Odette smiled and nodded when Lilly said, "Let me guess. You decided to go skinny-dipping."

"Good guess," Odette said, "except we weren't alone. Frankie was in the hot tub, listening to piped-in mood music and minding his own business. Paula and I decided to join him."

"You two had sex in a hot tub with the Don of the Bayou?" Lilly asked.

"We may as well have," Odette said. "We wrestled his bathing suit off of him, the three of us naked, when his wife Adele came out to join him. She began crying her eyes out when she saw us. Frankie chased after her."

"What did she do?" Lilly asked.

"It didn't help matters he was naked when he caught up with her. She slapped him, ran to the exit, and disappeared. Frankie was less than happy when he rejoined us in the hot tub."

"I can imagine," Avory said.

"Frankie's wife wasn't the only one pissed," Odette said. "Paula had to explain to her husband, Jimmie. Trust me when I tell you he thought the same thing about the incident as Frankie's wife."

"Nothing like a little indiscretion to spoil a vacation," Lilly said.

Odette sipped her rum and said, "Got that right! We were packing for home before the sun came up. When we returned, Frankie informed us he'd sold the island and the Majestic to a group from Chicago."

"That didn't take long," Avory said.

"Paula and I caught the blame for everything," Odette said. "We explained to Adele and Josie what had happened, and they seemed to believe us. It didn't matter to Frankie as he's determined to cut ties with the island."

Where does everything stand?" Lilly asked.

"Frankie's daughter Josie bought one of our canine trainees her son Jojo had fallen in love with. She paid us fifty grand. Eddie sued Frankie, and Josie's money has kept us afloat while this mess plays out in court."

"Fifty grand for a dog?" Lilly said.

"It's expensive to train a service dog. They sell for lots of money," Odette said.

"Fifty thousand dollars seems high to me," Lilly said.

"Josie is a successful real estate agent and has lots of money in her own right. Trust me when I tell you she didn't miss a penny though it pissed Frankie."

"I can imagine," Avory said. What's the story on Vixen?"

"She was stripping at a club on Bourbon Street," Odette said. "Jack and Chief visited the club to kick up their heels. No one has told me yet how or why Vixen ended up on Oyster Island."

"She looks like the proverbial deer in the headlights," Lilly said.

"Enough, already," Avory said. We have a movie to film, and things would go smoother if there were a resolution between Eddie and Frankie."

"Not going to happen anytime soon," Odette said.

Avory looked at Lilly and said, "You're a fiction writer. Dream up a way to facilitate patching the relationship between Eddie and Frankie."

Lilly saluted and said, "Yes, sir. I'll get on it right away, sir."

Another clap of thunder shook the Majestic shortly after lightning lit the darkened room. It rattled the chandeliers and the bottles behind the bar.

"That was a little too close," Avory said.

"These storms come and go, and this old building has been here almost a hundred years. It'll be here long after we're dead and gone."

"Let's hope that's later rather than sooner," Lilly said.

Seeing everyone's empty tumblers, Odette said, "More rum, or have you had enough?"

"More, please," Lilly said.

Avory held her cup so Odette could fill it. "Maybe we should check on Vixen," she said.

"If the storm ever slackens, I'd like to get my bags in the room. How long do these storms normally last?" Lilly asked.

"If I knew, I could get a job as a weathergirl

on TV in New Orleans. Come to think of it, I'm probably overqualified."

"Ain't that the truth?" Lilly said.

The candle flickered and died, the victim of a sudden chilly gust blowing through the old hotel.

"Damn!" Avory said. "It gets ghostly dark in here when the lights go out."

"And it's the middle of the day," Lilly said. "I had visions of sunbathing on the beach during our shooting breaks."

"It isn't always like this," Odette said. "We have more than our share of sunny days on the island."

"If you say so," Lilly said.

"You'll see," Odette said. "Let's take our drinks and check on Vixen. I'll bring the bottle."

"Lead the way," Avory said. "I can't see shit."

"Eddie had auxiliary lights installed in the stairwell," Odette said. "We'll be okay."

"If we ever get there," Lilly said.

"Piece of cake," Odette said. "I know the way."

When they reached the third floor, they found the door to Lilly's room ajar, the drop cloths gone. The room was spotless and magnificent, Avory was in awe.

"Oh my! I can't believe the expensive rugs, original art, and cut glass chandeliers. Everything's perfect."

"Wait till you see the bedroom," Odette said.

The bedroom had a four-poster bed, an intricately-carved armoire, and a dresser.

Odette smiled when Lilly said, "Do we have indoor plumbing?"

"Yes," Odette said. "I'll show you."

A door led into the bath, the floor tiled in black and white. An ornate brass tub shined like a new penny, and gold cast the plumbing fixtures.

"Glad someone else is paying for this and not

me," Lilly said.

"You're the first guest to occupy this suite in decades," Odette said. "Vixen did a great job."

"I'd say she deserves a raise," Lilly said.

"No doubt she's a hard worker," Odette said. "Too bad it's raining. The observation deck is a half-flight above us. It's my favorite place in this old lady."

"If it rains like this all the time, we'll never get to lie in the sun, much less get our movie filmed," Avory said.

"You kidding?" Lilly said. "The setting is perfect, and our interior shots are guaranteed to win us an Academy Award for best set design. Quit worrying, and let's check out your room."

"This bottle is heavy," Odette said. "Let me top up your tumblers and lighten it up."

"Hit me, sweet talker," Lilly said.

Avory held out her empty tumbler. "Me too," she said.

Intoxicated by Dominican rum and the mysterious ambiance of the old hotel, Lilly and Avory followed Odette into the adjacent suite.

Vixen was on her knees, her face buried in her hands. When she glanced up at them, they saw her face was red, puffy and streaked with tears.

Vixen didn't seem to know they were in the room. As they watched, she hoisted an oversized couch over her head and slammed it against the wall.

"Oh, my God!" Odette said.

When Odette moved to console Vixen and find out why she was crying, a force like a giant hand held her in place. The chandeliers rattled, the walls shaking as if they were experiencing an earthquake. As they watched, Vixen closed her eyes, spread her arms, and began levitating toward the ceiling.

Chapter 5

Jack had served a hearty breakfast of freshly sliced Creole tomatoes, scrambled eggs, and andouille sausage and grits. Eddie loosened his tie, enjoying the meal as J.P. stood at the open door watching the storm a moment before turning his attention to the cocker spaniel in the doggy bed by the crackling fireplace.

"What's the story on Vixen and the dog?" he asked.

"Yeah," Eddie said. "Where did they come from?"

"Chief and I decided to have dinner in the French Quarter last night and then take in the naked ladies at Rockie's."

"I like naked ladies. You could have waited until I was available," Eddie said.

"It was a spur-of-the-moment decision," Jack said. "We'll catch you next time."

"Guess I know how I rate around here," Eddie said.

"Don't be that way," Jack said. "You and J.P. were with us in spirit."

J.P. shook his head when Eddie said, "They didn't invite you either?"

"I'm telling you," J.P. said.

"I'm feeling abused," Eddie said.

"It's not stopping you from stuffing your face with my food," Jack said.

J.P. stood beside the doggie bed, looking at Mollie. "How did the cocker get hurt?" he asked.

"We were on our way back to the island when the car in front of us pushed the dog out the door," Jack said.

"Damn!" J.P. said. "Some people's cruelty and disregard for life never fail to amaze me."

"That's why lawyers are so rich," Chief said.

"Watch it, now," Eddie said. "I'm the only person between you and the homeless shelter on Camp Street in New Orleans."

"Just pulling your leg," Chief said. "You know I appreciate you. "What's the deal with the pink seersucker suit?"

"I'm searching for a brand so judges and opposing attorneys will remember me," Eddie said. "Something to scare them when I walk in the door."

Chief snickered. "Your appearance in that suit induces the opposite reaction."

"I did have a few curious looks," Eddie said.

"You have hippie hair. Isn't that branding enough?" Chief asked.

"Maybe," Eddie said. "I just get sick of wearing pin-striped suits."

"There's a reason lawyers wear expensive suits," Chief said.

"Not to mention there's a fine line between effective branding and comedy hour," Jack said.

"Are you a marketing expert?" Eddie asked.

"I know a bad idea when I see one," Jack said.

"I'll take your recommendation under consideration," Eddie said.

"How did you get a veterinarian to come to the island to put stitches in this beautiful dog?"

J.P. asked.

"We didn't," Chief said. "Vixen patched her up."

"Is she a vet?" J.P. asked.

"Hell no! Why would a vet be stripping at Rockie's?" Jack asked.

"You tell me," J.P. said. "Someone who knew what they were doing stitched the cocker's wound. Not an amateur."

"Lots of college girls strip to pay tuition and put food on the table," Eddie said.

"That's what Odette was doing," Jack said. "She's close to having her degree from L.S.U."

"Oh?" Eddie said. "What's her major?"

"Hotel and restaurant management," Chief said.

"You gotta be kidding me," Eddie said.

"Her daddy was a roughneck on offshore rigs," Jack said. "She worked summers and between semesters on the rigs as a cook. She can cook for a hundred as easily as for one or two people."

"Humph!" Eddie said.

"Vixen's too old to be a college girl," J.P. said. "My guess is she's in her mid-thirties."

"She's one beautiful woman," Jack said. "Exotic and a little strange."

"How so?" J.P. asked.

"She doesn't talk much," Jack said. "When she does, she has a funny accent."

"What kind of accent?"

"One I don't recognize," Jack said.

"We could use a good vet on this island," J.P. said. "If she can doctor dogs like she did this one, maybe we should talk to her."

"If she's not a college student, why would a veterinarian strip on Bourbon Street?"

"All I know is a degreed vet couldn't have patched the dog any better than Vixen did," J.P.

said. “Does the cocker have a name?”

“Mollie,” Chief said. “She has a tag.”

“Then we can track her owners. Maybe the people in the car stole her and tossed her out when she bit them.”

“If you’d seen how she chased after the car, you wouldn’t come to that conclusion,” Chief said.

Mollie wagged her tail when J.P. rubbed her head and said, “How you doing, Mollie?”

“Living the life of Riley right about now, I’d say,” Chief said.

“I still have contacts with the St. Bernard police,” J.P. said. “I’ll check out her tag. How did it go today at the courthouse?”

“Not good,” Eddie said. “Frankie isn’t stupid. He’s doing the same thing I’d do if I were him.”

“Which is?” Chief asked.

“He has hired every lawyer in the parish to prevent them from helping me. We have exactly zero allies,” Eddie said.

“What about a lawyer from out of the parish?” Jack asked.

“Bad idea. Judges hate outsiders.”

“Are we done for?” Chief said.

“Hell no!” Eddie said. “Though I’ll admit, I could use some help.”

“What about Heather Boudreaux’s boyfriend, Basil Doles?” J.P. said. “He’s smart, and his daddy’s rich. He has no allegiance to Frankie, and he likes the hell out of you.”

Heather Boudreaux was a waitress at Claws & Craws, a Cajun bar and restaurant on the outskirts of Chalmette. Her boyfriend, Basil Doles, had come looking for J.P. when he thought Heather had cheated on him. She hadn’t. Basil’s father was a state senator, and Basil a law student at L.S.U.

“I’d love his help though I can’t afford to pay

him much," Eddie said.

"Hell, Eddie," J.P. said. "Basil's daddy is the richest man in the parish, and Basil his only son. Call him. I'm guessing he'd love to help in exchange for your mentoring."

"Maybe," Eddie said. "I'll call him."

Chief stopped eating when his cell phone rang. He was almost smiling when he returned the phone to his pocket.

"That was my bank," he said. "There's a hundred grand in my account I never expected. How much money do you need?"

Eddie grinned. "Hopefully, not nearly that much."

"Think about it," Chief said. "Call Basil while you're at it."

"I'll do it right now," Eddie said. "Find out if he can help me or not."

Eddie stepped outside beneath the covered walkway and dialed Basil Dole's number as the rain splattered his pant legs.

"What's up, Eddie?" he said.

"I'll come right to the point. I think you probably already know I'm suing Frankie Castellano. He's a formidable foe and has hired every lawyer in the parish. I need help."

"Hell, Eddie. You had me at hello."

"You serious?"

"As a heart attack," Basil said. "Count me in."

"How much are you going to charge me for this gig?" Eddie asked.

"No money. I'm thinking of a trade," Basil said.

"What kind of trade?" Eddie asked.

"Heather and I are getting married."

"Wonderful. Let me be the first to congratulate you."

"We have a problem. We'd planned to have the wedding at Claws & Craws."

"What's the problem?" Eddie said.

"Claws & Craws is no longer an option. The Majestic is the only place large enough to accommodate everyone Heather wants to invite."

"What changed your mind about Claws & Craws? Sounds like the perfect place for the owner's daughter to tie the knot," Eddie said.

"Heather is fighting with her Dad. She's no longer working at Claws & Craws and needs a job and a place to live until after the wedding."

Eddie took a moment before answering. "I need help at the Majestic. I'll give her a job and a room at the hotel. I have to tell you, I've never hosted a wedding and have no idea how to pull it off."

"Heather knows what she wants. That's not all I need."

"Tell me," Eddie said.

"I graduated from law school at the end of the semester. I only have to pass the bar exam. I've quit my offshore job and need a secluded place to study for the test. Do you have a room for me at the Majestic?"

"You mean with Heather?"

"Not going to happen. Neither Heather's parents nor mine will go for that," Basil said. "I need a room of my own."

"You got it, big boy," Eddie said. "There's also office space you can use. When can you start?"

"Soon as we pack our bags," Basil said. "We'll be there later today."

"Thanks, Basil. See you when you get here," Eddie said.

Eddie had barely walked in the door to Jack's house when a clap of thunder rattled the dishes.

"Well," Chief said. "Is he going to help us?"

"He's all in," Eddie said.

"How much is it going to cost us?" Chief said.

"Heather and Basil are on their way to the island," Eddie said. "They're getting married, and Heather is fighting with her parents. She wants to have the wedding at the Majestic. I hired her."

"To do what? You have no business," Jack said.

"Maybe not this minute. Now that there's a major movie filming on the island, I'll make a fortune feeding and housing the crew. If Frankie doesn't hit us with a restraining order first."

"You don't sound too sure about that," Jack said.

"I'd be a lot surer if I had a mug of rum," Eddie said.

"Who's going to plan this wedding?" Jack said.

"Odette," Eddie said. "She has a degree, and you said she can cook for hundreds. If she needs it, maybe you can help her."

"Odette doesn't have her degree yet," Jack said.

"Close enough for government work," Eddie said. "What do you know about weddings?"

"Not much I didn't do during my stints in the Navy and Merchant Marines," Jack said. "I never planned a wedding."

"Neither have I."

"How many guests?" Jack said.

"Everyone in the parish," Eddie said.

"Good God Almighty!" Jack said. "Who's paying for all of this?"

"It's part of the trade I agreed to for Basil to help me with our lawsuit."

"Hell, Eddie. You're not as smart as I gave you credit for. A wedding that size could cost fifty grand," Jack said.

"No way," Eddie said.

"Why didn't you throw in a trip to the Bahamas for their honeymoon?" Jack said.

Jack flinched when Eddie slammed the mug of rum on the plank table.

"Okay, that's enough. Are you going to help or keep bitching about how badly I fucked up?"

"I'm in," Jack said. "Get your nuts out of the wringer."

Gone was Eddie's anger when he sipped the rum.

"What's the deal about the restraining order?" Chief asked.

Eddie glanced out the open door at the rain still drumming on the roof.

"Jesus!" he said. "When it rains, it pours."

"Just saying," Chief said.

"The ownership of Oyster Island is in the hands of the court," Eddie said. We're acting as if we're the actual owners. But are we? I guarantee Frankie will file a motion before long to have us kicked off the island."

"I've lived here all my life," Chief said. "He can't kick me off."

"The courts can," Eddie said.

"What are you going to do?" Chief asked.

"Beat Frankie to the punch."

"By doing what?" Chief asked.

"Don't know yet," Eddie said. "I'll think about it and discuss it with Basil."

"Should I start packing?" Chief asked.

"Hell no!" Eddie said. "This is a chess match, and it's my move. I'll think of something to pin Frankie's balls to the wall."

"You don't sound too sure about that," Chief said.

"Like I told Jack, are you going to keep bitching, or are you going to help?"

Chief stood at attention and saluted. "I'm all in, boss. Tell me what you need me to do."

"You can start by writing me a check for twenty grand," Eddie said. "That'll tide me over until I can get some accounting help and start billing the film crew. One more thing."

"Name it," Chief said.

"Though I'm a good-hearted soul, I can't work forever for nothing."

"You want all of the hundred grand?" Chief asked.

Eddie smiled and nodded when Jack topped up Eddie's mug with rum and coffee.

"Since we're horse trading around here," he said. "I propose a trade for my services.

"Hit me," Chief said.

"I had my heart set on owning and running the Majestic until Frankie pulled the plug on us. If I beat him in court, you get the island. I get the Majestic."

"Consider it yours, Eddie. I've got no use for that old firetrap."

"Then let's shake on it," Eddie said.

Chapter 6

Eddie had dozed off while sitting at Jack's plank table. When he opened his eyes, he saw the rain had finally stopped. Chief was asleep on the couch, and J.P. reading a news article on his cell phone.

"What time is it?" Eddie asked.

"You were asleep for about an hour," J.P. said.

"Where's Jack?"

"Outside feeding the dogs," J.P. said.

"I'm going to the hotel and get out of these clothes," Eddie said. "I don't believe pink is my color.

"I'm going with you," J.P. said. "I want to talk with Vixen and find out why she can stitch a wound like a pro."

"Doesn't matter," Eddie said. "She's working for me. You need to look elsewhere for a vet."

"She's worth more to this island as a veterinarian than a cleaning lady."

"Not to me," Eddie said. "I have guests to serve and a wedding that needs planning. If Vixen were a veterinarian, she wouldn't be working at a strip club."

"You'd think," J.P. said. "I'm an ex-cop, and

don't take anything for granted."

J.P. smiled when Eddie said, "Get over it."

"The clouds are still dark. Let's go before it starts raining again," J.P. said.

The sand beneath J.P. and Eddie's feet was wet as they hurried down the little hill from Jack's house to the Majestic. Like a wagon train, the film crew had circled their vehicles and formed a temporary camp on the sand near the hotel.

"This is only the advance group," J.P. said. "There'll be lots more people when the actors, cameramen, and everyone else involved in a movie gets here."

"You sound as if you know what you're talking about," Eddie said.

"Once they start filming, everything else on the island will grind to a halt. You'll see."

J.P. laughed when Eddie said, "They haven't dealt with me yet."

Directors and producers get pushy if they don't get their way," J.P. said.

"How do you know so much about it?"

"Film crews hire off-duty cops all the time for security purposes," J.P. said. "New Orleans is a movie mecca; I've worked my share of them."

"We'll make it work," Eddie said. "All businesses are the same."

"Good luck on that one."

"I'll admit I'm nervous as hell. I've never been married, much less involved in putting on a wedding. The movie is pushing me over the edge."

"It'll work out," J.P. said. "I'm here to advise you."

Eddie grinned. "Now, I am scared."

They found the front door of the hotel unlocked, the entrance dark. They made it to the lighted stairway without tripping over anything as panicked squeals issued from a room. Rushing up the stairs, J.P. pushed through the door, Eddie behind him.

Odette, Avory, and Lilly stared at Vixen floating near the ceiling. Her eyes were closed, arms and legs askew. When she opened her eyes and fell from near the ceiling, J.P. made a running dive. Though less than a perfect catch, he broke Vixen's fall and kept her from injury. Eddie and the three women hurried to help.

"Vixen, are you okay?" Odette asked.

"What happened?" she said.

Realizing J.P. had wrapped his arms around her, Vixen pushed him away, kicking him for good measure.

"Keep your hands off of me," she said,

Vixen sprang to her feet as Lilly, Odette, and Avory hovered around her.

"I don't believe what I just saw with my own eyes," Avory said.

"What happened?" Eddie asked.

"The furniture in the rooms I assigned to Avory and Lilly needed cleaning," Odette said. "We went downstairs for a drink to give Vixen a chance to work."

"When we checked on her, we heard a scream through the open door," Avory said. "We entered in time to see Vixen lift that couch off the floor and throw it against the wall. Then her eyes rolled back in her head, and she levitated to the ceiling."

Eddie went to the couch and tried to lift it. "You kidding me? J.P. and I would have trouble hoisting that antique behemoth off the floor."

"She did more than that," Lilly said. "She tossed it a good five feet."

"It's called hysterical strength," J.P. said. "Like when a mom sees her daughter trapped beneath a car's wheel and somehow has the strength to lift the vehicle off her. It's more common than you might think."

"There was no one else in the room," Odette said. "What scared her?"

"Abused or traumatized people often react violently to perceived demons. I can't explain the levitation."

"You were a cop. Not a psychologist," Avory said. "How do you know so much about disturbed individuals?"

"Cops are routinely sent to intervene in domestic disputes and often called on to do the job of a psychologist. If you don't know what to expect, you could kill an innocent person or get killed yourself."

"Damn!" Lilly said. "What else do you know about Vixen?"

J.P. grabbed her left hand and showed it to Lilly. "See the faint indention around her ring finger? She must have worn a wedding ring for years to develop that indention. She has stretch marks on her stomach."

"How do you know that?" Odette said.

"I saw her naked when you removed her towel and showed us her bruises. Remember?"

"If I were a man, the ring indention and stretch marks wouldn't be what I noticed when I looked at a naked woman," Lilly said.

"Good cops notice everything," J.P. said.

"And bad cops?" Avory said.

"They don't last long."

"That's what you were doing when we walked into the room this morning?" Avory said. "Vixen seemed passive as a lamb."

"Passive acceptance is what you do to avoid violent conflict," J.P. said. "It's common in battered wives and children."

"What else?" Odette said.

"She may be a missing person," J.P. said. He took a headshot of Vixen with his cell phone. "I'm sending her picture to the police. Have a missing person search done."

Odette had dropped the rum bottle when she saw Vixen floating toward the ceiling. It was now empty, the wasted rum pooling on the polished wood floor.

"I need a drink," she said. "Let's hit the bar downstairs."

"Now you're talking," Eddie said. "I'll join you once I get out of this suit."

Vixen's tears were gone as Avory, Lilly, and Odette helped her down the stairs and seated her at a table in the little bar on the ground floor of the Majestic. Odette scooted under the bar, returning to the table with tumblers and an unopened bottle of Dominican rum.

Vixen sipped the rum, impassive when Avory asked, "Did someone abuse you?"

"I'm good," Vixen said. "I hope you liked the way I cleaned your rooms."

"You did a wonderful job," Lilly said. "Hungry?"

Vixen shook her head.

"I'll fix us something," Odette said.

She returned with sandwiches and potato chips.

"Just what the doctor ordered," Lilly said.

They'd finished their sandwiches and were working on their second tumblers of rum when Eddie, dressed in shorts and an L.S.U. tee shirt joined them.

"Did you go to L.S.U.?" Avory asked.

"No," he said, "Though it's hard not to cheer for their football program."

"Did you play football?" Avory said.

Eddie shook his head. "I'm a nerd. As a kid, I was always the last one picked when they chose teams."

"You look pretty athletic to me," Lilly said.

Lilly almost blushed when Eddie said, "I've never had any complaints."

"Jack told me you stitched Mollie's wound," J.P. said. "We train service dogs here on the island. We have lots of dogs, and sometimes they need medical care. Are you a veterinarian?"

Vixen didn't respond to the question.

Eddie glanced at Odette and said, "Vixen needs a room of her own no matter what she decides to do."

"I have one for her," Odette said.

Vixen glanced at Eddie. "I'll pay you twenty bucks an hour and free room and board if you work for me. If you want to, you can help J.P. on the side."

"Thanks, Eddie," J.P. said.

Eddie smiled and said, "You owe me."

After situating Vixen in her room, Eddie tapped Odette's shoulder. "We have another topic of discussion before we rejoin the others," he said.

"About what?" she said.

"Jack and Chief said you have a hotel and restaurant management degree from L.S.U. Is it true?"

"Not quite. I had to drop out when my daddy died. I'm a semester short."

"Did you take accounting?" Eddie asked.

"Three semesters' worth," Odette said.

"Then you can keep books?"

"Like a pro," Odette said.

"I'm way over my head here," Eddie said. "I need help."

"What are you suggesting?" Odette said.

"I want you to manage the hotel," Eddie said.

"Everything?" Odette said.

"Pretty much. I'm playing this by the seat of my pants. We'll figure things out as we go along."

"Let's get one thing straight," Odette said. "I

don't like sexist men."

"Hell, neither do I," Eddie said. "Sometimes my balls try to take over from my brain. If that happens, you have my permission to slap the shit out of me."

Odette grinned. "At least you're honest. That's a breath of fresh air."

"Then you'll accept my offer?"

"Hell, Eddie, you're the craziest person I've ever met," Odette said. "I have no idea if I can work for you. I'll try it."

"Wonderful," Eddie said. "One last thing."

"Forget it. I'm not sleeping with you."

Eddie grinned. "What do you know about planning weddings?"

"I'm a female. I've thought about it all my life. So what?"

"You think you could put one together for us on a limited budget?"

"Who's getting married?"

"Heather Boudreaux and Basil Doles."

"The woman's family usually pays for the wedding," Odette said.

"There's a problem."

"Are they destitute?" Odette asked.

"Anything but," Eddie said. "Money isn't the problem here. Heather was a waitress at Claws & Craws," Eddie said. "The owner's only daughter."

Odette grinned. "Daughters have a way of working on their dads."

"That's part of the problem," Eddie said. "They're feuding, and neither is willing to admit they are wrong."

"I can relate," Odette said. "I worked with my dad. He could be a hard-headed son of a bitch."

"Then I guess you come by the trait honestly," Eddie said.

"Thanks," Odette said.

"Basil's going to help me with my lawsuit

against Frankie Castellano. I need him, and the wedding is a condition of his help. Because of Basil, Heather's going to be working for us. I'll let you take care of the details. One more thing."

"What?"

"The movie. J.P. tells me it will be more of a problem than I thought. Know anything about making movies?"

"Can you say cluster fuck?"

Odette nodded when Eddie said, "That bad?"

After squeezing Eddie's hand, she said, "Thanks for trusting me. I'll help you make things work."

Chapter 7

Odette and Eddie returned to the bar to find Lilly sitting in J.P.'s lap. Avory's ample bosom, emphasized by her low-cut blouse, blushed crimson. Lilly and J.P. stopped groping each other and laughed when Eddie and Odette joined them at the table.

"Thank God you returned," Avory said. "I thought they would start screwing like a couple of alley cats."

"When you spend the night together during a Goose Island hurricane, you form a bond that lasts forever," Lilly said.

"My imagination is working overtime," Eddie said.

"I failed to mention the mud, high winds, and rain falling in horizontal sheets," Lilly said. "We were catching up on missing out."

"Get a room," Eddie said.

Lilly was grinning as she climbed out of J.P.'s lap and moved to the other side of the table.

"Our movie star actor is getting here in a few days," she said. "He's going to be pissed when he learns you and J.P. are better looking than he is."

"Don't tell him," Eddie said. "He'll never know. Who is the actor?"

"Brett Andrews," Avory said.

"Damn!" Eddie said. "You do have a big budget for this movie. My price for the hotel just went up."

"The backers wanted to go long," Avory said. "Kate Monroe is the leading lady. She's closing in on forty and still has no Academy Award. We got her at a bargain because she thinks the script has serious potential."

"Can't wait to meet her," Eddie said.

"I guarantee you and J.P. will both meet her. She's a working nympho," Lilly said.

"My kind of woman," Eddie said.

"Every man's kind of woman," Avory said. "If you like perversion."

"She's truly never met a man she didn't like," Lilly said.

"It's in Brett's contract we have to hire a bodyguard for him," Avory said.

"He's a bit nutty and carries a loaded pistol everywhere he goes," Lilly said.

"I've seen his type," J.P. said

"If he weren't a famous movie star, he'd be in prison," Avory said. "An ex-police officer like J.P. would make him happy."

"Not gonna happen," J.P. said. "That's a part of my life I don't plan to revisit. There are a couple of young studs on the force in Chalmette who could fill the bill."

"Please give them a call," Avory said.

"I confess, I know little about filming a movie. What exactly do you need us to do?" Eddie asked.

"The two stars will stay in the Majestic. We have trailers for everyone else," Avory said.

"And the food?" Odette said.

"We have to break every six hours," Avory said. "Union rules. We'll need tables set out with drinks. Coffee, tea, soft drinks, and bottled water. No cakes, pies, or sugary desserts. Just healthy snacks.

"What about breakfast, lunch, and dinner?" Odette said.

"Hot meals and quality food," Avory said. "And no pizza. That's a rule you can't break."

"What about alcohol?" Odette said.

"Movie people tend to be drinkers. They're on their own when we stop shooting for the day. My advice is, don't let them run a tab."

"What else?" Eddie said.

"During the day and sometimes at night, the Majestic is ours. You need to work around us and not hinder the filming," Avory said. "I'll need reliable electricity. This darkness, while atmospheric, won't work. We'll create the atmosphere during the filming."

"We'll need the main kitchen to prepare the food," Odette said.

"That's a workaround," Avory said.

"What does that mean?" Odette asked.

"If we need to film a scene in the kitchen, you'll have to vacate the premises."

"I think I have a headache," Eddie said.

"Then maybe this will give you even more of a headache," Avory said. "You work at my convenience. If I say frog, you jump."

Eddie wasn't smiling as he rubbed his forehead. "Do you have a whip?" he said.

"This is no joke, so don't take it lightly," Avory said.

"I never take anything lightly," Eddie said.

"Then we'll get along just fine," Avory said.

"We're only now getting the hotel operational and, as yet, have no room service," Odette said. "Is that a problem?"

"Not for me," Avory said. "But movie stars tend to be prima donnas and expect people to cater to their every whim."

"Odette and I will figure something out,"

Eddie said. "None of this is going to be cheap."

"The production is fully funded," Avory said. "I'll pay whatever is reasonable, though not a penny more."

Eddie's cell phone rang before he could comment on Avory's demands. It was Basil Doles.

"Heather and I are in front of the Majestic," Basil said.

"I'm at the bar. Not far from the front door. It's unlocked. Bring your bags and join us. Sorry, I don't have a bellhop."

When Basil and Heather entered the front door, Basil called out.

"Where are you, Eddie? It's so dark in this place we can't see a damn thing."

"Wait there," Eddie said. "I'll come and get you."

Eddie returned with a handsome couple in their twenties. Both had dark hair and dark Cajun eyes. Heather's jeans were tight and displayed her long legs. Her Western shirt and casual attire clashed with Basil's dark suit, starched white shirt, and polished brogans. At least he'd loosened his expensive tie. Heather beamed when she saw J.P., immediately sitting in his lap and wrapping her arms around his neck.

"J.P.," she said. "Where you been?"

J.P. didn't answer her. Looking at Basil instead, he said, "Sorry, buddy. Please don't hit me."

"Heather has a mind of her own. If she were going to cheat on me, there'd be nothing I could do about it."

Heather kissed J.P. and then moved to Basil's lap. "You know I'd never cheat on you, Big Daddy," she said.

Basil was enormous, every bit of six-foot-three, and muscular enough to be a professional wrestler.

"Jealousy is no longer in my vocabulary," he said.

"Damn! Not even a little bit?" Heather said.

"This is Basil and Heather," Eddie said. "Heather will be working for the hotel. Basil's helping me with my lawsuit. They're getting married here."

"I'm Avory, the director of the movie we're shooting on the island."

"A female movie director?" Heather said.

"I'm proof such an animal exists," Avory said.

"How exciting," Heather said.

"And I'm Lilly. I wrote the script for the movie though Avory has already altered it so many times it may as well be her script."

"I've always wanted to act in a movie," Heather said.

"You and Basil are both very photogenic," Avory said. "I'll find bit parts for both of you if you like."

Heather squealed and hugged Basil until his face turned red.

"What are you drinking?" Odette asked.

"Whatever the rest of you are having," Basil said.

"Heather?" Odette said.

"A glass of chilled Chardonnay," she said.

Odette smiled. When she glanced at Eddie, she crossed her eyes. He pretended not to notice. Odette returned to the table with a tumbler for Basil and a bottle of Chardonnay in a silver wine chiller. Sometime later, someone else called from the front door.

"Anybody in here?"

"Who is it?" Eddie shouted.

"We have Avory and Lilly's baggage."

"I'll be right there," Eddie said.

Lilly and Avory smiled when six men appeared with their bags and trunks.

"See you later," Avory said. "We're going to get our rooms situated."

Basil watched them disappear into the darkness and said, "They look as if they plan to stay awhile."

"Thank God I'm not the bellhop," Eddie said.

"Me either," Basil said.

"Got that right," J.P. said. "I have paperwork to do at the training facility. I'll catch up with everyone later."

Heather frowned when Eddie said, "Odette is your supervisor. She'll assign you a room and train you in the coming days."

"I've waitressed since I was thirteen," she said. "I don't need any training."

Eddie appreciated Odette's diplomacy when she said, "We're just starting up operations. Avory and Lilly are our first guests at the Majestic. I know you're a professional, and I greatly value your input. Work with me, and we'll get the show on the road."

Heather pecked Basil's cheek and then followed Odette. Eddie poured Basil more rum.

"The hotel has a small office complex. There are desks, chairs, and file cabinets, though no computers or phones. I have no idea what else we might find," Eddie said. "Your room is on the second floor. Grab your bags, and let me show it to you."

"Heather has almost as many clothes as Avory and Lilly. They're in the car."

"You'll have lots of time to bring them in," Eddie said. Dust covers cloaked the room's furniture. "Sorry, I had no time to get your room ready."

"Not a problem," Basil said. He removed the dust cover and plopped his bags on the bed. "I'll finish here later. I'd like to see the offices."

They returned downstairs to the office

complex. The prior occupants had left in a huff, and the place was a jumble of tables and desks.

"At least I had electricity installed," he said. "The rest is a mess. Sorry."

"No problem," Basil said.

"We can work on the offices later," Eddie said.

"No way," Basil said. "I'll make a dent in it. I want to be up and running tomorrow."

"Oh, to be young again," Eddie said.

"You aren't that much older than me," Basil said.

"Maybe, though I feel like I'm ninety."

Basil clutched Eddie's hand and shook it. "I'm so grateful for this chance to learn from a master."

"Thanks, Basil. Frankie Castellano will throw everything at us, including the kitchen sink. It comforts me to know I have your help."

"Stop worrying. We're going to kick his ass."

When Eddie returned to the little bar, Odette brought him a ham and Swiss sandwich.

"Thought you might be hungry," she said.

"Give yourself a raise," Eddie said.

"I hope you're paying me well because this will not be easy. How much are you paying me?"

"I'll tell you soon as I find out how much I have to spend," he said. "Right now, we need to hire more help. I have a feeling this could get the best of us."

"Hell, Eddie. It's not like we're in New York City. Who are we going to hire?"

"Don't know," he said.

"Maybe Paula will have an idea. She and Jimmie will be back on the island tomorrow."

"You think Heather's going to work out?" Eddie asked.

"She resents me and wants to be the boss."

"A good manager knows how to handle truculent employees," Eddie said.

"Book learning and actual practice aren't the same things."

Eddie took another bite of his sandwich and said, "Anyone who can make a ham and Swiss this good will never fail."

"What'll we do if Frankie ends up owning the island?"

"We're nowhere near that happening," Eddie said. "Basil is a Godsend. That's why you need to help me manage Heather."

"She's a handful," Odette said. "Hope she doesn't end up doing more damage than good."

"I know," Eddie said. "I can read the signs. Just do your best with her."

"I will."

"One more thing," Eddie said. "I want you to move to the hotel."

"I have two dogs. Remember? One is just a puppy, though already so big he'll scare the guests."

Eddie squeezed Odette's hand. "This gig is turning out to be the hardest thing I've ever done. I need you. Please don't let me down."

Chapter 8

Jack and Chief were playing gin rummy at the plank table when J.P. walked in the door.

"Something smells good," he said.

"Got a pot of gumbo simmering on the stove," Jack said. "Want a bowl?"

"You kidding me? I'd love a bowl."

"Where you been?" Chief asked.

"Watching Eddie jump through hoops at the Majestic. Hope he's not in over his head."

"What are you talking about?" Chief asked.

"The movie director, Avory Dorean has so many requirements, Eddie doesn't know if he's coming or going."

"Such as?" Jack said.

"Catering requirements for feeding the movie crew. When it comes to preparing food, Eddie doesn't know squat from sic 'em."

"What requirements?" Jack asked.

"No sandwiches. Only hot, freshly prepared food. No sugary snacks. Things like that."

"Sounds like a piece of cake to me."

"You're a pro. Eddie isn't."

"He has Odette. She knows how to feed a crew."

"Not without more help, she doesn't," J.P. said.

Jack dished up a bowl of gumbo and mug of rum for J.P. and then returned to his game of gin with Chief. When J.P. finished the gumbo, he grabbed his cell phone.

"Chalmette Police Department, Sergeant Gebbia speaking," a man said.

"Wayne, it's J.P. Saucier."

"J.P., how you doing?"

"Happy as a three-peckered goat," J.P. said. "You?"

"Doing good," Sergeant Gebbia said. "You didn't call to socialize. How can I help you?"

"Can you check on someone for me?"

"Old girlfriend?"

J.P. chuckled. "A missing person."

"Description?"

"Female, thirties, five-ten, skinny, light-skinned, green eyes, short, naturally blond hair, speaks with a foreign accent and goes by the name of Vixen."

"Last name?"

"Unknown."

"Identifying marks?"

"No scars or tattoos. She was married and had a kid. Likely has a severe case of PTSD."

"That doesn't give me much to go on," Sergeant Gebbia said.

"She's a looker and was stripping at Rockie's on Bourbon Street. I have a picture of her on my cell phone I'll send you."

"Fingerprints or DNA?"

"Both," J.P. said. "I'll drop them off next time I'm in Chalmette."

"Good hearing from you. I'll start on this right now."

"Thanks, Wayne."

Jack and Chief were still playing gin when J.P.

refilled his mug from the bottle of rum on the plank table.

"What did you do with the towel Vixen used after taking her shower?"

"Why?" Jack said. "You planning to do something kinky with it?"

"Maybe," J.P. said. "Where is it?"

"It had blood all over it. I threw it away."

J.P. found the trashcan and began going through it.

"It's not in here," J.P. said.

"Outback in the dumpster," Jack said.

A commercial trash truck picked up the island's garbage once a week. The large dumpster was half full, and J.P. climbed into it. He returned to Jack's galley with a rumpled white towel.

"What the hell?" Jack said.

"Dumpster diving," J.P. said. "Got a grocery bag?"

Jack rummaged under a cabinet and found a plastic grocery baggie.

"Paper if you have it. Not plastic," J.P. said.

"You're weird," Jack said.

J.P. didn't respond to Jack's remark. "Have you washed the dishes today?"

"Not yet."

J.P. opened the dishwasher. "Which one of these did Vixen drink from?"

"That one," Jack said.

J.P. stopped him when he reached for the glass.

"Don't touch it. How do you know it's the one Vixen used?"

"The pink teddy bear," Jack said. "Vixen started crying when she saw it."

"Got a plastic baggie?"

J.P. slipped the baggie Jack gave him over the cup and sealed it."

"Where you going?" Jack asked.

"To put the towel and cup in my truck," J.P. said.

When he returned, he joined them at the plank table.

"What was that all about?" Chief said.

"A friend at the department is running a missing person's report on Vixen. Maybe I can find out who the hell she is."

Distant thunder rumbled as Odette hurried into the house and pulled up a chair.

"Why the long face?" Jack asked.

"Eddie hired me to manage the Majestic," Odette said.

"Hell, baby! That's cause for celebration, not a big 'ol frown on your pretty face."

"We already have a major problem. I'm unsure how to handle it."

"What problem?"

"Avory Dorean, the director of the movie they're filming on the island."

"What about her?"

Chief glanced up from his cards. "That woman looks like trouble," he said.

"Her rules for serving the film crew are so stringent, I don't know how to comply," Odette said.

"J.P. was telling us," Jack said.

"When I worked in the kitchen on the offshore rigs, warm food was available twenty-four hours a day. It was like running food service in a big hotel, except we might be a hundred miles from shore, and we only got resupplied once a week."

"What could be more challenging than that?" Jack asked.

"We served hot, healthy food in good portions."

"Do the same for the film crew," Jack said.

"The roughnecks weren't that picky. Avory won't settle for common meals. She said as much."

Jack scratched his chin. "Did you bring the ATV?"

"Parked outside," she said.

"Let's take a drive to the storage building. Seems I remember seeing a few things we can use there."

"What about our gin game?" Chief said.

"You owe me fifty cents. Leave it on the counter and come with us. We may need some muscle."

They met J.P. returning from his truck when they exited the house and shut the door.

"Where you going?" he asked.

"The storage building," Jack said.

"Can me and Lucky come?"

"Pile in," Jack said.

"Let me get some tools," J.P. said. "I'd like to see what's in some of those sealed crates."

"Hurry," Odette said. "It's starting to sprinkle."

The sand was still damp from the morning rainstorm as Odette steered the electric vehicle down the hill from the lighthouse. About a quarter mile from the Majestic, a large storage building occupied more than an acre of land.

Unopened storage containers sat stacked in the warehouse. There were also beds, stoves, building materials, and anything needed for the hotel. When Chief exited the ATV and opened the large metal door, Odette drove into the building.

The warehouse was dark, and there was no electricity. Jack shined his flashlight into the darkness as wind whistled through the rafters and rain drummed the metal roof.

"Creepy," Odette said. "What are we looking for?"

"Restaurant equipment," Jack said. "Seems I remember seeing some things we might be able to use."

They were a hundred feet into the dark and musty old building when Lucky halted and started barking. The chocolate Labrador retriever stopped barking and wagged his tail when J.P. rubbed his head.

"What is it, boy?" he asked.

"Bats," Chief said. "They have a colony up in the rafters."

"It's good almost everything is either covered with tarps are in crates," J.P. said.

"Got that right," Jack said. "Smells a little rank in here."

"Do bats bite?" Odette said.

"I'd worry more about guano in your hair than getting bitten," Chief said.

"There's an office complex up ahead. The wardrobe room is in there," Jack said. "Maybe we can find some hats."

The large complex had a standard ceiling protecting it from the bats in the rafters. It was also stuffy.

"Bet this place is unbearable during the summer," J.P. said.

"Whoever designed the building knew what they were doing," Jack said. "Some ventilation panels open and shut automatically, creating a circular air flow to cool and ventilate everything. Not quite like air conditioning, though better than nothing."

Problem is there's no electricity to activate it," Chief said.

"Frankie was going to install electricity," Jack said."

"Better not let Eddie hear you talking about what Frankie was going to do for the island," J.P. said.

"Jack's mad because he no longer gets a salary from Frankie," Chief said.

"We'll soon have steady profits from the canine training facility to offset your loss," J.P. said.

"Unless Frankie manages to kick us off the island," Jack said.

"Don't be like that," Chief said. "We were always victims to Frankie's every whim. We didn't know it at the time."

"You're right," Jack said.

"Eddie's like a junkyard dog, and Frankie's in for the fight of his life," Odette said.

"Uncle!" Jack said. "I'm on your side. Let's find the wardrobe room."

They'd visited the room once, intending to dress in costume while clubbing in the Quarter. Their excursion hadn't worked out the way they'd planned. Odette had almost forgotten the vintage clothing stored there.

"I love this place," she said. "I can't believe we haven't returned until now."

When Jack shined his light on a row of dresses, Odette squealed and started removing her clothes. She settled on a shiny red dress with shimmy tassels.

"Once a stripper, always a stripper," J.P. said.

"Once a voyeur, always a voyeur," she replied.

"We got work to do," Jack said. "Have your fun later."

"I love this dress. I'm wearing it." Odette found a sack to carry her jeans and blouse.

"The bats are going to love your dress," Jack said.

J.P. shined his light on another row of clothes.

"This looks like costumes for a Western movie," he said. "There's a whole row of dusters."

"What's a duster?" Odette said.

"Loose canvas coats that reach almost to the ground. Cowboys wore them to keep the dust off of their clothes. Bet they'll work the same for bat guano."

"Here's a rack of cowboy hats," Chief said. "We may look like shit when we leave the warehouse. At least it won't be all over us."

Even the shortest duster was too long for Odette. It didn't matter because she loved it, along with the black cowboy hat she had chosen.

"Where is the restaurant equipment?" Chief asked.

"The opposite end of the warehouse," Jack said.

Dressed like cowboys on a cattle drive, they made their way through the stacks of crates until they found the section where the hotel maintenance people had stored their spare restaurant equipment.

"What exactly are we looking for?" Chief asked.

"Buffet supplies," Jack said.

"For what?" Chief said.

"I have an idea," he said.

Jack began pulling out stainless steel pans along with other buffet paraphernalia.

"What are those things?" Chief asked.

"Chafing dishes. They keep food warm in a buffet line. There are enough warming dishes, pots, and ladles for one super fancy buffet," Jack said.

"But what are we going to serve in it?" Odette said.

"Cafeteria food," Jack said. "When I was cooking in the Merchant Marines, we'd have meat, vegetables, beans, and soup. Always something different to keep the sailors from mutinying."

"I don't think these movie people will be happy with salt pork and turnip greens," Odette said.

"Eddie will have a bigger budget than I had,"

Jack said. "You'll figure it out."

"Between cooking and serving, we won't have time to do anything else," Odette said.

"You need to hire a chef and enough workers to assist with the preparation."

"We can't offer anyone permanent employment," Odette said. "We may have no customers after the movie crew leaves."

"Then we'll have to figure a way to make this a must-visit destination," Jack said.

"We could start a strip club with Odette as the star performer," J.P. said.

"You know what?" Odette said. "You need your ass kicked, and I'm the girl to do it."

J.P. grinned. "Just pulling your chain," he said. "Don't get all bent out of shape."

"You wouldn't have said it if you didn't mean it," Odette said.

"I apologize," J.P. said. "In the dark and dressed in that long coat and hat, you could pass as one of the guys. I got carried away."

"You talk to guys differently when girls aren't around?"

"Why hell yes!" J.P. said. "Women are the same. I'll bet you tell Paula things you'd never tell me, Jack and Chief."

Though Odette shook her fist at him, she was smiling. "You watch it, mister. I can be as rough and crude as you boys are."

"You know I was joking," J.P. said.

"Knock it off, both of you," Jack said. "We have work to do."

"I'll get my truck," J.P. said. "There's lots of equipment that needs hauling.

"It's a long walk back to Jack's," Odette said. "I'll take you,"

"I'll open the bay door," Chief said. "Pull the truck around the warehouse."

"You got it," J.P. said.

"We should have a truckload ready to haul when you get here," Jack said.

The sky outside the warehouse had grown progressively darker as J.P., Odette, and Lucky returned to the main entrance.

"You aren't mad at me, are you?" J.P. asked.

"Hell, J.P., if women took offense at every sexist thing men say in front of them daily, there'd be no babies born."

"Ain't that the truth," he said.

Stopping, he shined his light into a partially-opened crate.

"What is it?" Odette said.

"Come see," he said.

Chapter 9

Hours had passed since Eddie had left Basil in the hotel's office complex, and he decided to check on him. The moment he walked in the door, he could see the transformation.

The dust and clutter were gone, and the reception area tidy. A welcoming couch and side chair sat across from the receptionist's desk. The pictures on the wall were originals, not knock-offs. Eddie was almost afraid to peek into the first office. Basil was sitting at the desk in the room, his feet propped on the desktop.

"Wow!" Eddie said. "This is nothing short of amazing. I'm impressed."

"Wait'll you see your office," Basil said.

"I can hardly wait."

Eddie followed Basil into an office down a short hallway. A leather couch and a large desk dominated the room.

Basil nodded when Eddie asked, "Were these desks in here? The furniture must have cost a small fortune."

"Nothing but the best for the new owner of the Majestic Hotel & Casino."

"Hope you're right about that," Eddie said.

"We'll need a phone system and computers, though we can get by with our cell phones and personal laptops for a while. The main thing we will need is central heat and air."

"The thought has crossed my mind. Window units won't work in interior rooms, and I imagine summer here can get hot and humid."

"That's a fact," Basil said.

"How much does it cost to install central heat and air?"

"You probably don't want to know. A complete renovation of the Majestic could cost millions."

"That's at least three zeroes more than I can afford," Eddie said. "We'll have to look for a cheaper short-term solution."

"Ms. Dorean can't film in a building with limited electricity."

Eddie and Basil glanced up at the door when someone spoke. It was Avory Dorean.

"My ears were burning. Were you talking about me?"

"Guilty," Eddie said. "Mr. Castellano only hooked up electricity for part of the hotel. Basil and I were discussing a possible short-term fix."

"The advance crew of carpenters and electricians are here. They're ready to prepare the location so we can begin filming."

"Seems like a tall task," Eddie said.

"My crew is the best in the business and equipped to handle all contingencies."

"Could be expensive," Eddie said.

"It's covered in the filming budget. Don't worry your pretty little head about it."

Basil wiped away his smile when Eddie turned to see his reaction to Avory's comment.

"When do they start?" Eddie asked.

"Any minute," she said.

Someone stuck their head in the door and said, "Knock, knock."

"Back here," Avory said.

A man with a swarthy complexion, dark hair, a bushy mustache, and a perpetual smile entered Eddie's office. Despite the chill in the air, he wore worn overalls with no shirt accentuating his hairy chest and muscular arms covered with tattoos.

"I'm Ben Biondo, the construction coordinator," he said.

Another man accompanied Ben. He was slightly built, well-dressed, and had an endless smile. He introduced himself in a British accent.

"I'm Colin Dane, Avory's set director. Lovely furniture," he said.

"This is Basil. I'm Eddie."

"Ben and Colin need a walkthrough of the hotel. I'll come with you. Please give as much detail as possible, including history, back story, whatever."

"Let's begin here," Eddie said. "This was the office complex the owners of the Majestic used to make hard decisions. They likely discussed smuggling, rum running, and murder in these offices."

Avory shook her head. "We have no scene set in an office. If we did, we'd film it on a back lot in L.A. Sorry."

"There are multiple offices in this complex. Eddie and I only need three," Basil said. "That leaves empty offices for the producer/director, the head writer, the construction coordinator, and the set director."

"I don't know," Avory said.

Basil was persistent. "Having an office is more efficient than making major decisions in your hotel room. When you shut your room door for the night, you can forget the day's worries and get a good night's sleep."

"Do you need an office, Ben?" Avory said.

"It's up to you, Ms. Dorean. I'm good either

way."

"Colin?"

"Yes, if I can get a table to lay out my designs," he said.

"How much trouble would it be to add electricity, heat, and air to the complex?"

"Piece of cake," Ben said.

"Is it a budget buster?" Avory asked.

"It would take more time to work around it than to include it in the overall plan," Ben said.

"Which office will I have?" Avory said.

"This one's the biggest," Eddie said. "Consider it yours."

"I'll requisition computers and a phone system," Ben said.

"We'll need fresh paint and Prohibition Era paintings on the wall," Colin said.

"You're going to need legal help from lawyers familiar with Louisiana law," Basil said. "Eddie and I can help if you furnish us with computers and let us share the phones."

Avory nodded. "Put them on the list, Ben."

"Yes, ma'am," Ben said.

"Let's look at the little bar off the office complex," Avory said.

Eddie watched Avory, Colin, and Ben exit the offices, then smiled and gave Basil a fist bump.

"Way to go, buddy. I'm glad you're on my side," he said.

"Never know what a free office will get you these days," Basil said.

"Maybe we can talk them into installing heat and air on the third floor."

They followed the three filmmakers to the cozy little bar where they'd had drinks earlier. Avory pointed to the elaborate woodwork.

"This bar has so much ambiance and atmosphere," Avory said. "We'll film at least three scenes here. Colin?"

"It's perfect just the way it is," he said.

"I'd like to make this bar available to the cast and crew after daily filming ends," Avory said.

Ben had a pencil and notepad and took notes. "Do all the appliances in the kitchen work?" he asked.

"I'll check with Odette, my manager, and find out," Eddie said.

Ben handed Eddie a card. "Have her call and set up a meeting with me. No use doing this piecemeal."

"This bar is cozy, though not big enough to accommodate your entire crew," Eddie said. "I suggest you reserve it for your execs and stars."

"What will everyone else use?" Avory asked.

"A larger bar and dining area down the hall will accommodate the rest of your crew. It's as beautiful as this bar, only more significant."

"I want to see it," Colin said.

"It's up a level," Eddie said. "We'll have to take the stairs."

The main dining room overlooked the casino, its bar reminiscent of the intimate one on the ground floor.

"This bar and restaurant seats a hundred and has all the ambiance of the smaller bar."

"The woodwork is simply gorgeous," Colin said. "Is it mahogany?"

"Teak, mahogany, and American walnut," Eddie said.

Seeing the happy expression on Colin's face, Avory smiled.

"I love it," she said.

"Frankie Castellano practically had an orgasm when he first visited the Majestic," Eddie said. "He called it the most beautiful bar and restaurant in the world."

"He would know," Avory said. "Colin?"

"It's as if I fell asleep and awakened on the set

of *Gone with the Wind*," he said.

Colin made a face when Avory said, "We need potted palms and ferns for atmosphere."

Noticing Colin's expression, Basil asked, "Did they decorate with potted palms and ferns during Prohibition?"

"I don't know," Avory said.

"Colin, what do you think?" Basil asked.

"I have no idea if they had potted palms and ferns in the bars," he said.

"Nor do most of the people who'll pay to see this movie," Avory said.

"But is it authentic?" Basil said.

"This is fictional entertainment and not a fucking documentary," Avory said. "Stick to the law and let me film this movie."

"Yes, ma'am," Basil said.

"Colin?" Avory said.

Eddie and Ben smiled when Colin said, "I'll order the potted palms and ferns."

Avory gazed over the railing overlooking the casino. "We'll do several shots from this vantage," she said. "Something is missing. What is it?"

"No casino equipment," Colin said. "We'll need craps, blackjack tables, and roulette wheels; they must be authentic."

"Can you find Prohibition Era casino equipment?" Avory asked.

"For the right price, you can find anything," he said. "The chandeliers are beautiful, and the woodwork extraordinary. This hotel is perfect, and the sets will be magnificent. What else?"

"There's not a lot of available history on the Majestic. The owners were secretive, as you might guess," Avory said. "What I was able to learn is interesting."

"Such as?" Colin asked.

"There are private dining areas with limited seating where the mob bosses could have dinner with their mistresses. Secret passages lace this old building," she said.

"That's something I didn't know," Eddie said.

"The passageways allowed the people in the inner circle to move from place to place in the hotel without being seen," Avory said. "There's also lots of two-way glass for spying on their guests."

"Sinister," Basil said.

"Too bad we don't have the original blueprints," Ben said.

"We'll have to make do without them," Avory said. "I'm taking Ben to the upstairs rooms. I have no scenes planned there. You're welcome to come along, Colin."

"I have other work calling my name. Please advise me when my office is ready."

Eddie showed Ben the rooms on the second and third floors. They finished their inspection in Avory's room.

"We'll electrify and duct both floors," Ben said. "We'll need extra rooms if the executive producers decide to visit the set."

"Good thinking, Ben. You may as well get back to your ballgame," Avory said. "We've accomplished a lot for today."

"Can you take a look at something before you go?" Basil asked.

"You bet," Ben said.

"It's downstairs in the complex of offices," Basil said.

"I'll come, too," Avory said. "Maybe I can get Odette to fix me a drink."

Basil touched a hidden button on the wall, and a door opened.

"One of your secret rooms," he said.

Avory pushed past Ben and Eddie. "What's in there?

"An old safe," Basil said. "It's locked. Any

ideas how we can open it short of a stick of dynamite?"

"Piece of cake," Ben said.

He squatted, blew on his fingers, closed his eyes, and began rotating the dial. He grinned when they heard a click, and the heavy door opened.

"I don't believe it," Basil said.

"Easy if you know how," Ben said. "Mind if I return to my football game?"

"Absolutely," Avory said. "Thanks, Ben."

Basil pulled out a stack of papers, put them on the desk, and thumbed through them.

"Anything interesting?" Eddie asked.

"An old ledger, a few thousand dollars in Prohibition Era currency, and a file folder containing miscellaneous documents," he said.

"An actual time capsule," Eddie said.

"I'll take a closer look at everything when I get a few extra moments," Basil said.

"Is that a map?" Avory asked.

"Maybe it's a treasure map," Eddie said.

"There's a signature and date at the bottom. Looks like whoever signed it used a quill," Basil said.

Basil opened the top drawer of the ornate desk and removed a Sherlock Holmes magnifying glass.

"Who signed it," Avory asked.

"Jean Lafitte. 1817."

"You gotta be kidding," Eddie said. "Must be a fake."

"It's a treasure map signed by the pirate Jean Lafitte. Why would you think it's a fake?" Avory said.

"If it isn't, it's a historical document that should be in a museum," Basil said.

"Maybe there's treasure buried on Oyster Island."

"What is it doing in the safe of a bunch of rumrunners?" Eddie asked.

"This could be a map of any place. There are hundreds of islands abutting Louisiana in the Gulf of Mexico," Basil said.

"Chief will know," Eddie said.

"The large man I met earlier today and paid a hundred grand?" Avory asked.

"Yes," Eddie said. "The real owner of Oyster Island."

"How can you be so sure?"

"American Indian Law. Chief is a full-blood Atakapa. Chief's grandfather sold the island. The transaction was invalid because he had no authority to sell it. I will get the courts to throw out the bill of sale because it circumvented Federal law."

"Mr. Castellano might have a say in how that goes down," Avory said.

"I was the Assistant Federal D.A. in New Orleans until about a year ago. Trust me when I tell you I'm personal friends with every Fed possibly involved in this case."

Eddie laughed when Avory said, "Sounds like a conflict of interest. Maybe all your friends should recuse themselves."

"Ain't going to happen," he said.

"What if they don't see it your way?" she said.

"Always a possibility," Eddie said. "It's why I have Basil, the best young attorney in south Louisiana, assisting me."

"Can we worry about it later?" Avory said. "I need a drink."

"Me too," Eddie said.

When Eddie started out the door to follow Avory, Basil grabbed his elbow and held up one finger.

"Are you boys coming?" Avory said.

"Grab a chair in the bar. Basil and I'll be there in five minutes." He turned to Basil and said, "What is it?"

"Lafitte's map wasn't the only thing interesting in the safe," Basil said.

"What else?"

"One of the documents is the deed to Oyster Island," Basil said.

"I thought you told me we have a copy of the deed," Eddie said.

"We do. This particular document looks as if it is the original deed."

"What's the significance?" Eddie asked.

"Don't know," Basil said. "I'll check it out."

"Later," Eddie said. "We both need a drink."

Chapter 10

When J.P. called to her, Odette turned to see him staring at a stack of crates. One of them was partially open.

"What are you looking at?" she asked.

"Slot machines," he said. "Antique slot machines."

"I'm not a gambler," Odette said. "How can you tell they're antiques?"

"New machines are digital. These are mechanical. They don't make them like this anymore."

"Then what are they good for?" Odette asked.

"Antique collectors probably love them," J.P. said.

"Forget the antiques and let's get out of here before it starts raining again," Odette said.

Lucky barked when J.P. saluted and said, "Aye, aye, captain."

Odette and J.P. were still wearing their long canvas coats and cowboy hats as they ran to the ATV.

"These dusters are great for reflecting the rain," Odette said.

"I'm keeping mine," J.P. said. "It'll come in handy on Oyster Island."

J.P., Lucky, and Odette bolted out of the ATV when they reached the top of the hill. J.P. took a long moment to find the keys to his truck.

"Hurry before we drown," Odette said. And don't get us stuck in the sand,"

Heavy rain had returned with a vengeance, the truck's wipers barely able to clear the water off the windshield as J.P. crept the truck down the gentle slope to the warehouse. The large bay door on the north side of the building was open, Jack and Chief waiting on them. J.P. backed the truck into the warehouse.

"The buffet equipment's going to get wet," he said.

"It's stainless," Jack said. "The rain won't hurt it."

"We're not stainless," Chief said. "Let's load the truck and wait for the rain to stop."

"We could be waiting here all day," J.P. said. "Let's take it to Jack's and enjoy dry clothes and mugs of rum. We can take the buffet equipment to the Majestic when it stops raining."

"Great idea," Chief said.

"Who's going to shut the bay door?" Jack asked.

"I'm driving," J.P. said. "I can't do it."

"I'll do it," Odette said.

"You're too little," Chief said. "I'll do it."

"I have the keys," Jack said. "It'll give me a chance to test our cowboy outfits."

"The dusters shed water pretty well," J.P. said. "That and the Stetson will keep you from drowning."

The rain had ended as Jack closed and locked the bay door. "May as well head to the Majestic," he said, "This is as dry as it has been in two days."

"Hope Eddie has rum in the place," Chief said.

"Quit carping," J.P. said. "Eddie has never been far from a bottle of booze. We'll get a drink, and our job will be complete."

It was still dry when J.P. backed up the truck to the floating ramp leading to the entrance of the Majestic. Odette followed behind the buffet platform with an armload of stainless steel buffet pans. Chief yelled after opening the door.

"Anybody here?" he said.

Eddie called to them from someplace in the darkness. "In the bar."

"Help," Chief called.

"I'm coming," Eddie said.

"Hurry. It's starting to rain again."

Eddie didn't immediately recognize the man inside the door wearing a floor-length duster and a black cowboy hat.

"Chief," he said. "Is that you?"

"It's me. Hold the door until we get this contraption out of the rain."

Eddie grabbed the door as three people dressed in the same garb as Chief maneuvered the stainless steel platform through the door. They were out of breath when they set it down with a thud. Odette removed her cowboy hat so Eddie could see who she was.

"What is this thing?" Eddie asked.

"A buffet," Odette said. "We found everything we need in the storage warehouse."

"Where are we going to put it?" Eddie asked.

"The little seating area outside the main dining room is perfect," Odette said.

Jack tossed Eddie a flashlight and said, "Can you lead the way?"

After several more trips to the truck, they had all the buffet equipment in the Majestic.

"I need a drink," Chief said.

"You're at the right place," Eddie said. "Put your hats back on. We'll play a trick on the others."

"Hope they don't have guns," J.P. said.

Eddie appeared from around the corner into the little bar. His hands extended toward the ceiling as if trying to avoid being shot. When the four people in dark cowboy hats and long dusters appeared behind him, everyone in the room reacted with squeals and moans. When Eddie started laughing, they realized they were the butt of a joke.

Odette, J.P., and Jack removed their hats and were also laughing. Avory and Basil sat on stools at the bar, conversing with Heather. Avory was clutching her heart.

"Not funny, Eddie. I almost had a heart attack thinking we were about to be victims of a home invasion."

J.P., Jack, Odette, and Chief hung their dusters and hats in the cloakroom. Eddie introduced everyone, and Odette went behind the bar to help Heather.

"Anybody hungry?" she asked.

"We all are," Eddie said.

"I'll see what we have in the kitchen."

Jack followed her. "I'll help," he said.

The lights flickered when thunder rumbled the old wooden building.

"Hope the rain doesn't wash my truck into the bay," J.P. said.

Lucky had found someone who liked chocolate Labs. Basil was rubbing his ears.

"Who is this beautiful dog?" he asked.

"Lucky," J.P. said. "You'll wear your fingers out before he moves."

"No problem," Basil said. "I had Labradors growing up. They're my favorite dog."

"You have a dog now?" J.P. asked.

Basil cast a glance at Heather. "Heather doesn't think we need one."

"Heather," J.P. said. "Don't be that way. A man needs his dog."

"Labs are too big," she said. "What if we have a baby, and the dog hurts it?"

J.P. grinned and said, "Lucky would never harm a baby. He'd take the arm off anyone who tried. You need a dog, girl."

"We have a wedding to plan," Heather said. "No time for pets."

"You and Basil are getting married?" Avory said?

"Eddie didn't tell you?"

"Tell me what?"

"Basil and I are getting married here at the hotel in the Grand Ballroom," Heather said.

Heather frowned when Avory said, "After the filming is complete?"

Heather didn't answer, her pretty smile disappearing and Basil looking at the floor when she glanced at him. Avory turned her gaze to Eddie.

"Like the movie, Heather and Basil's wedding is still in the planning stage," he said.

Avory let the matter drop when she heard Lilly coming down the stairs. Seeing Chief, she sat on a stool beside him. Chief quickly looked at her khaki shorts, tanned legs, and blue and gold sweatshirt emblazoned with the name U.C.L.A. School of Theater, Film & Television."

"I'm Lilly. What's your name?"

"Grogan La Tortue, though all my friends call me Chief."

"May I call you Chief?"

"I wouldn't have it any other way," he said.

"Has anyone ever told you that you're strikingly handsome?"

"No, though I think I like it. Are you trying to get into my breechcloth, Miss Lilly?"

Lilly didn't miss a beat when she said, "Do I

have a chance?"

"I'm big on friendship before sex," he said. "But I already like you a hell of a lot."

"You're funny, Grogan," she said.

"Please, call me Chief," he said. "The only three people who ever called me Grogan were my ex-wife and grandparents."

"Don't you think the nickname Chief has hurtful racial connotations?"

"Depends," Chief said.

"On what?"

"The way you say it. If I didn't like the tone of your voice, I might have to scalp you."

Chief was an imposing man. He wasn't smiling. Lilly sat straight up on the stool, crossed her legs, and folded her arms against her chest.

"You're joking, aren't you?" she said.

"I would never lay a finger on anyone in anger, Miss Lilly. I was only suggesting words often have many meanings, and it's up to intelligent people to decide if they should take offense."

Lilly uncrossed her arms and legs. "You are an intelligent man. I'm a writer and deal with taboos every day."

"Tell me how you do it," he said.

"There are only twenty-six letters in the English alphabet. Those letters comprise every word ever spoken. The world is walking a tightrope with no net when it starts banning words, books and free thought. It's only my opinion."

"You are a beautiful human being, Miss Lilly. I like you a lot. Do you have a room here?"

Lilly shook her head. "You're pulling my leg again, aren't you?"

"Metaphorically speaking," he said. "Though I wouldn't mind doing it for real."

"Do you ever smile?" she asked.

"High cheekbones," he said. "I'm smiling. It just doesn't look like it."

"Then I love your smile," she said. "Do you live on the island?"

"All my life," he said.

"You were at Jack's house this morning. Do you two live together?"

"Jack's my closest friend though I have my own place—a teepee on La Tortue Mountain.

"There are no mountains on Oyster Island," Lilly said

"La Tortue Mountain is almost twenty feet above sea level," Chief said. "For south Louisiana, that's a mountain."

"The only other island I ever visited in south Louisiana was flat. Why does this island have a twenty-foot mountain?"

"It sits atop a salt dome," Chief said. "There's probably an ocean of oil and natural gas below us."

"How do you know so much about the geology of this island?"

"I read a lot," Chief said.

"Where did you get your degree?" Lilly said.

"You mean high school?"

"You're college educated. Aren't you?"

"I have a master's degree in history from University of New Orleans," Chief said.

"Do you teach?"

"Jack says I spout off a lot," he said.

"I'd like to see your teepee," Lilly said.

"We'd drown getting there today," Chief said.

"Do you have a bearskin rug?"

"Now you are stereotyping me," Chief said.

Lilly clutched his big hand and squeezed. "Sorry," she said. "I'm only human."

"And a gorgeous one at that," he said.

"Chief, are you trying to get into my shorts?"

"Yes, Miss Lilly, I am. Do I have a chance?"

"You kidding?" she said. "I'm having a tough time not pulling you to the floor, tearing off our clothes, and then doing it in front of all these people."

"You're a writer, Miss Lilly. Like a glass of rum?"

"Avory and I tried some earlier. So smooth. It's my new favorite alcoholic drink."

Chief motioned Heather to bring Lilly a glass of rum. "It grows on you," he said.

"You're growing on me," she said. "Are you married?"

"No wife or girlfriend," he said. "Free as a bird. You?"

"I have a few close friends in L.A.," Lilly said. "Though no cages, and I love to fly."

Everyone was enjoying themselves as thunder shook the Majestic, rain peppering the roof. No one noticed Lilly and Chief holding hands and staring into each other's eyes like love-struck teenagers. Eddie could tell by Avory's serious expression she had something on her mind she wanted to discuss.

"What?" he said.

"Basil and Heather," Avory said.

"What about them?"

"Does Heather honestly believe there will be a major wedding in this hotel before finishing the movie? Answer me," she said when Eddie glanced away.

"She may have somehow gotten that impression," Eddie said.

"Were you in any way responsible for her mistaken impression?"

"I was hoping we could work something out," Eddie said.

"Like what?" she said.

"I haven't thought that far ahead," Eddie said.

"Then why did you agree to their wedding in the first place? You did agree to it, didn't you?"

"I need help with my lawsuit with Frankie. It was the only way to get Basil to help me."

"Then you're a liar, Mr. Toledo."

"What happened with Eddie?"

"You are a deceitful snake in the grass," Avory said. "I don't know how your clients could ever trust you."

"I'll work it out with Basil and Heather," Eddie said. "You can't plan a wedding overnight. The film will be a wrap before they marry."

Avory turned away from Eddie and sipped her rum. "Do you ever get frustrated trying to pound square pegs into round holes?"

"Frustration is every lawyer's middle name," Eddie said.

Avory shook her head. "Your middle name is trouble," she said.

Chapter 11

Veins of crimson tinted the pale blue sky as J.P. departed Oyster Island the following morning. He'd left Lucky at Jack's, the paper sack and a plastic baggie with Vixen's DNA sample and fingerprints in the passenger seat of his truck.

J.P.'s first planned stop was at the police station to deliver his samples to Officer Gebbia. He hadn't returned to the station since the Chief fired him, and he felt as if he were somehow trespassing on private property.

The feeling vanished when the office personnel began greeting him like a long-lost brother. His smile disappeared when he glanced up into the dark eyes of Captain Comier.

"How you doing, J.P.?" the head of the Chalmette Police Department said.

"Tolerable. How about you, Chief?"

"About the same. Can you stop by my office for a minute?"

The police officers surrounding J.P. melted away.

J.P. said, "You bet," and followed Captain Comier to his corner office.

Comier shut the door behind them, sat

behind his desk, and said, "Grab a chair."

J.P. had no idea what he was about to hear. His anxiety faded when Captain Comier smiled and said, "I'm glad to see you. You were my best cop. I had a hard time letting you go, though I know burn-out when I see it. You look more relaxed now than I remember in the past ten years."

"Thanks, Captain. Hearing it from you is a salve for my soul."

"That's all I have," Captain Comier said. "Next time, don't wait six months to drop by. Everyone in the department loves you and would give you the shirts off their backs. That includes me. You need help make me the first person you call."

When J.P. left Captain Comier's office, he saw Wayne Gebbia waiting outside his door.

"Good to see you, J.P.," he said. "Did the Chief ream your ass?"

"Captain Comier never really kicked my butt, though it sure felt like it sometimes. If you weren't in uniform, we could sneak out and get a beer."

"If this were ten years ago, I'd take you up on that offer. Things change when you have a wife and two kids."

"I hear you," J.P. said. "I appreciate you helping me."

"You doing a little private investigating now," Wayne asked.

"I'm a hundred percent in on the canine training facility. Two of my partners rescued a woman working at a strip club in the Quarter. I'm trying to find out who she is."

"Come into my office," Wayne said.

Sergeant Gebbia's office was tiny, a metal desk and computer dominating most of the space. The wooden visitor's chair in front of Wayne's desk was so rickety J.P. had to sit up straight to keep from tipping over.

"Sorry about the chair. I rescued it from down the hall. It's the only one I could find small enough to fit here."

"Hell, Wayne, at least you have an office. I never had one, and neither does most of the force."

"Sorry to complain."

"A sergeant I had in the army said when your men quit bitching, you better watch out."

Wayne let the subject drop as he thumbed through a stack of papers.

"The woman named Vixen was working as a prostitute in the Quarter for a notorious pimp named Antoine."

"Does she have an arrest sheet?" J.P. asked.

"Never arrested," Wayne said. "She wasn't working long when one of Antoine's enemies shot and killed him. Antoine was an abusive asshole and had lots of enemies."

"How did Vixen start stripping at Rockie's?"

"She's a striking woman, as you know. Someone spotted her wandering in the Quarter and hired her as a stripper."

"Any idea where she came from?"

"Lots of pimps buy sex slaves brought up by traffickers from the border," Wayne said. "I suspect Antoine was deep into sex trafficking. The woman probably crossed into this country illegally, was captured by traffickers, and transported to New Orleans for purposes of prostitution."

"And she didn't try to escape because of her mental problems," J.P. said.

"One of the many reasons some never escape the sex trade. Most of the sex slaves are homeless teens," Wayne said. "The pimps control them with drugs."

"Vixen is in her thirties and has no sign of

drug use." J.P. handed Wayne the glass and blood sample. "Maybe these will help identify her. Have any idea where she may have come from?"

"Many women who cross the border illegally are from Venezuela, Nicaragua, and Cuba. Countries experiencing war, suppression, and upheaval. Now, there's even an influx of illegal aliens from Ukraine. So far, that's all I have."

J.P. got out of the chair. "Thanks, Wayne. You've given me lots to chew on. I'll get out of your hair so you can get some real work done."

"I always have time to help a friend," Wayne said.

The weather was still sunny and clear when J.P. left the police station. He'd sold his house in Chalmette and had little reason to visit except for groceries and to stop by the animal shelter where he, Jack, and Chief had gotten all their candidates for the canine training facility. Today, he had other reasons for wanting to visit the animal shelter.

The head of the shelter was a woman named Susie Larsen. J.P. and Susie had had a rocky relationship since meeting and had recently won a two-step contest at a club and restaurant called Claws & Craws, the same Cajun restaurant Heather Boudreaux's father owned. Whenever J.P. went to the post office or grocery store, someone always asked him to dance a few steps for them. He'd already decided being known as the Cajun John Travolta didn't suit him.

Susie Larsen enamored J.P., though a long-term bond seemed doomed. Susie was in a relationship with a pretty waitress named Meika. It didn't stop him from dropping by the shelter to flirt with her. He found Susie behind her desk, doing paperwork.

"J.P.," she said. "You here for more dogs?"

"Not today. I dropped by to see your pretty

face."

Susie was more than pretty. She was a blond, blue-eyed beauty who had earned a reputation as a tough, no-nonsense administrator. Susie had turned a Texas animal shelter from a high-kill to a no-kill facility. She stood from her desk with a come-hither smile and hugged him.

"I've been down, and you just made my day," she said.

"What's the problem?"

"Meika and I broke up."

"What happened?" J.P. asked.

"Same old, same old," Susie said. "Among other things, Meika's afraid of long-term commitments."

"Sure it's only Meika to blame?" J.P. said.

"There's a new female in my life," she said.

"Oh?"

"She's down the hall," Susie said. "Want to meet her?"

"I don't want to intrude," J.P. said.

"No way. You're going to love Isabella."

"Where did you meet her?"

"Here at the shelter. She's getting groomed down the hall."

Susie laughed when J.P. rolled his eyes and said, "Excuse me?"

"Isabella's a German shepherd," she said. "A young couple surrendered her to the shelter."

"I hate that," J.P. said. "People shouldn't get a dog in the first place if it isn't for life."

"They had a reason. They lived on a busy street, and Isabella likes to chase cars."

"Why didn't they keep her on a leash?" J.P. asked.

"Isabella is strong and broke free practically every time they went walking."

"Proper training could have remedied that little problem," J.P. said. "People who surrender pets are taking the easy way out."

"My sentiments exactly," Susie said. "In this case, I'm glad they did because I fell in love when I saw her. We bonded almost immediately. I don't know what I'd do without her."

"Seems I remember you telling me you'd never had a pet."

"Things change."

"I'm happy for you," J.P. said.

Susie glanced at the clock on the wall. "Let's have lunch at Chico's. You can meet Isabella before we go."

"Is it Meika's day off? I don't want to cause trouble."

"Meika quit her job there," Susie said. "Isaac retired and gave the place to his son. Meika couldn't stand him."

"What's she doing now?" J.P. asked.

"Still living at my house, though she isn't speaking to me," Susie said. "Let's go. We can talk about Meika some other time."

They entered the grooming room down the hall, where two people were working on a beautiful German shepherd. One of the groomers was clipping Isabella's toenails.

"This is my doll, Isabella," Susie said.

J.P. rubbed Isabella's head. "How you doing, Miss Isabella? She's one beautiful dog."

Susie nodded and hugged the big dog. "You stay with Jason and Kathy, baby," she said. "Mama's going for a bowl of gumbo. I'll take you for a walk when we return."

Chico's was a little hole-in-the-wall café in the older part of Chalmette. It was where Meika had worked when J.P. had first met her and Susie. The wonderful aroma of gumbo and seafood wafted from the kitchen behind the bar of the crowded cafe.

"Looks like we'll have to sit at the bar," J.P.

said.

"Suits me," Susie said. "I'm a sit-at-the-bar kind of a girl."

They were soon drinking cold Abita beer straight from the can and enjoying bowls of gumbo while listening to Zydeco music from the jukebox and the crack of pool balls from the adjacent game room.

"Maybe there's a chance for me now that you and Meika broke up," J.P. said.

"I was thinking the same thing," Susie said.

"Why don't you and Isabella come to the island when you get off work? Spend the weekend with me and Lucky."

"I don't know," Susie said. "I'm worried about Meika. I hate to leave her alone all weekend."

"Then there's still something between you two?"

"I love her, though more like a sister. She's hurting, and it makes me sad."

"Would a new job change things for her?" J.P. asked.

"She needs another job and a change of location. She wanted to move to Biloxi because she loves the beach. Her family lives here in Chalmette, and she couldn't commit to moving away."

"Things have changed on Oyster Island," J.P. said. "Eddie and Frankie Castellano are going at each other tooth and nail."

"Why?" Susie said.

"Long story. The bottom line is Eddie has taken sole control of the Majestic, a film crew is on the island to film a movie, and Basil Doles and Heather Boudreaux have moved there to help. They're planning to marry at the Majestic."

"By a justice of the peace?"

"A full-blown wedding with at least half the people in the parish on the guest list."

"While a movie is filming? How are they going to pull that one off?"

"Beats the hell out of me," J.P. said. "I'm glad it's Eddie's problem and not mine."

"Poor Eddie," Susie said.

"He's hired Odette as his manager, Heather as a waitress-bartender, and a woman Jack and Chief rescued from a strip bar in the French Quarter named Vixen. He needs to hire even more help."

"Vixen? What's the woman's last name?"

"That's the sixty-four dollar question. We don't know, and I'm not sure she does."

"She was a stripper?"

"I think she's suffering from traumatic amnesia. I filed a missing person's report and just left the police station. A friend there is helping me find out who she is and where she's from."

"You think Eddie might hire Meika?"

"I'll ask him," J.P. said.

"What's up," Eddie said when he answered his cell phone.

"Meika and Susie broke up. Meika needs a job and a place to stay. You interested?"

"Give me her number. I'll call her right now. I'll even drive into town and help her pack," Eddie said.

"Call her," J.P. said. "I'm in Chalmette. If she takes the job, I'll bring her to the island."

"I heard most of your conversation," Susie said. "Isabella and I will spend the weekend with you on Oyster Island."

"To rub it in Meika's face?" J.P. said.

"To celebrate. Meika and I are exes. Neither of us is going back. Not ever."

"Sure about that?"

"Positive," she said.

"My heart's still tender from the last time you

broke it."

Susie laughed so hard she almost blew Abita out her nose.

"You're the biggest bullshitter I've ever come across. No woman will ever own your heart."

"Never say never," J.P. said. "I have feelings, too."

"Only in your dick," Susie said.

"That's a low blow."

"I still love you," Susie said, kissing him between bites of gumbo.

They stopped talking when the telephone rang. It was Eddie.

"Meika's taking the job," he said. "She's already packed and ready to go. Can you give her a ride to the island?"

Chapter 12

Meika was waiting on the porch when J.P. reached Susie's house. She began loading her bags into the backseat before he'd turned off the truck's engine.

"That it?" he asked.

"I don't have much," she said.

"Need to stop anyplace in Chalmette? There's not much business once we get out of town."

"I'm ready. Don't wait on me."

J.P. turned the truck south, and they were soon out of town, Meika staring out the passenger window.

"You okay?" J.P. finally said.

"Nervous," she said. "Except for occasional trips to New Orleans, I've never really gone far from Chalmette."

"Oyster Island is in the middle of nowhere. It isn't far from Chalmette. You can visit anytime you like."

Though both were exceptionally attractive, Meika was the antithesis of Susie. While Susie had short blond hair and blue eyes, Meika's hair was dark, like her eyes, and draped to her shoulders.

"I don't even have a car," she said.

"Don't like to drive?'

"Didn't need one. Susie drove me everywhere I wanted to go. How did you hear about our problem?"

"I was in town today on other business and stopped by the shelter to say hi. Susie told me," J.P. said.

"I'll bet she did. She's always had the hots for you."

"Susie never cheated on you with me," J.P. said.

"Don't sound so defensive. Our relationship is over. I'm moving on with my life. What Susie does is her business." When J.P. didn't respond, she said, "Something you want to tell me?"

"Susie and Isabella are coming tonight to spend the weekend with me," J.P. said.

"More power to you," Meika said. "Hope you two have a wonderful time. That's always been part of our problem."

"Me?"

"Not you. Men in general."

"Was Susie cheating on you with another man?"

"We didn't break up because of cheating," Meika said. "We have a basic difference, and it finally raised its ugly head."

By now, they were well out of town, with low-lying marshlands bordering both sides of the narrow blacktop. J.P. slowed the truck when an alligator sunning on the road slid into the coffee-colored water.

"What difference?" he asked.

"I'm a lesbian. I've known it since I was a little girl. I like men, though not as sexual partners. I would never even think of having sex with a man. At least not consensually. Susie is different. She was even married once.

Meika grinned when J.P. said, "I didn't know

that."

"There are many things you don't know about Susie."

"You broke up with Susie because she likes men?"

"One of the many reasons. Susie has a college degree, a house, and a professional job. I don't. Let's stop talking about Susie. Tell me about my new job on Oyster Island."

"Mostly catering to a film crew. The producer and director is a woman named Avory Dorean. She's savvy in an aggressive sort of way, and I think even Eddie is having trouble fielding her commands."

"What does she look like?" Meika asked.

"Blond hair. Blue eyes."

"Does she look like Susie?"

"Nowhere close. Susie's taller and more athletic. Avory's hair is more platinum, and she has...?"

"Big tits?" Meika said.

"Big gorgeous tits," J.P. said. "She wears revealing blouses so everyone notices."

"Love it," Meika said. "Big tits are damn sure one thing Susie doesn't have."

"What are you smiling about?" J.P. asked.

"Susie used to get so pissed when I ogled chicks with great hooters."

"Hell, Meika. We ought to go drinking sometime. You like women as much as I do."

"Sounds like fun to me, long as you don't get drunk and try to cop a feel. I'll knock you on your ass."

J.P. grinned again. "I'll bet you would. Have you ever been to Rockie's on Bourbon Street?"

"What about it?"

"It's a strip club. Jack and Chief like to go there, sit at the pussy bar and watch the naked ladies. They keep sneaking off without me."

"Take me when you go. I love watching naked ladies."

"Hell, Meika, if you weren't a woman, we could have been best friends."

"Keep your hands to yourself, and we can be great friends," Meika said. "Enough about that. Tell me more about this gig I'm getting into."

"You're so pretty. Avory might give you a shot as an actress. If you could only act."

"I can act," Meika said. "My dad still doesn't know I'm a lesbian."

"You got the looks. Like a cross between Angelina Jolie and that woman who starred in *Gone with the Wind.*"

"Vivien Leigh?"

"Way before both our times," J.P. said. "I'm surprised you even know what I'm talking about."

"I watched the movie with my mama and grandmother. They both loved it."

"Well, you're as pretty as she was," J.P. said.

"Stop wasting your time. You're nowhere close to having sex with me. Avory Dorean's a different story."

"The old casting couch trick might get you in the door," J.P. said. "If you can act, you got the body and good looks to go with it. You could be a movie star."

"Shut the hell up," Meika said. "You're wearing me out. Avory's probably straight as an arrow."

"Her friend Lilly isn't," J.P. said.

"Lilly?"

"Lilly Bliss. I met her a few years ago when I was still a cop. She's a writer and was on a sabbatical at Goose Island, a resort for artists and actors."

"Never heard of it," Meika said.

"Not far from here, in Plaquemines Parish. Lilly likes men and women. She and an actress had a little thing going."

"What actress?"

"Stormie Chambers."

"She's old," Meika said.

"She looked pretty damn good when I met her," J.P. said.

"Is she a lesbian?"

"Stormie is anything you want her to be," J.P. said.

"You had sex with her?"

"I don't kiss and tell."

"Lilly Bliss?"

"Lilly and I spent the night together during a hurricane. Believe me when I tell you no sex was involved."

The wooden bridge to the island wobbled when J.P. drove across it. Meika had once visited the island with Susie and spent an eventful night in the old hotel. The sky had turned dark when Eddie met them at the front door to the Majestic.

"Meika," Eddie said. "So glad to see you. We are drinking down the hall in the little bar."

Avory, Lilly, Chief, Jack, and Basil sat around the circular bar as Heather and Odette mixed drinks. Eddie introduced Meika to Avory, Lilly, and Basil. She'd already met everyone else. Meika had Chief move so she could sit between Avory and Lilly. J.P. grinned when he noticed Meika admiring Avory's abundant cleavage.

"See something you like?" Avory said.

Meika grinned and said, "You caught me looking."

"No problem," Avory said. "I'm a bit of an exhibitionist. I like them looked at."

"Then you'll love me," Meika said. "I can't take my eyes off of them. Hope it turns you on."

"Don't know about Avory," Lilly said. "I'm getting hot just listening to you two,"

There were no more stools, so J.P. grabbed a

glass of rum from Heather and found an empty table. He noticed Vixen standing alone in the dark a few tables away. She turned when he called her name.

"Can I talk with you for a minute?" Vixen ignored him. "I spoke to the police about you today."

She had crossed her arms when she bent over the table and said, "I've done nothing to hurt you. Please, leave me alone."

"I wouldn't hurt you for the world. I promise. I was a police officer before moving to the island. I have the feeling you're in trouble. I'm trying to help."

"I don't need your help," Vixen said.

Vixen started to move away when J.P.'s cell phone rang. The distressed look on his face kept her from disappearing into the darkness. Susie was sobbing so loudly on the phone, Vixen could hear it.

"Susie, calm down and tell me what's the matter," J.P. said.

"I stopped to take pictures of a gator in the swamp by the road. When a truck raced past, Isabella chased after it. It ran over her."

"Is she dead?" J.P. asked.

"Barely breathing. There's blood all over the place. The fucking truck driver dragged her and never stopped."

"Where are you? I'll come get you."

"No, I have her in the truck. Can you help her?"

"Hurry. I'll be waiting by Jack's house at the top of the hill." J.P. hung up the phone and said, "Jack, throw me the key to the clinic. We got a casualty coming in."

"We'll come with you," Jack said.

The three men hurried out the door and jumped into J.P.'s truck. Vixen followed them, sliding into the backseat beside Chief. When Jack opened the door to the clinic, she took charge.

"Get washed up," she said.

When Susie raced to a stop in front of the clinic, Jack and Chief followed Vixen with a stretcher.

"Careful," Vixen said. "She may have internal damage."

Dressed in surgical gowns, caps, and masks, Jack and Chief laid Isabella on the operating table. J.P. clutched Susie's arm, trying to hold her back. Vixen stopped her.

"You need to leave. I'll save your dog. I can't do it with you watching." She glanced at J.P. and said, "Take her to Jack's and keep her there."

Vixen shut the door in their faces and hurried to the operating table.

"She is bleeding out. I need to suture her. Do you have Ketamine?"

"What does it do?" Jack said.

"An anesthetic," Vixen said.

Jack brought her a syringe with the Ketamine. Isabella's eyes closed, and her breathing slowed as Vixen began suturing her lacerated veins. She was soon lying in a pool of blood but no longer bleeding."

"What'll we do? We've got no blood," Jack said.

"We'll have to direct transfuse her. Bring your big German shepherd."

"Do dogs all have the same blood type?" Chief asked.

Vixen shook her head. "Some breeds tend to be universal donors. German shepherds are one of those breeds."

"What if he's not?" Chief said.

"This dog is going to die without a transfusion. Please bring your dog. It's the only chance we have."

J.P. was sitting on the couch, trying to console a near-hysterical Susie, when Chief burst through the door and whistled.

"Ol' Joe, I need you."

"How's it going?" J.P. asked.

Chief didn't answer as he and Ol' Joe hurried out the door.

"I can't take this," Susie said. "I'm helping."

"No, you're not. Vixen will save her."

"Vixen, the stripper?"

"I don't know why she was stripping on Bourbon Street. Whatever her name is, I'm pretty sure she's an experienced surgical vet. Give her a chance."

Jack and Vixen had rigged a table for Ol' Joe to lie on and needles to tap into the two dog's veins.

"Can you lift him?" Vixen said.

Ol' Joe didn't resist when Chief put him on the makeshift table. He lay still when Vixen patted the dog's head and put pressure on his neck. She quickly found a vein and inserted a needle into it.

"How is this going to work?" Chief asked.

"Gravity," Vixen said.

She only nodded when Chief asked, "You sure about this?"

The direct transfusion was soon dripping blood into Isabella's vein. As it did, Vixen and Jack cleaned the dog's wounds.

"Do you have antibiotics?" Vixen asked.

Chief brought her a syringe without answering and watched as Vixen injected Isabella.

"What else?" Jack said.

"Cover her with a warm blanket," Vixen said. "Let me see what drugs you have."

Vixen loaded another syringe and used it to inject Isabella.

"What did you inject her with?" Jack asked.

"A drug to help prevent her from going into shock," Vixen said.

"What now?" Chief asked.

"We wait," Vixen said.

"Is she going to make it?" Jack asked.

"We have done all we can. Isabella is in the hand of God."

The transfusion was completed and Ol' Joe lay on the floor beside the operating table, refusing to move. Jack, Chief, and Vixen pulled up chairs. They were half asleep when Isabella opened her eyes. Vixen smiled for the first time.

"She is going to be okay," Vixen said.

"How do you know?" Jack asked.

"I know. Go get J.P. and Susie."

Susie's eyes were red, her face puffy when Jack motioned them to come with him.

"I can't go in there," Susie said.

J.P. followed Jack into the operating room and said, "Is Isabella going to make it?"

Vixen nodded, "No broken bones, only contusions and lacerations. She lost lots of blood. We transfused her with the help of Ol' Joe."

"Will she be...?"

"Up and walking in a few days. In a few weeks, as good as new."

"Thank God!" J.P. said.

Vixen began removing her medical gear. When she reached the door, she turned around.

"I'll return tomorrow to check on her."

Vixen walked down the hill toward the Majestic without covering her head. Another storm was moving across the island, the rain falling again.

Chapter 13

Isabella slept peacefully, a funnel collar around her neck to prevent her from biting at her stitches.

"Isabella survived," J.P. said. "She'll be here in the morning."

"I saw how far the truck dragged her," Susie said. "You don't have to lie to me. I know she's dead."

Sensing Susie was in shock, J.P. patted her hand.

"Ol' Joe is with Isabella," Chief said. "He'll come and get us if she takes a turn for the worse. I need a drink."

Chief poured himself a mug of rum and one for Susie. She sat the cup on the plank table.

"I'm going to sit on Jack's couch, close my eyes and try to get some sleep," she said.

"Let's get your bag out of the car," J.P. said. "You can sleep in my Airstream. I'll take the couch for the night."

"You don't have to do that," Susie said."

"Get some rest," he said. "You'll feel better in the morning."

J.P. grabbed a couple of the western dusters and handed one to Susie. They were both already wearing cowboy hats.

"Put this on. It'll keep us dry until we get your bags."

Jack and Chief were still drinking rum at the plank table when J.P. returned from situating Susie in his trailer. The crackling fire in the stone fireplace provided a sense of warmth, even if the weather was only chilly and not frigid. The dogs were asleep in their beds in front of the fire.

"You boys did a wonderful job with Isabella. Thank you," he said.

"It's Vixen you need to thank. If she isn't a fully trained vet, I don't know who is," Chief said.

"She saved Susie's dog's life," Jack said. "That's a fact. This accident spoiled your weekend of pleasure."

"Won't be the first time. I can feel a trip to Pauline's coming on."

"Take me with you this time," Chief said.

"What are you talking about?" Jack said. "Lilly Bliss was all over you earlier tonight."

"She probably won't remember who I am next time I see her."

"She'll remember," Jack said.

The rain had returned with a vengeance, thunder rattling the windows as Jack poured more rum.

"What did you find out about Vixen?" Chief asked.

"Officer Gebbia said she was working in the French Quarter as a prostitute for a pimp named Antoine."

"No way!" Jack said.

"He thinks she got abducted by sex traffickers," J.P. said. "When someone shot and killed Antoine, Vixen wandered the French Quarter until someone hired her to strip at Rockie's."

"Why would she be crossing the border from

Mexico?" Chief asked.

"Don't know," J.P. said.

"You'll have to share the couch with me," Chief said. "It's too wet to make it back to my teepee."

"You take it, Chief. The seat reclines in my truck. I'll sleep in it."

"Better have more rum before you go."

"It has been a long day, and I'm half asleep. Catch you two tomorrow."

When J.P. climbed into his truck and out of the rain, he realized he was more tired than he'd thought. He was about to recline the seat and turn in for the night when lightning flashed by the beach, and he saw something. Although far down the hill, it looked like someone walking toward the surf."

"Can't be," he said.

Despite his retirement from the police force, J.P. couldn't quit acting like a cop. Cranking the truck, he started down the hill to get a closer look at someone walking across the beach. He had always had better than 20-20 vision.

It was Vixen. She waded into the breaking waves and didn't stop when he yelled at her. Her head had already disappeared beneath the water when he rushed in after her.

When J.P. reached the spot in the choppy water where Vixen had disappeared, he dived beneath the storm-charged waves. His lungs were about to explode when he grabbed a hank of hair and pulled her to the surface.

Vixen was unconscious when J.P. dragged her out of the water, laid her on the sand, and began administering CPR. He could feel a slight pulse and kept after it. Finally, she coughed and blew saltwater out her nose and mouth. Her tears quickly became hysterical.

"Why did you save me? I want to die."

"Not on my watch, you're not," J.P. said.

She began pounding his chest with her fists. "Get off of me," she said.

J.P. stood and said, "You're not returning to the water."

When she began screaming hysterically, J.P. yanked her to her feet, grabbed her shoulders, and shook her.

"Get control," he said. "Your family doesn't want you dead."

She gasped for air and asked, "What do you know about my family?"

"I was a police officer. I'm going to find them for you."

"They're all dead," Vixen said.

"How do you know?" When Vixen didn't answer, he said, "You're coming with me."

J.P. pulled her gently to his truck. Vixen mumbled something in a language he didn't understand.

"I'm not going to hurt you. Can't you trust me for a little bit?"

"Take me to my room," Vixen said.

"Ain't gonna happen," he said. "You're going to spend the night in Jack's recliner, and I'm going to be there to ensure you do."

Jack and Chief were still awake and playing gin when J.P. entered the house, pulling Vixen behind him.

"What the hell!" Jack said.

"Vixen tried to drown herself," J.P. said. "We're staying the night with you."

"She can have the couch," Chief said. "I've slept on the floor plenty of times."

"She's taking the recliner," J.P. said. "Do you have any dry clothes we can wear?"

Jack threw them both towels. "There are robes in the bathroom," Jack said.

J.P. reached inside the bathroom door and

grabbed a robe.

"Change out of those wet clothes," he said. "If you're in the bathroom more than five minutes, I'm busting the door down,"

Vixen was dressed in the robe, her hair dry when she exited the bathroom. When she sat at the plank table, Jack quickly slid a steaming bowl of gumbo in front of her. Vixen stared at it as if she'd never eaten gumbo.

"Let me put a dollop of rice in it for you," Jack said. "Chief?"

"Why not?" Chief said, sitting beside Vixen.

Vixen stared at him when he began pouring hot sauce on his gumbo.

"What is that?" she asked.

"Louisiana hot sauce," he said. He put some on the tip of his finger and held it to her lips. "Taste it."

When Vixen pointed to her gumbo, Chief laced it with hot sauce and watched as she took a bite.

"More," she said.

Jack and J.P. grinned. "You're going to burn all the hair off your tongue," J.P. said.

"Damn!" Jack said. "That girl's hardcore."

"Good," she said.

The rescued cocker Mollie had exited her bed by the fire and approached the recliner. J.P. held his breath, hoping Jack's hot bowl of gumbo had vanquished Vixen's suicidal tendencies. As if to make sure, Jack gave her another bowl which she laced with plenty of Louisiana hot sauce. She went to the recliner, raised the footrest, and closed her eyes. Jack covered her with a blanket.

Chief lifted the cocker and placed her in Vixen's lap.

"She wants to sleep with you," he said.

"She is afraid of me," Vixen said.

"I don't think so," Chief said. "Mollie knows who saved her life."

"She's family now," J.P. said.

"I have no family," Vixen said.

"Mollie, Jack, Chief, and me are your family. You're stuck with us."

Chief had sprawled on the couch, a colorful blanket pulled up to his neck. Mollie relaxed in Vixen's lap, and her eyes closed. Vixen rubbed the dog's head and then shut her own eyes.

"I'm hitting the sack," Jack said. "Sorry I have no more beds."

"I'm going back to the truck," J.P. said. "Hope you don't mind me wearing your robe until my clothes dry."

"No problem," Jack said. "I've learned to keep several in the bathroom."

J.P.'s clothes, except for his boots and cowboy hat, were drenched, and it was still raining outside. Pulling his boots over his bare feet, he put on his hat and ran for the truck. When he got in, he realized the seat was uncomfortably wet. Cranking the engine, he started down the hill to the Majestic.

It was late, and the hotel dark when he arrived. Eddie had a couch in his room and would let him sleep there for the night. He would have stayed in the truck if it were anyone other than Eddie. Eddie would understand his predicament without being judgmental.

A scream pierced the silence as he entered the front door. With his cop persona kicking in again, he raced up the stairs and found the lights on in Eddie's suite.

"What's the screaming about?" he said.

Eddie was wrapped in a sheet and sitting on the side of his bed. Avory and Lilly stood beside him when J.P. burst through the door. Avory looked resplendent in her blue nightgown, Lilly's red nightgown even more striking. J.P.'s face turned the color of Lilly's gown when he realized his robe had opened, and Lilly and Avory were staring at his private parts. He quickly corrected the wardrobe malfunction.

"What the hell happened?"

"A strange woman with vampire fangs came through the wall in my room," Avory said. "I ran to Lilly's. The ghostly woman followed us into the hall. We woke Eddie, and he let us in."

"Eddie sleeps in the nude," Lilly said.

"Sorry," Eddie said. "I don't usually have people pounding on my door at two in the morning."

"Who was that woman?" Avory said.

"Laurel, the hotel's resident ghost," Eddie said.

"She has fangs," Lilly said.

"She was a vampire before gangsters drove a stake through her heart. Now, she's a ghost."

"And what are you doing here with your dick hanging out?" Avory said.

J.P.'s face flushed again. "I got drenched," he said. "Jack lent me this robe. The seat in my truck is wringing wet, so I drove here to sleep on Eddie's couch."

"You have a beautiful Airstream trailer. Why don't you sleep there?" Lilly said.

"Susie Larsen's using it," J.P. said.

"Who is Susie Larsen?" Avory asked.

"My ex-roommate," a person at the door said.

It was Meika and Odette dressed in revealing nighties.

"We heard the screams," Odette said. "Sounded like someone was getting murdered."

"They had a visit from Laurel," Eddie said.

"Who is Laurel?" Meika asked.

"The ghost of a vampire who lives here at the hotel. She's benevolent and wouldn't harm a soul."

"Susie's on the island to see you," Meika said. "Why aren't you in the trailer with her?"

"Her dog got run over on their way to the island. Vixen saved the dog. Susie was so upset I let her sleep in the trailer alone."

"Vixen, the housekeeper?" Avory said.

"She's more than a housekeeper," J.P. said. "I believe she's suffering from traumatic amnesia and is a skilled surgical veterinarian."

"A surgical vet was stripping at Rockie's?" Odette said. "What's her story?"

"I'm trying to find out," J.P. said.

"Where is this stripper/surgical vet?" Meika asked.

"Asleep at Jack's," J.P. said. "She tried to drown herself, and I had to fish her out of the Gulf. It's how my clothes and truck got wet. Can I sleep on your couch, Eddie?"

"Be my guest," Eddie said.

"I'm not returning to my room," Avory said.

"Me either," Lilly said.

Odette grinned and said, "Slumber party. Break out the booze."

Meika sat on the couch, and Odette joined her.

Eddie broke out the rum. "Help yourself," he said. "I'm going back to sleep."

Before Eddie could return to his bed, Heather, dressed as scantily as Odette and Meika, pushed through the door.

"I heard screams," she said.

Chapter 14

The storm had passed over the island sometime during the night. Eddie awoke when the sun shined into his eyes, the aroma of the coffee he brewed wafting from the little kitchenette, soon waking J.P.

"Where'd everybody go?" J.P. asked.

"After you dozed off, Avory ripped me up one side and down the other for letting a ghost invade her room. When she finally ran out of breath, she and Lilly stomped off."

"What about Heather, Meika, and Odette?"

"Meika and Odette could hear what was coming down and had the good sense to clear out before Avory started in on them," Eddie said. "That woman's going to be a major pain in the ass until she gets her movie filmed."

"What the hell were you supposed to do about a ghost in her room?" J.P. asked.

"Beats the hell out of me," Eddie said.

"What about Heather?" J.P. asked.

"She tried to talk to me about her wedding when Avory got in her face. I told her there would be no wedding until Avory concluded filming. Heather ran out of here in tears."

"How long will it take to make the movie?" J.P.

asked.

"No earthly idea," Eddie said. "When I tried to broach the subject with Avory, she got even shittier with me."

"I can tell you're in a bad mood," J.P. said.

"What was your first clue?"

Someone knocked on the door. It was Odette, and she had a bottle of rum with which she laced Eddie's coffee.

"Thought you might need this," she said.

"Thanks, Odette. I believe you're going to make a hand."

"I couldn't help overhearing you and Avory last night. Can't Heather wait an extra week or two for her wedding?" she said.

"Apparently not, and it has put me in an untenable situation."

J.P. laced his coffee with the rum. "How so?"

"I promised Basil he and Heather could host their wedding here. I made the promise because I need Basil's help fighting Frankie."

"What difference can a few weeks make?" J.P. asked.

Eddie poured more rum into his coffee. "Heather's feuding with her dad, who sounds as if he's as hard-headed as she is. She's hell-bent on having the biggest wedding St. Bernard Parish has ever seen."

"You're going to have to lay down the law," Odette said.

"And take the chance of losing Basil's legal assistance? I don't think so. Frankie has hired every lawyer in Chalmette. Basil is the only help I have. I need him."

"Basil's a smart man," J.P. said. "Maybe he can talk some sense into Heather."

"He's already tried."

"Glad it's your problem and not mine and Odette's," J.P. said.

"You're wrong. Frankie is determined to kick everyone off this island," Eddie said. "If that happens, I lose the Majestic, you lose the canine training facility, and Odette loses her dream job."

"I thought you said our chance of winning is as good as a slam dunk," J.P. said.

"I was shooting off my mouth," Eddie said. "Trying to convince me and everyone else. Trouble is bravado doesn't win lawsuits."

"There's a chance we can lose?" J.P. said.

"Maybe fifty-fifty. Frankie has more resources than we do, and he plays dirty."

"How so?" J.P. asked.

Odette had left the door ajar. Basil entered and answered J.P.'s question.

"Our case involves American Indian Law and should properly be heard in Federal Court. Frankie is suing us in state court," Basil said,

"Talk to the judge," J.P. said.

"Not that simple," Eddie said. "Frankie's lawyers have raised enough questions regarding state law to muddy the water. We're stuck with answering all their complaints even though there's only one correct answer in the scheme of things."

"I know all the parish judges. They're honest and don't take bribes. Can't the presiding judge see the problem?" J.P. said.

"It's not just the law," Basil said. "Political pressure, popular opinion, and even personalities come into play. Eddie and I are trying to plug a hole in the dike while Frankie's exploding sticks of dynamite in the water."

"Damn!" J.P. said. "Don't sound good. Anything I can do to help?"

"Thanks," Eddie said. "Basil and I have everything under control."

Odette started for the door. "I'm going downstairs and slit my wrist," she said.

"It's not that bad," Eddie said.

"Tell it to Heather," Basil said. "I ran into her in the hall downstairs, and she unloaded on me."

"She's upset," Odette said. "Meika and I will keep her busy today and take her mind off the wedding."

"Thanks," Basil said.

"As Eddie says, we're all in on this together. You and Eddie concentrate on defending the island. We have reinforcements coming today."

"Who?" Eddie asked.

"Paula and Jimmie are on their way here. Paula will think of something."

Paula and Jimmie Boutet were part owners of the canine training facility. Jimmie owned a hardware store in Chalmette, and they were spending their weekdays in town and weekends on the island.

Paula was a Cajun traiteur, and practically everyone in Chalmette thought she was a witch. Everyone was right. Odette was barely down the stairs when her cell phone rang. It was Paula.

"Lady and I took a walk across the beach. We're at your tent. Where are you?"

Odette had lived in a pop tent on the beach with her dog Mudbug for nearly a year. She'd only moved into the Majestic after Eddie had hired her and made it a requirement of her employment. Lady was Paula's beautiful golden retriever.

"Eddie hired me to manage the Majestic. He had me move to the hotel as part of the deal," Odette said.

"When did this happen?"

"A few days ago."

"And you didn't call to let me know?"

"I wanted to tell you in person," Odette said. "This is a lifetime opportunity, and I'm so happy."

"I'm happy for you and so proud of you."

"Thank you, sister. Stay right there. Bruiser

and Mudbug have been cooped up in the room and are dying to go for a walk."

Paula and Lady were waiting on the beach when Odette and her two dogs came jogging across the sand. Odette hugged Paula and then held her at arm's length.

"I love your hair," she said. "When did you decide to lighten it?"

"Last week," Paula said. "I'm never going to be a blond like you."

"But why? Your dark hair was beautiful."

"I've had dark hair all my life. I wanted to try something different."

Paula blushed when Odette asked, "Does Jimmie like it?"

"You kidding me? We haven't had sex as good since our honeymoon."

"Maybe he pretended he was getting a little strange."

"Exactly," Paula said. "I let the thought pass and enjoyed myself."

"You're okay with it?"

"Jimmie can't keep his big mouth shut. I'd be the first to know if he ever had an affair."

"Did you leave Jimmie at Jack's?" Odette asked.

"He got a call from the hardware store. He dropped me off and returned to Chalmette to take care of a problem," Paula said.

Paula shook her head when Odette said, "Something serious?"

"He'll be back on the island later. Who is the short-haired blond at Jack's?"

"Her name is Vixen. She was stripping at Rockie's and sleeping beside the dumpster. Chief and Jack rescued her when the bouncer threw her out the door," Odette said.

"Vixen? Is that her real name?"

"Probably not. She doesn't talk much and has

a foreign accent. J.P. thinks she has traumatic amnesia. Last night, he fished her out of the Gulf when she tried to drown herself."

"My God!" Paula said. "I didn't see J.P. at Jack's."

"Susie Larsen broke up with her squeeze Meika, who's working here at the Majestic now. Susie and J.P. planned to shack up for the weekend. It didn't work out because her dog got run over. Vixen performed surgery and saved Susie's dog."

"Excuse me? Vixen's a vet?"

Odette nodded. "And a damn good one."

"How did J.P. know she is a vet? Did she tell him?"

"Vixen, Jack, and Chief rescued a dog on their way from New Orleans to the island," Odette said. "The cocker was injured, and Vixen patched her. J.P. said you could tell she was no amateur."

"Things have been busy. What else has happened since Jimmie and I were here last?"

"A bunch," Odette said. "There's a crew here filming a Prohibition Era movie with the Majestic as the backdrop. Eddie hired Heather Boudreaux, and she and her fiancée Basil Doles have moved to the island."

"How did Heather's dad let her escape Craws & Claws?"

"Eddie said he and Heather had a falling out."

"Because?" Paula said.

"Don't know. Basil is helping Eddie with the lawsuit on the island ownership. Part of the deal to get Basil to help him was to promise to host their wedding at the Majestic."

"Does Eddie know what he's getting into?"

"Need you even ask? Eddie's never been married and probably knows less about weddings than most men."

"I hear that," Paula said. "Jimmie and I almost broke up over ours. My mom and I were so stressed."

"If I ever get married, it'll be in Vegas," Odette said.

"Just as long as Jimmie and I are invited," Paula said.

"You have to be there. You're going to be my maid of honor."

"I can hardly wait. Tell me about this movie."

"A blond named Avory Dorean is the producer/director. She has bigger balls than most men I know. She informed Heather there would be no wedding until her crew completed filming."

"How did Heather react?"

"Not well," Odette said.

"I can imagine. The sand is damp. Did it rain here last night?

"All day and most of the night. I love this sunshine."

So did the dogs, all three romping in the breaking waves.

"Wish we could join them. It's too nippy for me," Paula said.

"I can't wait until the weather gets warmer," Odette said.

"Me either," Paula said. "What else have I missed?"

"A bimbo named Lilly Bliss."

"An airhead?" Paula asked.

"She's the writer of the movie and no airhead."

"What does she look like, and why did you call her a bimbo?"

"She's attractive in a bookish sort of way. Curly black hair, though not Cajun black. Short with a good figure. She's Avory's best friend."

"Are they. . . ?"

"They might like each other. Lilly Bliss loves men. We were drinking in the little bar last night, and she had her hands all over Chief. I was afraid she would grab his dick in front of everyone. She told us she knew J.P., and they'd hooked up."

"Doesn't surprise me," Paula said. "J.P. isn't selective."

"That's a fact," Odette said. "He's finally stopped making passes at me. Have any idea why Heather and her dad are fighting?"

"Harvey thinks the sun rises and sets over him. His wife Carol allows him to get away with it."

"How well do you know them?" Odette asked.

"They're my parent's best friends. Heather was a change-of-life baby. Almost ten years younger than me. Her brother, Matt, is my age."

"Matt?"

"He's dreamy," Paula said. "Don't ever mention his name around Jimmie."

"Why is that?" Odette said,

"Matt and I grew up together. While our parents played cards, Matt and I played doctor in the woodshed. No telling what would have happened if we hadn't got caught."

"Who caught you?"

"Mom and Carol," Paula said. "Our dads would have killed us both. It was the last time they ever brought Matt when they came to play cards."

"Does Jimmie know?"

Paula nodded. "When he found out I wasn't a virgin, he kept after me until I told him everything."

"How old were you?" Odette said.

"Old enough to know better."

"You can't hold grudges about something that happened in high school."

"Tell it to Jimmie," Paula said.

"I don't think so," Odette said. "Maybe your mom can talk to Heather's mom about the wedding. Find out what the problem is."

"Maybe," Paula said. "Sounds as if it's been a three-ring circus on Oyster Island."

"Thank God you're here. It's going to take a little witchcraft to straighten out things."

"Hope I'm up to it," Paula said.

Chapter 15

When Odette and Paula finished their visit and entered the kitchen of the Majestic, they found Heather crying and Meika red in the face.

"What's the matter?" Paula asked.

"That bitch, Avory, just ate our asses out because we don't have lunch prepared."

"She never told me she expected us to start providing meals today," Odette said.

"She's on her way upstairs to report us to Eddie," Meika said.

"Don't panic. It isn't lunch yet. Let's see what we have to work with." After looking around the kitchen, Paula said, "This equipment looks new. It can't be original."

"Frankie updated the kitchen with modern appliances," Odette said.

"Well, he spared no expense," Paula said.

Eddie burst through the kitchen doors. "I hope that bitch Avory wasn't as nasty to you as she was to me," he said.

"She was," Meika said.

"Don't give her the satisfaction of knowing she upset you."

"You're one to talk," Odette said. "You could

light a match on your forehead."

"I've dealt with hanging judges that weren't as vicious as she is," Eddie said.

Paula didn't stop her search to listen to Eddie's ranting.

"Appliances weren't the only things Frankie bought. There's both French and flat loaf bread, and it's fresh," Paula said.

"Before Frankie and I got into a pissing match, he hired a commercial produce company to deliver food. I got a bill on Friday and was going to cancel the service," Eddie said.

"Good thing you didn't," Paula said. "We'll need everything here if we're supposed to start today. It looks as though someone knew what they were doing."

"Frankie's wife Adele ran a successful Italian restaurant in Metairie for years. I'll bet she told Frankie what to order or prepared the list herself. Hope someone knows how to cook Italian." Meika, Heather, and Odette raised their hands. "What about Muffulettas and po'boys?"

"All of us," Odette said. "We all have Cajun parents."

Paula shut the door of one of the commercial refrigerators.

"Frankie stocked the fridge with Italian cold cuts, fresh oysters, and shrimp," she said. "Even jars of olive salad. How many people are we feeding?"

"Twenty to thirty," Eddie said. "They're in a union; the union bylaws govern their breaks and meals. Avory informed me they'll be ready to eat in thirty minutes."

"Meika, fry some shrimp and make ten oyster po'boys. Heather, you prepare ten shrimp po'boys. Odette and I will knock out twenty Muffulettas. There are commercial tea makers and coffee urns still in boxes. Can you get them ready for us, Eddie?"

"I'm on it," he said.

"You're going to need help," Odette said. "I'll call Jack and Chief."

Eddie was frustrated trying to assemble the tea and coffee makers. Jack got the equipment into working order and brewing on the buffet line when he and Chief appeared with a steaming aluminum kettle.

"What is it?" Paula asked.

"It was our dinner," Chief said.

"Gumbo," Odette said. "Thanks, Chief."

"Thank Jack. He started the pot last night."

"We have lots of food. You won't go hungry," Odette said.

Avory watched as Ben Biondo's construction crew began appearing for lunch. Meika and Heather smiled as they served the workers. Paula made sure they dined using antique dishes and silverware and that there was bottled water and soft drinks for those who desired something other than coffee or tea.

Like a proper restaurant host, Eddie stood at the end of the buffet and introduced himself to everyone. All the workers were smiling and satisfied when they returned to work.

"I'm impressed," Avory said. "That's as slick a catering operation as I've seen on a movie set." Before leaving, she added. "Don't let it go to your heads. The crew breaks at three; some will want dinner by six."

"Do we have anything to give them for snacks?" Meika asked.

"Avory said no sugar," Eddie said.

"We have dates, olives, trail mix, and fresh fruit," Paula said. "The three o'clock break will take no time to prepare."

"What about dinner?" Heather said.

"Don't give them a big choice," Jack said. "Two different entrées max. Steam some vegetables and warm the rest of the gumbo."

"We have no menus," Odette said.

"Don't need them," Jack said. "Chalkboard. There's a big one still in the box against the wall."

"No alcohol," Eddie said. "If they want to imbibe, they can do it at the bar and pay for it themselves. Avory said not to let them run a tab."

Paula smiled when she noticed Chief eyeing the leftover Muffulettas. "Help yourself, Chief. We can't serve the leftover food again."

"That goes for everyone," Odette said. "No use letting our good work go to waste."

They were soon sitting around a kitchen table enjoying leftover po'boys and muffulettas.

"I'm exhausted, and we've only served one meal," Meika said. "Two breaks and three meals daily will be a real pain in the butt."

"Especially if we have to waitress and then mix drinks until all hours," Heather said.

"We need a chef," Eddie said.

"You serious?" Meika asked.

"I'm not sure how I would compensate a chef," Eddie said. "If I had someone in mind, I'd figure it out."

"Just add it to Avory's tab," Paula said.

"What if we have no business after the production crew leaves?" Eddie said.

"You'll have to worry about it later. Right now, we need someone," Odette said.

"Isaac Guillot is available," Meika said.

"Who's that?" Eddie asked.

"You know him," Meika said. "He owned Chico's in Chalmette. He gave the little café to his son when he retired. He called me last night and said he was dying of boredom. He'd cook for you in a heartbeat."

"Is he reliable?" Eddie asked.

"You kidding? He cooked for everyone in Chalmette for thirty years. He could do all the cooking and free up Heather and me to do the waitressing and bartending."

"I wonder how much money he'll need," Eddie said.

"He lived over the café. Money was never his thing. He'll probably work for free to get out of the apartment he's in," Meika said.

"Give him a place to live and a purpose in life," Paula said. "As Meika said, Isaac isn't fixated on money. He's probably saved every dime he ever made and has no idea what to do with it."

"What about his wife?" Eddie asked.

"She left the old man years ago," Meika said. "Without his Chico's customers, he's grown lonely."

"I'm running out of rooms to house the staff," Eddie said.

"I have the answer to that problem," Chief said. "A dozen houses are on the other side of the storage warehouse. No one has occupied them in decades. They have a great view of the bay."

"Can you call Isaac for me, Meika?"

Meika was smiling when she got off the phone. "He's on his way," she said. "He'll be here in time to help us cook dinner."

"Must not have had much to pack," Eddie said.

"He probably never unpacked," Meika said.

"Thanks, Meika." Eddie shook Jack and Chief's hands. "You were all a big help to me."

"Does that mean Jack and I get to eat here for free?" Chief asked.

"Free food and drinks for the rest of your lives," Eddie said. "Unless Frankie prevails in court."

"Don't say that," Jack said.

"Basil and I won't let that happen. I'll find

Ben Biondo and see if he'll look at the vacant houses and tell me what it'll take to make them livable."

"I'll come with you," Odette said. "If Mr. Biondo wants to see the houses, I'll drive you in the ATV."

"You won't know where to look unless I go too," Chief said.

"Then let's do it," Eddie said. "Ben's probably in the office complex. I'm anxious to see what progress they've made there."

"I'll stay and help the girls," Paula said.

"Thanks, Paula," Eddie said. "I owe you one."

"Don't worry," she said. "I won't let you forget."

Eddie couldn't believe it when they entered the office complex. Everyone's office, including his own, was up and running. There were even computers, desk phones, and a large printer shared by all. A young woman he didn't recognize occupied a desk in the reception area and looked as if she worked there.

"Help you?" she asked.

"I'm Eddie Toledo. I have an office here."

The young woman said, "I'm Sara, the receptionist for the film crew. I'll be here every day until filming is complete."

With sun-bleached hair and a California surfer girl's tan, Sara looked more like a would-be starlet than a receptionist. She noticed and smiled when Eddie checked her hand for a wedding ring.

"We're all having drinks later in the little bar down the hall," Eddie said. "Join us when you get off work, and you can tell me all your Hollywood secrets."

Sara grinned and said, "You have a deal. The little travel trailer I'm staying in gets pretty boring."

"I'll see to it we liven things up for you," Eddie said.

Odette was shaking her head when Eddie finally released Sara's hand. Ben Biondo had heard them talking and peeked into the reception area.

"Your office is ready," he said. "Want to see it?"

"You bet I do," Eddie said.

Avory had gotten the biggest office though Eddie's was nothing to complain about.

"Like it?" Ben asked.

"You kidding? I never expected polished wood floors and mahogany paneling."

"We pulled up the old carpeting and wallpaper," Ben said. "Let me show you the other offices."

Ben knew who approved his paycheck, and no one was surprised Avory's office was the plushest with Oriental carpets and original paintings on the wall. They found Basil keyboarding in his office.

"Love the digs," Eddie said. "I wasn't expecting as much."

"You'll get used to it," Basil said. I'm working on answers to Frankie's petition."

"Keep at it. I have questions for Ben," Eddie said.

"Hit me," Ben said.

"Is there some other place to talk?" Eddie asked. "I don't want to interrupt a man with a head of steam."

Ben nodded. "Let's go to the conference room."

"We have a conference room?" Eddie asked.

"Nothing but the finest," Ben said.

They followed the construction manager down the hall to a paneled room with a mahogany conference table and plush antique chairs that looked like no one had ever sat in them. Plans and blueprints covered the table.

"Nice," Eddie said.

"What can I help you with?"

"You've met Odette. Chief tells me some vacant houses are close by. Could you take a look and tell me what it might take to make them livable?"

"No problem," Ben said.

Eddie made sure he spoke to Sara on the way out the door.

"See you later for drinks?" he said.

Sara smiled and said, "Wouldn't miss it."

When they were out the door, Odette said, "Don't you ever take a break from chasing pussy?"

"Be kind," he said.

Eddie's reply didn't wash away Odette's frown as they motored past the warehouse to the houses overlooking the bay.

"They're gorgeous and so unusual," Odette said.

Decks surrounded the one-storied structures, their oversized roofs covering the decking. They all had large picture windows affording great views of the scenic bay.

"They look like vacation bungalows on an island paradise," Eddie said.

"Exactly how the planners meant them to appear," Chief said.

"Let's have a look inside," Ben said.

They soon visited all of the houses. Behind the homes, a walking garden had grown up around the cobblestone paths winding through it, fountains and statuary conveying the appearance of a French Quarter courtyard.

"The houses are all electrified and run on a common generator," Ben said.

"They used generators back then?" Odette

asked.

"Since the early 1900s," Ben said. "The old generator is an antique and needs replacing with a modern, more powerful, and efficient unit."

"So you think they're useable?" Eddie asked.

"They will be when my crew finishes with them. One thing, though," Ben said.

"What's that?" Eddie said.

"My crew is cramped and getting grumpy. We'll get the houses up and running if you let us occupy however many we need until filming is complete."

"Save a couple for my staff. You're welcome to the rest," Eddie said.

Ben shook Eddie's hand and said, "Plenty of houses here for everyone. We'll begin tomorrow."

"Any idea when they'll be ready?"

"My crew is the best in the business. We'll sleep in these lovely structures tomorrow night if we get an early start."

Eddie gave Chief and Odette a wink and said, "Wonderful."

Chapter 16

When J.P. returned from the Majestic the morning after rescuing Vixen, he noticed Susie's car was gone. Still dressed in Jack's bathrobe, he knocked on the door of the Airstream. When no one answered, he entered the trailer, showered, and changed into clean jeans and a dark blue Western shirt.

Smoke was curling out of Jack's chimney when he left the trailer. Jack was at the stove cooking, and Vixen on the couch, Mollie's head in her lap.

"Where's Chief?" J.P. asked.

"Left earlier to feed his chickens and scrawny cat," Jack said. "You're late for breakfast. You probably need some bacon and eggs and hot coffee."

"You're reading my mind," J.P. said.

"Didn't have to," Jack said. "I could hear your stomach growling over here. What did you do with Susie?"

"She isn't in the trailer, and her car is gone. She was so upset about Isabella it wouldn't surprise me if she returned to Chalmette."

"Without checking on Isabella? That dog has been looking for her all morning," Jack said. "Her ears perked up when you walked in the door."

"Why isn't she in the clinic?" J.P. asked.

"Chief brought her here and fixed a bed for her in front of the fireplace. She likes being with the other dogs, though she is too gimpy to play outside with them."

"Hell, she was hit by a truck and lucky to be alive."

"You can thank Miss Vixen for that. I never saw a better surgeon during my time in the Merchant Marines."

Vixen remained impassive on the couch as if she hadn't heard Jack's compliment. J.P. turned his attention to Isabella.

The dog was alert, her tail thumping the floor when J.P. patted her head. Vixen continued to stare out the window when J.P. sat beside her on the couch.

"You okay?" he asked.

Vixen remained silent.

Rain storms had blown over the island, leaving sunshine and warmer weather in their wake. J.P. sat at the plank table, eating bacon and eggs and drinking Jack's hot coffee.

"Know anything about training dogs, Miss Vixen?"

Vixen didn't answer. When a vehicle pulled outside, J.P. got up to see if it was Susie. It wasn't.

"I had a problem at the hardware store and had to return to Chalmette to take care of it," Jimmie said as he pushed through the door. "Paula's with Odette."

"Glad you're back," J.P. said.

Vixen nodded when J.P. introduced her to Jimmie. Feeling the chill in the air, Jimmie patted Isabella's head.

"What happened to you, girl?" he asked.

"She's Susie Larsen's dog. Susie was on her

way to the island last night. A truck ran over her when she stopped to take a picture of an alligator."

"I passed Susie up the road sitting on the hood of her car," Jimmie said. "When I stopped to see what was wrong, she said she was okay."

"She was upset about Isabella," J.P. said. "Vixen patched her up and saved her life."

Jack didn't allow Jimmie to ask about Vixen's surgical ability.

"Want some breakfast?" he asked.

"Had breakfast in Chalmette. Late night?"

"Very late," J.P. said. "You ready to work some dogs?"

"Raring to go," Jimmie said.

The Oyster Island Canine Training Facility had taken shape. There were offices, kennels, a grooming room, training arenas, and a fully equipped medical clinic, except with no vet. Jimmie and J.P. worked with a few dogs at a time, both exercising and training them.

"What's the deal with Vixen?" Jimmie asked.

"She was stripping at Rockie's on Bourbon Street. When she had a physical altercation with the bouncer, Chief and Jack intervened and brought her to the island."

"Why was a vet stripping on Bourbon Street?" Jimmie asked.

"First of all, her name's probably not Vixen. I think she has amnesia," J.P. said.

"Have you tried to find out who she is and where she's from?" Jimmie asked.

"I filed a missing person's report with the police department in Chalmette. We'll know something soon. Meantime, I'm trying to talk her into helping us with our vet work."

"She doesn't want to?" Jimmie asked.

"Though I'm not sure what caused her amnesia, I'm betting she suffered one hell of a traumatic experience," J.P. said.

"Such as?"

"You know as much about her right now as I do," J.P. said.

It was almost lunchtime when Jimmie said, "I need a nap. These dogs are never going to run out of energy."

"Get something to eat and take that nap. I'm going to work the dogs for a few more hours."

It was late afternoon when J.P. returned the dogs to the kennel. He already knew which candidates would make good service dogs and which ones they'd adopt to people as family pets. He was hungry and in need of a nap himself when he returned to Jack's.

J.P. found Jimmie sitting alone at the plank table, drinking a beer. Vixen hadn't moved from the couch.

"Where's Jack?" J.P. asked.

"He and Chief left to help Eddie at the Majestic. I had to make a sandwich because they took the pot of gumbo Jack had cooked."

J.P. grinned and said, "How inconsiderate of them."

"There's plenty of bread, cheese, and bologna," Jimmie said.

J.P. ate a sandwich before turning his attention to Vixen.

"You did an amazing job with Isabella last night," he said. "Our dogs always need vaccinations or someone to patch them when they get scraped up. We need a vet. Would you be interested in taking the job until I find out who you are?"

"I am not a veterinarian," Vixen said.

"You could fool me. Whether you are degreed or not, you're damned good at doctoring dogs. We need someone with your skills."

Vixen shook her head. "I cannot," she said.

J.P. said, "Why not?"

Vixen didn't have a chance to answer as Susie Larsen entered the house without knocking. Susie was tall, Vixen taller. From her red and puffy face, it was easy to see she'd been crying. Something in Susie's sorrow caused Vixen to leave the couch and put her arms around her. Vixen remained silent as Susie sobbed on her shoulder.

"I can't take this," Susie said. "Isabella is the only dog I ever owned. She wouldn't be dead if it weren't for me."

"Isabella isn't dead," Vixen said.

"She has to be. The truck ran directly over her."

"She's stiff, sore, and anxious to see you."

"Please don't tell me this is all a cruel joke," Susie said.

Susie turned when Vixen cocked her head toward the fireplace. Isabella didn't leave the doggie bed, though her tail thumped against the floor, her head held high. Susie continued to cry when she knelt beside Isabella and hugged her. J.P. and Vixen watched until Susie kissed the dog and returned to face Vixen.

"Thank you, thank you, thank you," she said, hugging Vixen again.

Vixen finally broke away. "I have to go," she said. "I have shirked my job all morning."

She halted when J.P. said, "If you take a step toward the beach, I'm coming after you."

J.P. and Susie stood at the door, watching Vixen walk down the hill to the old hotel.

"What was that all about?" Susie asked.

"Vixen tried to kill herself last night."

"Are you making this up?" Susie asked.

J.P. shook his head. "You know how bad you felt when you thought Isabella was dead?" Susie nodded. "Multiply that by ten, and you'd approach Vixen's pain."

"What's causing it?" Susie said.

"Wish I knew," J.P. said.

"And why is she working as a housekeeper when she's a wonderful surgeon?" Susie asked.

"I don't know. What were you doing all morning? Jimmie said he saw you up the road sitting on the hood of your car."

"Thinking," Susie said. "It was the spot where the truck hit Isabella. I thought she was dead. I didn't want to return to Chalmette or face seeing her broken body."

"God was looking out for her. Vixen says she'll be good as new in a few weeks."

"I'm not much company. I'm going to take Isabella and return to Chalmette," Susie said.

"Don't go," J.P. said. "You need to be around people for a while and not home alone. You and Isabella can take the Airstream. Lucky can stay with Jack and the other dogs. I'll find some other place to sleep."

"I'm so sorry. I know you're pissed off at me," Susie said.

"I'm not," J.P. said. "Life has a way of changing the best-laid plans. This is one of those times. I'm okay with it."

"You sure?"

"There'll be other weekends, or maybe not. I'm pretty good at rolling with the punches."

"We'll stay," Susie said. "It'll let me spend some time alone with Isabella."

"If I can get a few things from the Airstream, I'll go to the Majestic and see if Eddie will let me bunk on his couch. You and Isabella will have the whole house except for Jack and the other dogs."

J.P. exited the Airstream, loaded his shaving kit and change of clothes into his truck, and then started down the hill to the Majestic. He stopped along the way to answer his cell phone. It was Sergeant Gebbia.

"What's up, Wayne?"

"I have some info on your missing person," Wayne said.

"Hit me."

"She got separated from a group that was granted amnesty and legally crossed the Mexican border. I have a lead on them."

"Are they local?" J.P. asked.

"Hardly," Wayne said. "Try North Dakota."

"What else?" J.P. asked.

"Too much to discuss over the phone," Wayne said. "Tomorrow's my day off. Can you come on Monday morning?"

"You bet? What time?"

"Anytime before ten," Wayne said. "I get to work early."

"I'll be waiting at the door when you get there. Thanks, Wayne."

J.P. called Eddie while he had the phone in his hand. Eddie answered on the first ring.

"What's up?" he asked.

"I'm homeless again. Can I bunk on your couch tonight?" J.P. asked.

"I may have to start charging rent," Eddie said.

"Why not?" J.P. said. "Everyone else does."

"I'm up to my neck in alligators right now. The door's open. Go up and make yourself at home."

The Majestic was abuzz with activity as J.P. ascended the stairs to Eddie's suite with his change of clothes and shaving kit.

The same pillow and blanket he'd used the previous night were still askew on the couch. He thought about fixing a drink. Instead, he pulled off his boots, curled up on the couch, and pulled the blanket over his shoulders. When he awoke sometime later and glanced out the window, he saw it was dark outside.

J.P.'s growling stomach reminded him he hadn't eaten since awakening on the same couch. After peeking into Eddie's refrigerator and finding little to eat except a jar of pickles, he decided to go downstairs and see if anyone was still drinking.

He found Meika tending bar, Avory on a stool nursing a martini. Lilly and Chief sat alone at a table in a dark corner. Eddie and a young woman he didn't recognize were on a couch. J.P. pulled up a stool at the bar beside Avory.

"How did things go today?" he asked.

"The construction crew is making headway," Avory said. "Everything should be ready to begin filming sometime next week."

"Is that when the actors arrive?"

"If your friend Eddie gets his head on straight and concentrates on the business at hand instead of his roaming hand's business."

"Do I detect a hint of jealousy?" J.P. asked.

"Hah!" Avory said.

Before they could continue the conversation, someone walked into the dark little bar. It was Susie.

Chapter 17

Meika's reaction to seeing Susie was immediate. Dropping the tumbler she was polishing, she watched it bounce across the floor until it shattered in an explosion of splintering glass. Susie acted as if she didn't notice.

Susie's tight jeans, white Stetson, expensive snakeskin boots, and flashy Western shirt implied she'd gotten over worrying about Isabella and was ready to party. When she planted a sultry kiss on J.P.'s lips, he could tell she'd been drinking.

"You okay?" he asked.

"Isabella is doing great. She has an appetite and even walked a few steps. I've mistreated you and decided we should celebrate."

J.P. glanced at Meika, who'd finished cleaning up the broken glass and was frowning at him.

"Seems I've already ridden in this rodeo," J.P. said. "Meika, bring Susie a dirty martini and put it on my tab."

When J.P. got off his stool, Susie said, "Where are you going?"

"Calling it a night," he said.

Before he could leave, Eddie joined them at

the bar.

"Where are you going?" he asked.

"Up to the room and get some sleep," J.P. said.

"Meika, get J.P. a tall scotch and put it on my tab. You can't leave yet."

"What happened to the pretty girl you were sitting with?"

"She's the receptionist of our new office and has to be at work at seven." Eddie grasped Susie's hand and said, "It's been a while."

Susie's beaming smile almost lighted the dim room. "What a lucky girl I am to have two handsome men to talk to."

"I'm the lucky one," Eddie said. "Two gorgeous blonds drinking at my bar."

Eddie was laying it on thick, even by his standards. He even had J.P. grinning. Susie was basking in the attention when Odette appeared from the back with a short, nearly bald man. She had sliced a tray of po'boys and Muffalettas into finger-sized bites. Avory turned her back on Eddie and held up a finger to signal Meika to bring her another dirty martini.

"Free food," Odette said. "Anybody hungry?"

J.P. raised his hand. "Isaac," he said. "What the hell are you doing here? I thought you had retired."

"I was going crazy staying in that damn apartment alone. When Meika called and said Eddie needed a chef, I got in my truck and drove down."

"You must not have had much to pack," J.P. said.

"I never unpacked," Isaac said.

"Avory Dorean, this is Isaac Guillot, our new chef," Odette said. "Dinner tonight was the first meal he has cooked for the Majestic."

"Pleased to meet you, Miss Avory," Isaac said. "I hope you enjoyed your étouffée."

"I've never tasted better," Avory said.

J.P. didn't have to be asked twice and was munching on a Muffaletta and sipping his scotch. Neither he nor Eddie noticed Meika whisper something into Odette's ear. Susie did.

"Take off," Odette said. "I'll close for you. And give you your tips tomorrow."

Meika smiled, hugged Odette, and hurried away. Susie followed her down the hall and didn't return to the bar.

"What's wrong with her?" Eddie asked.

"Lover's quarrel," J.P. said.

"Then why was she here with you?"

"Not for sexual reasons; that's for sure," J.P. said.

"Mind if we join you at the bar?" Eddie asked.

"Why not?" Avory said. "Just save your bullshit for someone else. I'm not playing your game."

Eddie didn't know how to respond to Avory's rebuff, so he stuffed a bite-sized oyster po'boy into his mouth and raised a finger for Odette to bring him another scotch. When Avory excused herself to go to the ladies' room, J.P. punched Eddie's shoulder.

"That beautiful woman holds the keys to the success of the Majestic. You need to concentrate on her and forget about Susie and the twenty-year-old you were romancing on the couch."

Isaac had taken the tray of small sandwiches to Lilly and Chief's table, while Odette was eavesdropping on J.P. and Eddie's conversation.

"I agree with J.P.," she said. "We need Avory. You could make things easier for us if you'd pay her more attention."

"You kidding?" Eddie said. "She doesn't even like me."

"You don't always have to like someone," J.P. said.

"J.P.'s right," Odette said. "Liking someone isn't always mutually compatible with lusting for them."

"You think Avory is lusting for me?" Eddie said.

"She's hot for your body," Odette said.

"What do you think, J.P.?"

"It won't hurt anything to pay her some attention."

Odette nodded when Eddie asked, "Do we have any raw oysters?"

"We got a shipment today," Odette said. "Isaac and I shucked a couple of dozen."

When Avory returned, Eddie said, "Odette, bring us a round of oyster shooters."

"What's that?" Avory said.

"I'll tell you after you've had one," Eddie said.

"How about the rest of us?" Odette said.

"You got it," Eddie said. "Shots for everyone. Two if Avory likes them."

Isaac had returned from serving finger sandwiches to Lilly and Chief's table.

"Can you help me fix a dozen oyster shooters?" Odette said.

"Does that mean we're included in the round?" he asked.

"Of course," she said.

Everyone watched as Avory downed one of the oyster shooters.

"Wonderful," she said. "Now tell me what's in an oyster shooter."

"Every bartender has their recipe," Odette said. "I put a raw oyster in the shot glass, add cocktail sauce, horseradish, lemon, and black pepper, stir, and then enjoy.

"Are you supposed to chew the oyster?" Avory asked.

"Nope," Isaac said. "Just toss it back in one swallow."

"Keep them coming until we run out of oysters," Eddie said.

After the second oyster shooter, Lilly and Chief started for the door. When Lilly was a few steps ahead, Chief tapped J.P.'s shoulder.

"You can sleep on Jack's couch tonight," he said. "I don't need it."

"Lucky you," J.P. said after Chief followed Lilly upstairs.

"I better go," Avory said. "Early day tomorrow."

"One more?" Eddie said. "Odette's oyster shooters are the best I've ever had."

Avory didn't answer, though she remained on the stool. "I suppose one more won't kill me."

"I guarantee it won't," Eddie said. "Have you seen the upper deck yet?"

"Odette showed it to us."

"It's lovely during the day and magical at night," Eddie said. "I believe it's a full moon outside. The sky is clear, and the vista over the Gulf during a full moon is spectacular."

"Maybe you can show me," Avory said.

Eddie took Avory's hand and led her away from the bar.

The oysters were gone. Isaac excused himself and returned the tray to the kitchen, leaving Odette and J.P. alone at the bar.

"Sounds like I'm going to need the couch at Jack's," he said.

"Avory has a room," Odette said. "I'd take a chance and stay here. It's a long walk back to Jack's."

"Have any sandwiches left?" he asked.

"I'll get you a sack. I'm shutting down the bar before someone else walks in."

J.P. fished one of the little sandwiches out of the paper bag and ate it as he walked up the stairs. He was on the couch when the door opened. It was Eddie.

"What happened?" J.P. said. "Odette and I were betting you'd spend the night with Avory."

"Everything was going great until I mentioned Heather's wedding. The temperature cooled off fast after that. Are those sandwiches on the kitchen counter?"

"All yours," J.P. said. "I already ate my share."

Eddie grabbed a sandwich and poured himself a scotch.

"I'm not ready to go to sleep," he said. "Want a drink?"

J.P. got off the couch, joined him, and said, "Why not? I slept before hitting the bar. I was tossing on the couch when you came in."

"Is Susie Meika's girlfriend?"

"What was your first clue?" J.P. said.

"Guess she ruined your weekend."

"I should have known better. Susie pulled the same trick on me already. She had me convinced her relationship with Meika was permanently over. Who was the blond you were sitting on the couch with?"

"Her name is Sara, and she works for the construction crew. She has aspirations of being an actress."

"She has the looks," J.P. said. "Avory sure noticed. She has a thing for you."

"You think?" Eddie said.

"It's obvious."

"She's attractive and intelligent and closer to my age."

"You never let a little thing like age stop you," J.P. said.

"You're the pot calling the kettle black," Eddie said. "Were you ever married?"

"Came close a time or two," J.P. said.

"What stopped you?"

"Police work," J.P. said. "It's tough on a wife

never knowing if her husband will make it home at night. What about you? If you had married Josie, you'd be set for life."

"And we wouldn't be fighting Frankie in court right now," Eddie said. "Trust me, I've thought about it."

"Your hotel business is going well."

"Odette is a lifesaver. She's intelligent, savvy, and knows the business better than I ever will. Paula's not bad, either. I'd give her a shot if she weren't already married."

"She's the most happily married person I know," J.P. said.

"She and Odette got Meika and Heather to work together, and I don't deserve to have a chef as good as Isaac."

"Where do you intend to put all your help?" J.P. said. "Chalmette's twenty miles away, and you're going to run out of rooms for the paying guests."

"Some vacation bungalows are on the other side of the storage warehouse."

"I didn't know that," J.P. said.

"Neither did I. Chief informed me about them earlier today. He and Odette went with Ben Biondo and me to check them out."

"Who's Ben?"

"The construction superintendent for the movie crew. The houses are in good shape. Ben will make them livable in exchange for letting his people occupy some of them. Isaac has a house and Odette, Heather, and Meika decided to share one."

"How do they look?" J.P. asked.

"They're beautiful. We were barely back to the hotel before Odette began lobbying me for one," Eddie said.

"Everything's going your way. Your food service will take shape with Isaac working for you," J.P. said. "Now I know why they call you Lucky Eddie.

"Not quite everything. Vixen worries me. She's doing a great job, though it's clear she's not a long-term solution to my problem."

"You need more than one housekeeper," J.P. said. "I'm stealing Vixen from you if I can."

"Don't do it. I need her," Eddie said.

"She's more valuable to me as a veterinarian than to you as a housekeeper," J.P. said. "The training facility needs her."

"Then why are you trying to find out who she is? She won't stay on the island for either of us if she resolves her amnesia."

"Maybe," J.P. said.

"You talked with the police. What do you know about Vixen?"

"Sex traffickers kidnapped her at the Mexican border. They sold her to a French Quarter pimp. When someone murdered the pimp, she wandered the streets until someone from Rockie's noticed her and hired her to strip."

"I understand that. Vixen's one gorgeous woman," Eddie said. "She was probably making good money. Why was she still living on the streets?"

"She once was married, had a child, and too old to be stripping. Massive trauma caused her amnesia and left her mentally unstable," J.P. said.

Eddie poured them a drink and ate another slice of a po'boy.

"Any idea where she's from?" he asked.

"I had a call from Wayne tonight."

"Who is that?"

"A Chalmette police officer working the missing person's case for me," J.P. said. "He says she was with political dissidents who crossed the border seeking asylum. They relocated to North Dakota."

J.P. smiled when Eddie said, "It's colder than a witch's tit in a brass brassiere this time of year in North Dakota. Are you planning to go there and talk to the people in the group?"

"Don't know yet. Wayne has more info on Vixen. I'm meeting with him Monday morning."

"Let me know what he says," Eddie said.

"I'm worried," J.P. said.

"You're doing all you can," Eddie said.

"I'm not talking about Vixen. I'm worried about you and me and everyone else on the island. I was a police officer for too many years not to know how shaky a decision in a court of law can be."

"Me too, Buddy. Don't tell anybody," Eddie said. "If it weren't for Basil, we'd already be in trouble. Let's hope he doesn't bail on us."

"He wouldn't do that."

"If Heather can't have her wedding here before the movie wraps, it's a definite possibility," Eddie said.

J.P. finished his scotch in a single swallow and poured more.

"This is damn good scotch," he said.

"Frankie stocked the hotel with it. Nothing but the best for Frankie," Eddie said.

After another taste of the scotch, J.P. said, "Seems to me you have three options."

Eddie laughed and said, "Tell me."

"You can kick Frankie's ass in court."

"Our first court appearance is this week," Eddie said. "What are my other two options?"

"Convince Avory to let Heather have her wedding before the movie wraps."

"If tonight on the observation deck was any indication, getting her to go along with the wedding isn't happening. What's my third option?"

"Marry Josie."

Chapter 18

When Eddie and Odette entered the office complex the following morning, Sara wasn't at her desk. Basil was already at work. He nodded when Eddie knocked on his door.

"You don't have to knock," he said.

"Where's Sara?" Eddie asked.

"Shut the door, and I'll tell you," Basil said.

"Am I invited?" Odette said.

Basil motioned them in. "You bet," he said.

"What happened?" Eddie asked.

"I was working late and decided to turn off the lights and nap," Basil said. "When I woke up, it was morning, and Avory and Ben Biondo were in a heated discussion outside my office."

"They didn't know you were listening?" Odette asked.

"My lights were off," Basil said.

"What were they arguing about?" Eddie asked.

"Sara," Basil said. "Avory wanted Sara gone. Problem is, Sara is Ben's daughter."

"You're kidding," Odette said.

"Ben was pissed and told Avory so," Basil said. "He had her backpedaling. She called one of her friends and got Sara a part in a movie filming in Hollywood. Ben and Avory shook on it. An hour later, Sara was gone. Any idea what it was all about?"

"Avory's hot on Eddie; he had drinks with Sara last night in the bar."

"Avory isn't hot on me," Eddie said.

"The hell she isn't," Odette said.

"Who's our receptionist now?" Eddie asked.

"Guess we're answering our own phones," Basil said.

"Don't look at me," Odette said.

"You're too valuable," Eddie said. "I'm going to miss a gorgeous nineteen-year-old hanging on my every word."

"Weirdo!" Odette said.

"Don't slander your boss," Eddie said.

"I have to check the kitchen and see how the ten o'clock break planning is coming."

After Odette had exited Basil's office, Basil said, "Keep the door shut."

"Why the secrecy?"

"Frankie filed a new pleading last Friday at five."

"It's Sunday," Eddie said. "How do you know about the pleading already?"

"A friend in the clerk's office emailed me a copy," Basil said. "Frankie's trying to change the jurisdiction to St. Tammany Parish."

"He can't do that," Eddie said. "St. Bernard Parish is the proper venue."

"I've already prepared our answer. I'll file it when we get service. Frankie's just delaying because he doesn't have a case."

"Or maybe he has someone in St. Tammany he can influence."

"I don't think so," Basil said. "The St. Tammany judges are honest."

"Frankie has a big pocketbook," Eddie said.

"Doesn't matter," Basil said.

Eddie tapped Basil's shoulder and said, "Good work. Take a break and get something to eat."

"I will. The food's becoming world-class around here."

"Tell me about it," Eddie said. "I'm going to gain twenty pounds if I'm not careful."

"Can we talk about something else before you go?" Basil asked.

Eddie said. "What's up?"

"Heather," Basil said. "We have a problem."

"One we haven't discussed?"

"Before Heather and her dad got into it, her mom planned to help her with the wedding. Now, she has no idea where to begin."

"What about Paula, Odette and Meika?" Eddie said. "I'll bet they know all the ins and outs."

"I know Paula does. She's from a large family, and I'll bet she's helped plan a dozen or more."

"I'll speak to Paula about it," Eddie said.

"Heather can't know we discussed this. She's very prideful," Basil said.

"Paula will handle it. Heather will never know we talked."

"Thanks, Eddie," Basil said.

"No problem. Now, take a break."

Eddie left the office complex and couldn't help but smile when he opened the kitchen door, the aroma piquing his appetite. Isaac, Meika, and Heather were busily working in front of one of the kitchen's commercial stoves. Odette and Paula watched from a corner table."

"May I join you?" Eddie asked.

"You're the boss," Odette said. "You don't have to ask."

"The break went like clockwork," Paula said. "Isaac and the girls could feed twice as many people if they had to."

"There'll be more than that once filming starts," Eddie said.

"We'll be ready," Odette said. "What's up?"

"How did you know I had something else on my mind?" Eddie asked.

Odette and Paula shared a knowing smile. "You men are so transparent," Odette said. "Women know what you're thinking before the words pour out of your mouths."

"Now that's a bit sexist, don't you think?"

"But true," Odette said.

"Well, you're right. Do either of you know anything about planning a wedding?"

"Paula could be a professional wedding planner. She's helped plan so many," Odette said.

"You getting married?" Paula said.

"Hope not," Eddie said. "It's Heather. She was counting on her mother to help her plan her wedding, and she doesn't have the foggiest clue where to begin."

When Paula stood from the table, Eddie grabbed her arm.

"We can't let this be so obvious," Eddie said. "Heather needs your help, though she doesn't know yet that she does."

"Got you," Paula said. "Odette and I can handle this. She'll never know you were involved."

"Or Basil," Eddie said. "We'll help every way we can, though we must remain anonymous. What's for lunch?"

"Jimmie went fishing beyond the barrier islands this morning and caught grouper and redfish," Paula said.

"Smells wonderful," Eddie said. "Is there enough for Basil and me?"

"We'll serve you in your offices," Odette said.

"Can't wait," Eddie said.

After lunch, Meika, Heather, and Isaac

relaxed at the large table with Odette and Paula, eating grouper, redfish, and sides of rice pilaf, green beans, and roasted Greek potatoes.

"We've only worked together for a few days, though it feels I've known you and Meika all my life," Odette said.

"Sisters," Meika said, hoisting her glass of white wine.

"What about me?" Isaac asked.

"You're one of us," Meika said. "Even if your anatomy doesn't match."

Isaac was sipping a glass of ouzo instead of the wine the others were drinking. He clicked glasses with them.

"I know you probably have your wedding plans under control," Paula said. "I love planning weddings if you need any help."

"You've planned weddings?" Heather asked.

"A few," Paula said.

"More like a dozen," Odette said. "She gets calls all the time from people she doesn't even know wanting her to help them."

"You serious? How much do you charge?" Heather asked.

"Nothing for you," Paula said. "Tell me where I need to start."

Heather's eyes began to tear, one rolling down her face. Odette put her arms around her.

"What's wrong?"

"My mom was going to help me plan the wedding. Now, I have no clue where to begin."

Heather shook her head when Paula asked, "Have you registered at any stores?"

"Why do I need to do that?" Heather asked.

"You and Basil want to have nice china and silverware. The price per place setting is high, and no one is likely to buy you the entire set, even if they knew what you wanted," Paula said.

"How will I know?" Heather asked.

"We'll get you registered where you can choose what plates and silverware you want," Paula said. "We'll print the store's name on the invitation. The store keeps a record of place settings sold. They'll direct the customer to another item when your set is complete. That way, you don't wind up with four toasters and six waffle irons. When do you plan to wed?"

"Valentine's Day," Heather said.

"That's coming up in a few weeks," Paula said. "I'm not sure we have enough time. Can you put it off until March?"

Heather shook her head. "Basil and I met on Valentine's Day. It's when I want to marry him."

"You sure?" Odette said. "Once we print the invitations, the wedding date is set in stone."

"You sound like my dad," Heather said. "He told me Valentine's Day was the best day of the year for Craws & Claws and that he wasn't going to ruin it because I was too stubborn to change the date."

Paula glared at Isaac when he said, "What an asshole!" When Meika, Odette, and Heather gave him dirty looks, he said, "What?"

"You don't call a girl's dad an asshole," Paula said.

"Isaac's right," Heather said. "I plan to marry only once. Dad shouldn't be more interested in making money than his daughter's happiness."

"Then Valentine's Day it is," Paula said. "Take tomorrow off and go with me to Chalmette and New Orleans. We'll get you registered and visit the printer."

"I can't," Heather said. "Odette needs me."

"Meika and I will cover for you," Odette said. "You and Paula need to move fast if you plan to marry on Valentine's."

"You sure about this?" When Heather nodded, Paula said, "Valentine's Day it is."

Odette glanced at the kitchen clock. "We have to get back to work." When Paula headed for the door, Odette said, "Where are you going?"

"To talk with Eddie and get him to cut us a check for the printer."

"He won't pay for Heather's wedding invitations," Odette said.

"He will after I talk to him," Paula said.

Paula found Eddie in his office. Expecting lunch, he glanced up from his computer with a smile. Paula shut the door behind her.

Eddie's smile disappeared when he realized she had no food.

"We discovered why Heather and her dad argued, and we've settled on a wedding date."

"When?" Eddie asked.

"Valentine's Day."

"That won't work. It's right in the middle of filming. Avory will go ballistic."

"It's Valentine's Day or not at all," Paula said.

"Unacceptable," Eddie said. "Where are you going?"

Paula didn't answer. Instead, she walked down the hall and returned with Basil. Basil was smiling, with no idea what was going on.

"What's up, boss?"

Realizing Paula had ambushed him, Eddie said nothing. She wasn't going to let him off the hook.

"Tell Basil what you just told me," she said.

"We're having the wedding on Valentine's Day," Eddie said.

"I knew it was the day Heather picked. I didn't tell you because I never thought you'd agree," Basil said. "What's Avory going to say?"

"I'll handle Avory," Eddie said. "Our lunch is on the way. Get back to work."

Heather and Meika were both beaming when they delivered meals.

"Grouper or redfish?" Meika asked.

"They both look wonderful," Eddie said.

"You can't have them both," Meika said.

"Then either is fine."

Heather placed the steaming dish in front of Eddie and then put her arms around his neck, hugging him so hard she almost strangled him.

"Thank you," she said. "I can't imagine there's any nicer boss in the world than you."

Meika had already left the office to deliver Basil's meal. When Heather followed her, Paula shut the door again.

"I need a check to pay for the invitations," she said.

"Why does the Majestic have to pay?" Eddie asked.

"Because we're going to use this occasion to publicize the hotel."

"We're not even officially open yet," Eddie said.

"Think of all the goodwill you'll receive. You'll be a hero in Chalmette. Your contribution won't go unnoticed by whichever judge handles your case."

"Damn it, Paula! Why didn't you get a law degree? I could use another good lawyer right now."

"I don't have to be a lawyer to help you win in the court of public opinion. You may even want to run for mayor of Chalmette someday."

"I need all the help I can get," Eddie said.

"I hope having the wedding on Valentine's Day won't anger Avory."

"She'll be angry," Eddie said. "That's a fact. You must help me stem the tide when Avory lowers the boom on me."

"You know I'm a witch," Paula said.

"No, you aren't," Eddie said. "You're a lovely person."

"You misunderstand. I'm a witch, a Cajun traiteur. Though I don't know how I'll do it, Avory will be happy about Heather's decision to get married on Valentine's Day. I promise."

"I hope you're right and this wedding doesn't become another Valentine's Day massacre."

Chapter 19

When Susie Larsen returned to Chalmette, J.P. had his Airstream back and looked forward to sleeping in his bed for the first time in two nights. He decided to drink at the Majestic and found Lilly Bliss alone at the bar.

"You look lonely," he said. "Mind if I join you?"

"Please do," Lilly said. "I hate drinking alone."

Meika leaned over the bar. "What are you drinking, J.P.?"

"Scotch; straight. Did you and Susie kiss and make up?"

"Nothing has changed," Meika said. "I'm not returning to Chalmette, and Susie's not moving to the island." Meika smiled. "Last night, we had one last swing at the piñata, and we both missed. We cried our eyes out when Susie returned to your trailer."

Meika's sleeveless purple blouse tied in a knot at the waist highlighted her cutoff jeans and long legs.

"Kind of nippy outside," J.P. said.

"The construction crew will arrive in about an hour." Meika pirouetted. "They love my outfits. I love their tips." Meika pushed the scotch toward him. “Want another, Miss Lilly?”

“Thanks, sweetie,” Lilly said with a smile.

When Meika moved away to mix Lilly’s martini, J.P. asked, “Where’s Chief? You two were thick as thieves last night.”

“I’m working late,” she said.

J.P. said, “I got it. You want to socialize with the construction crew too.”

Lilly shook her head. “Just taking a break.”

“From what?”

“Script problems,” Lilly said.

“I thought you were ready to start filming.”

“Should be close,” Lilly said. “We’re not.”

“What’s the problem?”

“I’ve redone the script three times in the past few days,” Lilly said. “Avory hates all three.”

“Aren’t you supposed to have a finished product when you reach this production stage?”

“Doesn’t always work that way,” Lilly said.

“Why not?”

“The investors are interested in a finished product and need a movie in the can. Avory and I rushed things a bit to accommodate them.”

Lilly nodded when J.P. said, “You’re saying you haven’t written the movie?”

“Oh, it’s written all right. We don’t have much of a plot yet.”

“What do you have?”

“A piece of shit. Avory and I can’t agree on how to fix it. I’m about to pull my hair out,” Lilly said.

“What’s the movie about?” J.P. asked.

“It started as a vampire flick set during the Prohibition Era.”

“A horror picture?” J.P. said.

“A horror flick that has morphed into a paranormal romance with horror undertones.”

“What’s the storyline?”

“The hero is the son of a bootlegger, the

heroine a naïve country girl who becomes the object of affection of the crime boss who runs the casino. Both our stars are too old for their parts. I'm only now realizing it. Avory's trying to think of a way to make it work."

Lilly nodded when J.P. said, "Is that why she's so cranky?"

"And getting worse every day. I told her she needed to get laid to relieve some of her stress."

"Guess you'll have to give the money back," J.P. said.

Lilly sipped her martini and said, "Not going to happen."

"What then? Kind of late to start over," J.P. said. "You've written lots of scripts. Can't you fix this one?"

"My inspiration has flown out the window," Lilly said.

"When are the actors getting here?"

"The two stars are arriving in a couple of days," "Lilly said.

"And the rest of the cast?"

"New Orleans has an abundance of experienced actors. We intend to draw from that pool to complete the cast."

"Because?" J.P. asked.

"Two reasons: budget and local accents. Avory wants to make this film as authentic as possible."

"Sounds like she got the cart ahead of the horse. She should have had her script finalized and casting done before arriving on the island."

"Don't tell her unless you want your head torn off," Lilly said.

"I'll help any way I can," J.P. said.

"Then take her to bed and screw her brains out," Lilly said.

"Avory has eyes for Eddie though he struck out last night."

"She's lusting after him. Problem is, she thinks he's a pompous asshole."

"Can't you do anything to change her mind?" J.P. asked.

"The only person who changes Avory's mind is Avory. She's one hard-headed woman."

"Is this her first time directing?" J.P. asked.

"She's directed a dozen or more films. That's not the problem."

"Then what is?" J.P. asked.

"This is the first movie she has directed and produced. We're talking a different ballgame, and she's terrified of failure."

The men from the construction crew had begun trickling into the dark little bar. J.P. and Lilly finished their drinks. Meika was in her element.

"One more?" Meika said.

"Tab me out, sweetie," Lilly said. "Hard work is calling, and the buzz I already have is all I need."

"Same here," J.P. said. "Have fun."

"Oh, I will," Meika said.

The wind had picked up as J.P. hurried up the hill to Jack's house. Distant thunder rumbled over the Gulf, lightning rippling across the dark sky. Another storm approached the island, and J.P. was thankful he wasn't spending the night in his truck.

The dogs were asleep in front of a roaring fireplace, and Chief was sitting alone on the couch. Jack poured J.P. a mug of Dominican rum.

"Where've you been?" Jack asked.

"At the Majestic, having a drink with Lilly Bliss."

"Better watch it," Jack said. "Lilly is Chief's honey."

"She's working and was taking a break," J.P. said. "I wouldn't try to beat Chief's time with Miss

Lilly."

"What was she working on?" Paula asked.

"The movie script isn't quite written."

"That's crazy," Odette said. "Filming is about to begin."

"In a few days," J.P. said.

"Lilly told you that?" Paula asked.

"Among other things," J.P. said. "Avory has directed lots of movies. This is the first one she has put together from scratch."

"What does that mean?" Jimmie asked.

"An executive producer is like a homebuilder. The general contractor doesn't build houses. He hires sub-contractors. Concrete companies to lay the foundation, carpenters to frame and roof the house, and plumbers to install the plumbing."

"I still don't see what you mean?" Jimmie said.

"The executive producer hires writers to develop a script, a director to direct the movie, and a casting director to hire the actors. The job of an executive producer is to ensure the work gets done and the film is successful."

"Sounds crazy to me," Jimmie said.

"Avory's frightened her first project as an executive producer will flop and cause her Hollywood connections to blacklist her," J.P. said.

"No wonder she's so out of sorts," Odette said.

"Lilly told her she needs to get laid to relieve her stress so she can make better decisions," J.P. said.

"What a sexist thing to say," Odette said.

"Don't give me a dirty look," J.P. said. "I didn't say it. I'm only telling you what Lilly told me."

"What happened with her and Eddie last night?" Odette asked. "They left the bar together."

"Avory's hot for Eddie, though she thinks he's a pompous asshole. Lilly's words. Not mine. It's Sunday night. Why are you and Jimmie still on the island?"

"I'm helping Heather and Basil with their wedding. Heather didn't have the foggiest idea where to begin. I'm getting them registered at several department stores and then taking them to have invitations printed."

"At least she has a guest list," J.P. said. "How will you start the printer if you don't know the wedding date?"

"Valentine's Day," Paula said.

"You're shitting me!" J.P. said. "Avory won't allow it."

"Eddie has agreed on the date and is even paying for the printing," Paula said.

"No way!" J.P. said.

"He needs Basil to help him defend Frankie's lawsuit. I convinced him Basil would walk unless the wedding happens on Valentine's Day."

"Basil won't hold him to that date."

"He will if he wants to marry Heather," Paula said.

"That's just crazy," J.P. said. "How's Eddie going to convince Avory to take a break in filming to accommodate a wedding?"

"I don't know yet. Odette and I are working on that little detail."

"Good luck with that! Lilly Bliss is Avory's best friend, and she's afraid of her," J.P. said.

Thunder shook Jack's little house, the rain drumming the roof. Jack topped up everyone's rum and started a fresh pot of coffee. No one seemed to notice Chief napping on the couch.

Chief's eyes popped open in time for him to see a ghostly figure pass through the wall. The person standing before him was less human and more of a flickering image.

"Grandpa," Chief said. "Is that you?"

The old man's garb was from a different time and place. His scrawny old chest was bare except for a buckskin vest. His big toe peeked through a hole in his well-worn moccasins, and a lone feather decorated his braided gray hair.

"It's me, Grogan," the ghostly presence said.

"What are you doing here?" Chief asked.

"There's something I need to tell you."

"Tell me what?" Chief asked.

"I made a horrible mistake many years before you were born. Because of the mistake, my soul has never passed, and I've roamed the island's backside since I died. I want to cross over and join the Great Spirit. I need your help to do it."

"Why did you wait so long to come to me?"

"I couldn't face you. Now, you may lose the island, and my soul will be trapped here forever with many white men. The notion causes me great pain."

"What did you do so horrible your soul can't pass?" Chief asked.

"I sold the island," Grandpa's ghost said.

"For what?"

"A Model T Ford."

"You sold the island for a Model T Ford?" Chief said.

"I couldn't help myself. It was the most beautiful thing I'd ever seen in my life. The white men took me for a ride in it and then taught me how to drive it. I had to have it."

"There was no bridge back then. How did the men get it to the island?"

"Floated it over on a barge along with gasoline drums and a pump to fill the tank."

"Where is this Model T? I've never seen it?"

"I drove it all over the place. It would go anywhere. I loved that car. It finally ran out of gas on the backside of the island. That's where I left it."

"I've been all over this island," Chief said. I can't believe I never saw it."

"It's just a pile of rusty metal now. Trees and underbrush have grown up around it. It's near a big old oak tree on the north side of the swamp. I carved my name and your grandmother's on the tree."

The storm had intensified, and Grandpa's image flickered when thunder shook the house.

"Are you a ghost, Grandpa?"

"Yes. Do you forgive me?"

"Of course I do," Chief said. "Eddie says you couldn't have sold the island because it wasn't yours to sell."

"Eddie is a smart man. You must help him save the island, or else I'll roam it forever."

The old man nodded when Chief said, "Even in a storm like this?"

"There's no shelter for a lost soul," the ghost said. "I must go."

"Wait, Grandpa. . ."

Chief sprang up from the couch as the wandering spirit passed through the wall. When a plaintive cry burst from his mouth, everyone stopped what they were doing and stared at him in horror.

Chapter 20

Rain pounded Jack's roof as Chief flung open the door and barreled down the hill into the brunt of the storm.

"What the hell is that all about?" J.P. said

They could hear Chief shouting something. The fury of the storm drowned out the single word.

"Grandpa!"

"Maybe I better go after him," J.P. said.

Paula reached across the table, grasping J.P.'s wrist.

"He's in no danger," she said.

"How do you know?" J.P. asked.

"I'm tuned in to his feelings."

She nodded when J.P. said, "You can do that?"

"Chief needs his space right now," she said.

Ten minutes later, Chief pushed through the door, his clothes drenched and his long gray hair soaked. Sensing something was wrong, Coco, Chief's Chihuahua, got out of his bed by the fire and jumped into his arms.

"What the hell were you doing?" Jack asked.

"You didn't see him?" Chief said.

"See who?" Jack said.

"My grandpa."

"Your grandfather is deceased. Was it his ghost you saw?" Paula asked.

Chief nodded and said, "He looked so real. For a minute, I thought he'd come back to life. I realized he was a spirit when his image flickered."

"What did he want?" Paula asked.

"To confess. Grandpa told me he'd sold the island to a bunch of white men. He said he was sorry."

Chief shook his head when Jimmie said, "Did they get him drunk first?"

"I don't like how you asked that," Chief said. "I'm an Indian and can drink you under the table. Forget the stereotypes."

"Sorry," Jimmie said.

"I'm in a forgiving mood. Just don't do it again," Chief said. "The white men traded Grandpa something for the island."

"Like what?" J.P. asked.

"A Model T Ford."

"Your grandpa traded the island for an antique vehicle?" J.P. asked.

"It wasn't an antique in 1919. Grandpa begged my forgiveness and pleaded for me to help Eddie make things right again."

"Your grandfather knows Eddie?" Paula said.

"Grandpa's ghost knows everyone on the island and everything about it. His destiny is to walk it night and day. Right now, his spirit is wandering on a lonely path through the storm."

"Damn!" Jack said. "If that's his fate for trading for an old Ford, I can only imagine what I have to look forward to when I croak."

"Chief's grandfather's plight is self-inflicted," Paula said. "I can give him a little nudge to help him cross over."

"Get out of those wet clothes," Jack said. "A

cup of grog will warm you up and soothe your jangled nerves."

Chief had spent so many nights on Jack's couch he kept his own terrycloth robe in the bathroom. His hair was still damp when he emerged dressed in the robe.

"Jimmie and I are going to the camping trailer," Paula said. "We're leaving early tomorrow."

"Forgive me, Chief?" Jimmie asked.

"You're my friend. I didn't take what you said personally. You still needed to know you were out of line."

"Thanks," Jimmie said.

When Jimmie whistled for Lady, the big dog's tail wagged as they hurried out the door.

"Me and Lucky are also turning in early," J.P. said. "I'm going to Chalmette tomorrow to see what Sergeant Gebbia has learned about Vixen."

Jack and Chief were soon alone and began a game of gin rummy while they sipped their rum.

"What are your plans?" Jack asked.

"If it's not raining tomorrow, I will find Grandpa's Model T."

Jack never slept late, the morning sun barely over the horizon when he shuffled into the kitchen. Chief was already at the plank table and dressed in his dried clothes.

"Were you up all night?" Jack asked.

"I tossed and turned until about an hour ago," Chief said. "I'm going to look for Grandpa's Ford."

"It's barely light outside. I'll fix us some breakfast and then go with you."

"Grandpa's visit has left me with a sense of unease. Let's look for the car. We can eat later."

"His visit must have upset you," Jack said. "I've never known you to skip a meal."

"And it has me worried."

"Let's take a few things with us," Jack said.

"Like what?"

"You'll see," Jack said.

Jack returned from his tool shed with a backpack, a gallon of motor oil, a can of gasoline, and a drain pan.

"What's in the bag?" Chief asked.

"Tools, tire patches, and an air pump."

"Grandpa said nothing's left of the car except a pile of rusted metal."

"Never trust a ghost," Jack said. "I've seen too many videos on the Internet of people starting old vehicles that have sat for decades."

"You believe that horseshit?" Chief said.

"You want to chance having to return for tools? It won't hurt a damn thing to take everything now."

"Fine," Chief said.

The dogs followed them out the door, jumping into the backseat of the ATV beside the tools and other equipment Jack had brought. Though the rain had moved past the island, the day was gloomy and dark. Jack removed the charger from the ATV and started down the hill toward the island's backside.

The farther away they got from the beach, the more trees and vegetation they encountered. They soon reached shallow, tea-colored water abutting a briny estuary, eventually leading to the Gulf of Mexico. Mangrove trees with root systems looking like the bony fingers of old men jutted into the water.

"Strange-looking trees," Jack said. "We had nothing like them in Massachusetts."

"Because they're subtropical," Chief said. "Grandpa used to say mangrove fingers hold South Louisiana together."

"I see why," Jack said. "I've never seen a tree

with such a root system. Kind of creepy looking if you ask me."

"Creepy and beautiful at the same time," Chief said.

"I wouldn't want to be lost out here after dark. Why is it so quiet?"

"It's winter; the snakes and gators hibernating."

"It's not that cold," Jack said.

"Not that hot, either," Chief said.

"What are we looking for?"

"A giant oak tree," Chief said.

"That's a tall task. The forest around the swamp is full of trees. How will you know which is which?"

"Grandpa carved his initials into the tree," Chief said.

"That's a big help," Jack said.

"There's a trail up ahead," Chief said.

"I don't see a trail."

The three dogs were raising a ruckus in the backseat.

"Let them out," Chief said.

The dogs bounded out of the ATV and disappeared into the forest.

Chief showed Jack a machete. "We may need it," he said.

"Hope they don't meet a bobcat," Chief said.

"You think there are bobcats in there?" Jack said.

"Now, who's stewing?" Chief said. "Let's hurry, or they'll get away from us."

Jack pointed the nose of the ATV into the trees.

"This is little more than a trail," Jack said.

"It's the door into the swamp," Chief said.

"How do you know?"

"Grandpa taught me how to track when I was only knee-high. Even the dogs sense it."

The sound of the dogs had grown louder, Coco yapping, Oscar and Ol' Joe howling.

"There's nothing to track except trees," Jack said.

"You don't see the tire tracks?" Chief said.

"What tracks?" Jack said.

The dogs continued barking as they entered the trees. Careful not to get stuck, Jack kept the ATV moving forward. Soon, even he could see the ruts in the sandy loam.

"If your grandpa's Model T is in here, we'll never find it," Jack said.

"Good thing it's the middle of winter. Can you imagine getting through this vegetation if it were in full flush?"

Jack grabbed Chief's arm and hit the brakes. "The dogs quit barking," he said.

"They found it," Chief said.

"How could they have found it? They don't even know what they're looking for."

"They found it," Chief said. "You'll see."

The trail led them into a clearing, the dogs sitting in front of a large oak tree.

Chief stepped out of the ATV and said, "That's Grandpa's tree. Come see."

Jack followed Chief to the base of a giant oak. The tree had grown since Chief's grandpa carved his initials. Chief had to gaze upward to see them.

"Where's the car?" Jack said.

The hardwoods had parted, revealing a giant clump of mangrove trees growing in a circle. The exposed woody roots formed a fort-like wall, and the umbrella-shaped mangrove trees' leafy canopy created the roof. A cave-like opening large enough to drive a car through bade them to enter, and Jack started forward.

The structure's interior formed by the mangroves was like a cave forcing Jack to turn on the lights of the ATV, the dogs running ahead of the beams. When the dogs slowed to a stop, Jack had to slam on the brakes. Leaving the headlights on, he and Chief got out of the ATV. The old black car they stared at was Grandpa's Model T. For a moment, they were both speechless.

"Grandpa said the car was a pile of rust."

"Looks like it just rolled off the assembly line," Jack said.

Chief climbed in behind the wheel. "The mangrove trees must have grown up around it after Grandpa ran out of gas. He parked it here and never returned to check on it," he said.

"The mangrove canopy kept the rain from turning it to rust," Jack said. "I'll bet it'll start if we put some gas in the tank."

"Let's find out. Get the tools," Chief said.

"The tires are flat, and I forgot to bring a jack."

"This old bucket probably has one," Chief said.

"Look in the box in the rear," Jack said. "Must have been where they kept the luggage."

"And everything else. There weren't many filling stations back then."

"Or paved roads," Jack said.

Jack removed a tire and separated it from the inner tube with a crowbar.

"You know what you're doing?" Chief said.

"Piece of cake," Jack said. "When I was a kid, I fixed flats on my bicycle. Throw me one of those spare inner tubes."

It took them a while to reinstall and inflate all four tires.

"That's the hardest part," Jack said. "I'll change the oil. You prime the carburetor."

Jack slid under the old car and began draining the oil. Chief opened the hood, priming the carburetor with gasoline. When Jack started filling the crankcase with fresh oil, Chief had already finished his part of the task.

"Hope we brought enough gas," Chief said.

"We can get more if it isn't," Jack said. "Let's hope it starts. The car has sat here for more than a hundred years."

"Only one way to find out," Chief said. Jack was standing in front of the car and already had his hand on the crank.

"Crank this baby and see what happens," Chief said.

Jack only had to turn the crank once before it sputtered and started.

"Amazing," Jack said. "What now?"

The lights of the old Model T cast a bright beam through the darkness.

"Put the tools and dogs into the ATV and try to keep up. I'm driving Grandpa's Ford back to your house."

Chapter 21

Chief drove the car out of the mangrove swamp and headed across the island toward Jack's house. Deciding he wanted to show the vehicle to Lilly, he slowed to let Jack and the dogs catch up to him.

A Gulf breeze whipped Chief's shoulder-length hair. For a moment, he felt the same exhilaration he knew his grandfather must have felt so many decades ago.

"I'm going to stop by the Majestic for a drink. Want to go with me?" he said.

"I have things to do," Jack said. "Are you sleeping on the couch tonight?"

"Depends," Chief said.

"On what?"

"I'm taking Lilly for a ride in Grandpa's Model T. Have a few drinks with her and then see what happens."

"I'll take care of the dogs," Jack said. "Don't do anything I wouldn't do."

Meika, Odette, and Heather were leaving the Majestic. When Chief pulled to a stop, they came running.

"Where'd you get the car?" Odette asked.

"It was my grandpa's. When I saw his spirit

last night, he told me where to find it."

"Where was it?" Odette asked.

"In the mangrove swamp on the island's backside," Chief said.

Heather stroked the black fender with the palm of her hand. "It's beautiful and looks brand new."

"It is brand new," Meika said.

"Nope," Chief said. "More than a hundred-years old."

"And it still runs? No way," Meika said.

Chief nodded when Odette said, "Are you here to see Lilly?"

"Have you seen her?"

"She and Avory are locked in a room upstairs. Avory said they aren't coming out until they've worked all the bugs out of their script."

"What are you ladies doing?" Chief asked.

"Moving into our new house," Meika said.

"What are you using for furniture?"

"There's plenty of furniture in the storage warehouse. We picked out what we wanted this morning. Ben and his men moved it for us. We're on our way to see if we need to do any rearranging," Odette said.

"Need some muscle?" Chief asked.

"Sure," Odette said. "Can you give us a ride?"

"I thought you'd never ask," Chief said. "Hop in."

When Odette climbed into the passenger seat, Meika and Heather realized they had no room.

"You can come back for us," Heather said.

Chief stepped out of the car. "There's room for everybody," he said. "This baby has a rumble seat.

Chief opened the trunk of the old roadster that doubled as a backseat.

"How the hell do we get up there?" Meika asked.

Chief lifted her into the car, everyone laughing when he performed the same maneuver with Heather.

"Hang on," he said. "I don't have insurance."

Chief took off across the island, everyone squealing when he began cutting doughnuts in the sand. Tired of acting like a teenager with the family car, he drove to the cluster of vacation homes. When they arrived, he was surprised at what he saw.

The bungalows surrounded a communal garden with cobblestone pathways, marble sculptures, and a rock fountain with water spewing from a gargoyle's mouth. A live oak with branches draping to the ground highlighted the garden. Ben Biondo's workers were busy trimming hedges and trees, weeding flowerbeds, and planting fresh flowers. Ben met them when they exited the Model T.

"Love your car," he said. "Want to sell it?"

"It was my grandpa's," Chief said. "His ghost would never give me a moment's peace if I ever did."

"Let me know if you change your mind," Ben said.

"Your crew has done wonders," Odette said. "The garden is beautiful. How did it get so lush in this sand?"

"The builders must have hauled in a trainload of topsoil," Ben said.

Ben smiled when Meika said, "Where did you get the goldfish?"

"New Orleans," he said. "They arrived this morning."

"We're here to help move furniture," Odette said.

"Too late," Ben said. "It's all in already. Check your house. See if you like everything. If not, we'll change it out."

"Thanks, Ben," Odette said.

"No problem. Call if you need me."

Chief followed the three women to a corner house facing the bay.

"Looks like you have the best house in the complex," Chief said.

"We had the first choice," Odette said.

A porch swing and three rocking chairs occupied the covered porch facing the bay.

"I know where I'll be spending lots of time," Meika said.

"Me too," Odette said.

Three bedrooms and the kitchen opened up into the sunken living room. The furniture looked expensive and brand new, albeit nearly a century old. Odette's bedroom overlooked the garden.

"Odette had the first choice of bedrooms," Heather said. "She chose this one instead of the one with the best bay view."

"I can sit on the front porch and see the bay," Odette said. "Or I can gaze out my window and see the garden. It's the best of both worlds."

Chief sat on the front porch alone, drinking rum Odette had given him while she, Meika, and Heather put away their clothes. They joined him on the porch when they'd finished unpacking.

"Come on, girls," Odette finally said. "Let's get back to the hotel and prepare for dinner."

"No, Mommy, no," Meika said. "I love it here."

"It's a long walk from the hotel. I'm going to hit up Eddie to get us another ATV," Odette said.

"He's so grumpy. I think he needs a blowjob," Meika said.

"Don't look at me," Odette said.

"Not my job," Heather said. "I'm engaged."

"Your suggestion, Miss Meika," Odette said.

"Sorry," Meika said, "I'm not inclined in that direction."

"Then that settles it," Odette said. "He'll have

to stay grumpy."

Chief returned them to the Majestic without cutting any doughnuts in the Model T. He followed the three women into the hotel and to the kitchen, where Paula was helping Isaac.

"Thank God!" she said. "I thought you three had abandoned ship."

"No way," Odette said. "Thanks, Paula."

Paula hung her apron on a rack and started for the door. "Did they get you to volunteer?"

"Ben's workers had everything in order. All I did was drink rum, and it's about to wear off."

"Let's stop by the little bar," Paula said. "I'll fix you one."

The bar was empty as Chief sat on a stool. When Paula handed him his drink, he said, "Have you seen Lilly?"

"They didn't leave the room for lunch," Paula said. "I took them sandwiches. They're having script problems. Avory said they weren't leaving the room until they solved them. Lilly is fit to be tied."

"I'll bet," Chief said.

"I haven't returned to the camping trailer all morning," Paula said. "I'm leaving before Jimmie comes looking for me. Will you be okay?"

"I may as well go with you," Chief said. "Got a go cup?"

Paula handed him a red plastic cup and said, "Will this do?"

Chief was pouring the rum into the cup when he signaled a thumbs-up.

When Paula saw the Model T, she asked, "Whose car is that?"

"Mine," Chief said. "It was my grandpa's."

"It's beautiful. Does it run?"

"Hop in, and I'll show you," he said.

Paula held on tight as Chief sped up the hill toward the lighthouse.

"I love it," she said as she exited the car. "Thanks for the ride."

After parking the Model T beneath the protective overhang, the aroma of something cooking collided with Chief's senses.

"Smells wonderful," he said.

"Chicken fried steak and mashed potatoes," Jack said. "You always know the right time to show up."

Jack's perfectly-breaded chicken fries were almost as big as the dish they occupied.

"Man, that was good," Chief said after finishing his last bite of Texas toast."

"They'll weigh you down. Who's counting?"

"Not me," Chief said.

"That's a fact. Where's Miss Lilly?"

"Avory has her nose to the grindstone," Chief said. "It's okay. I have to go to the teepee and check on the chickens and my cat."

Chief nodded when Jack said, "And spend the whole night there? My couch is going to miss you."

"It'll get over it," Chief said. "Looks like rain out over the Gulf. I'm leaving Grandpa's car beneath the overhang."

"Want to play some gin or pinochle before you go?"

"I'm heading out before it starts raining."

"Suit yourself. I can take your money now, or take it later," Jack said.

"Later is better for me," Chief said. "See you tomorrow."

It was dark when Chief, Coco, and Ol' Joe left Jack's and headed toward the island's backside on foot. Raindrops sprinkled Chief's shoulders as they walked up the path to his teepee. A nip in the air invigorated Coco and Ol' Joe, and they ran in circles from sheer exhilaration.

Chief's cat Buttercup waited patiently,

rubbing his legs as he filled her food and water bowls. Already fed, Ol' Joe and Coco went straight to the pallet in the teepee. Chief grabbed a towel and cleaned up in his cold water shower.

It was dark, puffy clouds covering the stars and moon when he reentered the teepee and placed kindling and another log on the fire pit. He soon fell asleep after joining his animals on the sleeping pallet. He was lost in the land of dreams, chasing a bear through the forest, when something awakened him.

Chief sat up straight, gazing around the teepee in the dim light cast by gentle flames licking up from the fire pit. Whatever had awakened him hadn't disturbed his cat or two dogs. For a moment, he thought he had imagined the commotion. Then, he not only heard it again, he felt it. The pallet shook, and it wasn't his imagination.

The wind had whipped up outside the teepee, the door flap blowing. The rain had returned. Perfect sleeping weather if all his senses weren't suddenly working overtime. Chief couldn't explain why the chaotic movement he'd felt hadn't awakened his dogs and cat. His animals didn't stir when he crawled from under the blanket.

Chief didn't bother dressing or putting on his moccasins as he stepped through the door flap. Dressed in only his loincloth, he glanced upward as lightning danced across the sky. He knew it wasn't the thunder when another quake rocked La Tortue Mountain. Chief had never experienced an earthquake, though he knew one had just shaken him. He started along the trail toward the Magic Fountain, not knowing what to expect when he got there.

Except for an occasional burst of lightning, the path was as dark as the interior of a tomb. It didn't matter. Chief had walked up the hill so many times he could do it in total darkness.

When he reached the Magic Fountain, he knew something had changed. The pool of crystal water no longer occupied the highest part of La Tortue Mountain. The path continued upward at a steep rate. Chief sensed something else.

"Grandfather, is that you?"

An unearthly glow emanated from a breach in the rock wall before him, and Chief had to crouch to enter the opening. The swell had increased the island's elevation by at least fifty feet. After looking around, he backed out of the narrow entrance and returned down the steep trail to his teepee.

Coco, Ol' Joe, and Buttercup were still asleep when Chief entered the teepee. After dropping his loincloth to the floor, he used a towel to dry himself, crawled beneath the blanket, and returned to sleep.

Chapter 22

Jack, Chief, and their dogs were gone when J.P. dropped Lucky off. J.P. left Lucky in the communal playpen with the dogs in training.

"Sorry, big boy. We'll go for a walk on the beach when I return."

J.P. was waiting in the Chalmette police station when Wayne Gebbia arrived. He led J.P. down the hall. After chatting briefly with the cops around the coffee pot, they went to Sergeant Gebbia's office. Wayne shut the door behind them.

"I have some information about your missing person. I don't know how much it's going to help."

"You've already told me more than I could have learned on my own," J.P. said.

"Sex traffickers kidnapped your missing person before she crossed the Mexican border. Her group, three Ukrainians and a Russian man were granted asylum and crossed the border legally into the United States. The Ukrainians relocated to Bismarck, North Dakota. The Russian man seems to have dropped off the face of the earth."

"Do you have a name for Vixen?"

"I couldn't get the couple to tell me much over the phone," Wayne said.

"Because?"

"They're scared," Wayne said.

"Of what?" J.P. asked.

"Retribution."

"From who?"

"The Russians."

"Is it possible Russians could come looking for them?" J.P. asked.

"Anything's possible. The husband was a schoolteacher in one of the Russian-occupied provinces. The fighting destroyed their town. They'd lost everything, have relatives in North Dakota, and decided to move there."

"Why did they go through Mexico?" J.P. asked.

"A sponsor advised them if they reached the Mexican border, the U.S. would likely grant them asylum," Wayne said.

"Do you mind sharing their number with me?"

"I don't mind, though I doubt they'll tell you any more than they told me."

"What do you suggest?" J.P. asked.

"You know personal interviews are the best. They're afraid of the police, and I doubt the boys on the force in Bismarck could get much out of them. I'm sorry, J.P. That's all I got."

"You've been a big help. I'd know nothing right now if it weren't for you."

J.P.'s mind reeled after leaving the police station. He knew what he needed to do, though he was unsure how to get there. The Chalmette Animal Shelter was close, and he stopped and got Susie Larsen's help. She gave him a distressed look when he stuck his head in the door.

"I hope you aren't here to give me a ration of shit about this past weekend."

"Not why I'm here," he said. "I could see you were upset because of Isabella. How is she?"

"She's behind the desk. See for yourself."

Isabella licked his hand when he patted her head.

"Looking good," he said.

"I took her to the vet who vaccinated her. He said he could tell an accomplished surgeon had stitched her wounds."

"That's one of the reasons I'm here," J.P. said. "I'm trying to find who Vixen is and where she came from. Sergeant Gebbia at the police station found a couple who were with her in Mexico."

"She's from Mexico?"

"I believe she's from Ukraine," J.P. said.

"So, how can I help you?"

"The couple I need to interview lives in Bismarck, North Dakota. Can you check and see if any flights are going there today?"

"It's the dead of winter and cold in North Dakota."

"Have you been there?"

"A cousin of mine worked there as a roughneck," Susie said. "He married a North Dakota girl, has two kids, and lives in Bismarck."

"There's oil in North Dakota?"

"Lots of it," Susie said. "Sammie spent a winter in a man camp."

"What the hell is a man camp?"

"There weren't enough places to rent in North Dakota when the oil boom began. Big oil companies built modular housing. Sammie got rich because his room and board were free. He bought a hardware store which he still runs."

Susie was already searching the Internet while telling J.P. about her cousin Sammie.

"Find anything?" he asked.

"You have choices," she said. "Nothing direct. One-way or round trip?"

"Better do a one-way. I have no idea how long this is going to take."

Susie quickly had J.P. booked on a flight to Bismarck, and printed out his itinerary.

"Your plane leaves in less than two hours," Susie said. "Better get moving."

J.P. thanked her and started for the door.

"Wait a minute. I want to apologize for the weekend that wasn't."

"It's all good," J.P. said.

"Can we try again?"

"You and I are the Parish two-step champs," J.P. said. "I can't remember having so much fun as we did the night of the contest. Maybe we could go dancing when I get back from North Dakota. Never know what it might lead to."

Susie came around the desk and gave him the biggest hug.

"Don't freeze your balls off," she said. "We might need them later."

J.P. made the twenty miles to Louis Armstrong New Orleans International Airport in record time—a good thing, as he arrived not long before the plane began boarding. J.P. loved the airport. New Orleans is the birthplace of jazz, and no artist embodies that musical genre better than Louis Armstrong. He had no time to enjoy the airport's ambiance or beautiful architecture as he raced to the boarding plane.

Seeing his white Stetson, a flight attendant asked, "Where's your coat, cowboy?"

"Hopefully, I can buy something when we get there," he said.

"I'll check for you," she said. "Better stay inside until then."

J.P. realized what a long flight he was in for when he read the itinerary Susie had printed for him. It included a long layover in Minneapolis. The flight attendant smiled at him as he prepared to exit the plane.

"I found a place in the terminal where you can purchase warmer clothes," she said.

J.P. was wearing thermal socks and insulated underwear when he returned to the plane for the last leg of his flight. He also had warm gloves, and a purple and gold goose down jacket with Vikings embroidered on the back. As the plane descended to the Bismarck Municipal Airport, he saw the snow covering the ground.

J.P. didn't know what he would do with his new clothing when he returned to Louisiana. As he hailed a cab outside the terminal, he decided not to worry about it.

J.P. gave the cab driver the address of the Ukrainian couple. The roads were dry, though snow piled high on either side. It was late afternoon when he exited the cab and knocked on the door of a small house in a working-class neighborhood.

"Who is it?" a woman behind the closed door asked.

"J.P. Saucier," he said. "Can we talk?"

"I don't know you," she said.

"I'm from Chalmette, Louisiana. You spoke with Sergeant Gebbia with the Chalmette Police Department. He gave me your address. Call and ask him if you don't believe me."

"Are you a policeman?" the woman asked.

"Used to be," he said. "Now, I train service dogs."

"What do you want?"

"A woman was with you in Mexico. She has traumatic amnesia and has no clue who she is or where she's from. She helped me with my dogs, and now I'm trying to help her. Won't you please talk to me?"

"He's a cowboy," a small voice said. "Let him in, Mama."

The door opened, and a little boy smiled as he clutched his mother's leg.

"I'm J.P. What's your name?"

"Bo," the little boy said.

J.P. shook Bo's hand. "Happy to meet you, young fella. What's your mama's name?"

J.P. smiled when Bo said, "Mama."

"Hanna Kosenko," the woman said. "My husband is still at work."

"What does your husband do?"

"Bohdan teaches high school. He'll be home soon. I have coffee in the kitchen. Would you like a cup?"

Hanna nodded when J.P. said, "Love some. It's like a meat locker out there."

"Bohdan and I love this place. It reminds us of home, and relatives here helped us establish."

Hanna was tall, probably five-seven or eight, her dark shag-styled hair framing her blue eyes. Bo also had dark hair and blue eyes.

"How old is Bo?" J.P. asked.

"Four," the little boy said. "Are you a real cowboy?"

"I ride horses and used to compete in rodeos," J.P. said.

"I want a horse," Bo said.

"If you ever visit me in Louisiana, I'll take you horse riding."

"Can I, Mama?"

"Sure," Hanna said.

When the front door opened, Bo ran to hug his father's leg. Bohdan smiled as he lifted his son, twirling him in a circle. His smile disappeared when he saw J.P. sitting at the kitchen table.

"Bohdan," Hanna said. "This is J.P."

"Hanna didn't let me in, Bohdan," J.P. said. "Bo did. I'm sorry to disturb you and your beautiful family. I only want to ask a few questions, and then I promise you'll never see me again."

"Please, Bohdan," Hanna said. "Sit with us."

Bo was still hugging his father's leg. "J.P.'s a cowboy," he said.

Hanna frowned when Bohdan said something in a language J.P. didn't recognize.

"I'm sorry," J.P. said. "I don't understand Ukrainian."

"It's not Ukrainian," Hanna said. "Bohdan called you a killer in Russian."

"I'm one-hundred-percent coon-ass Cajun from south Louisiana. I've never even met a person from Russia."

Realizing J.P. had no idea what he had said, Bohdan sat at the table and let Hanna pour him a cup of coffee.

"What is it you wish to know?" he asked.

"My partners and I run a canine training facility on an island south of New Orleans. Jack and Chief rescued a woman from a bar in the French Quarter. She has traumatic amnesia. I'm trying to find out who she is. I believe she may have accompanied you to the Mexican border."

"Her first name is Renata," Bohdan said. "A Russian was part of our group. Renata was with him."

"What was a Russian doing with you?"

"He was a deserter from the Russian army," Hanna said.

"What was Renata doing with a Russian deserter?" J.P. asked.

"Renata didn't communicate," Bohdan said. "I don't believe I ever heard her speak."

"What's the Russian's name?" J.P. asked.

"Alex Pavlovich," Hanna said.

Hanna shook her head when J.P. asked, "Did Pavlovich tell you why Renata was with him, Bohdan?" J.P. said.

"I never spoke to the man except in passing," Bohdan said. "I didn't trust him." He gave his wife a look and said, "Hanna was friendly with him."

"He reminded me of my brother. I felt sorry for him because he had lost everything like us and could never return to Russia."

"What happened to him?" J.P. asked.

"He was flown here to Bismarck with us," Bohdan said. "We have no idea where he is now."

J.P. was a trained interrogator and noticed the glance Hanna gave her husband after hearing his remark.

"The taxi is waiting outside for me," J.P. said. "Thanks for your help."

"I'll walk you to the door," Hanna said.

Bo was sitting in his father's lap, and J.P. said. "So long, Bo. Don't forget about the horse ride I promised you."

Bo remained with his father, waving as Hanna accompanied J.P. out of the room.

When Hanna opened the door, J.P. said, "You know where Alex is, don't you?"

"He moved to Tioga and got a job drilling oil wells. He lives in the Lone Wolf Lodge, a man camp outside the town."

"What's he look like?" J.P. asked.

"Shorter than I am," Hanna said. "He has dark receding hair and a shiny forehead."

"Thanks, Hanna."

The cab driver was blowing on his hands when J.P. climbed into the back seat.

"Can you drive me to Tioga?" J.P. asked.

"Tioga's two hundred miles north. You think the roads are bad here? You don't want to go to Tioga."

"Then take me back to the airport," J.P. said.

J.P. grinned when the man said, "Returning to Texas?"

"Nope. I'm renting a car and driving to Tioga."

Chapter 23

Snow fell in clumps when the cab driver dropped J.P. in front of the Bismarck airport. Once inside the terminal, he called Jack.

"Where are you?" Jack asked."

"The airport in Bismarck, North Dakota."

"What the hell are you doing there?"

"Following up on some leads. I know what Vixen's real first name is."

"What?" Jack asked.

"Renata. I spoke with a couple who were with her before crossing the Mexican border."

"When are you coming home?" Jack asked.

"After I interview a Russian man who accompanied her to Mexico," J.P. said.

"Is he in Bismarck?"

"A little town north of here. The roads are bad, and I don't know how long it will take to drive there."

"It's already getting dark. Find a motel and go tomorrow," Jack said.

"I'll think about it," J.P. said.

"When was the last time you drove on ice and snow?"

"In the army," J.P. said. "Don't worry about

me. It's like riding a bicycle. You don't forget."

J.P. laughed when Jack said, "I grew up in snowy Massachusetts, and those are famous last words."

"Will you watch out for Lucky until I return?"

"You know you don't have to ask," Jack said.

"Thanks, buddy. I didn't bring my phone charger. I need to get off the line before it goes dead."

"Be careful," Jack said.

"I will. If you see Susie Larsen, tell her it's so damn cold, I'm about to freeze my balls off."

"Then keep your pants on," Jack said.

J.P. bought a phone charger in a terminal gift shop. His stomach was growling. He hadn't eaten all day except for some pretzels on the plane. The burger and fries he purchased before heading for the rental car kiosks helped.

It felt like the temperature had dropped another ten degrees when J.P. found his rental car in an unheated parking garage. He was soon heading north, the wipers working overtime to keep the windshield clear of snow.

It was late when J.P. reached Tioga and pulled into an all-night filling station. The man behind the counter had a handlebar mustache and a red stocking cap pulled over his ears.

"Can you give me directions to the Lone Wolf Lodge?" J.P. asked.

"You looking for a job?"

"Maybe," J.P. said.

"I need help here. I pay good. You interested?"

"Does it pay as much as the oil rigs?" J.P. asked.

"Not even close. You don't have to work twelve to sixteen-hour shifts and weeks at a time with no days off."

"You have quite the liquor store. I didn't realize you could sell alcohol at a filling station in

North Dakota," J.P. said.

"As long as I ring up the sale on a different register. Don't ask. It don't make any sense to me, either. The Lone Wolf Lodge is about twenty miles north of here."

"What's a man camp like?" J.P. asked.

"Modular housing. The oil companies pay for the lodge. You get a bed, a T.V. set, a table, and a chair. The cafeteria is open from four in the morning until nine at night. No pets, women, guns, or alcohol in your room."

"Picky, picky," J.P. said with a grin.

"Good thing they never search the rooms, or they'd probably find lots of things that aren't allowed," the man said.

"If the road is as bad as the one I just came off of, I think I'll find a motel here in town and head out tomorrow morning," J.P. said.

"The company that owns the man camp keeps the road clear. You'll have an easier trip than on the state highway."

"It's late and too damn cold to sleep in the car," J.P. said.

"The reception center is run like a motel. They'll give you a room because you'll be working by tomorrow."

"You sound as if you know what you're talking about," J.P. said. "Did you work the rigs for a while?"

"Ten years. The last oil bust shut everything down and ended my oil career. No rigs running to speak of for almost two years. I got hitched, had a kid, and needed work. I had enough money saved to buy this place. It's profitable, though good help is hard to find. I'm Mack, by the way."

"I was never good at retail, Mack, or I'd take you up on your offer."

"You on the run?" Mack asked.

J.P. smiled. "If I were, I wouldn't tell you, now

would I?"

"Don't mind me," Mack said. "I did a little time once myself."

"How's your liquor prices?" J.P. asked.

"Best in town," Mack said.

"Got any Russian vodka?"

"A little hard to come by with the war and all," Mack said. "I got a bottle of Zyr. Is that Russian enough for you?"

J.P. left Mack's with a full tank of gas, a bottle of Zyr vodka, and directions to the man camp. The road was clear of ice and snow, and he soon reached the facility where oil crews lived when they weren't working.

The Lone Wolf Lodge was a mélange of large modular structures, with florescent lighting imparting a hollow feeling of security. A van stopped in front of one of the larger modular buildings. The weather had grown frigid as J.P. stepped out of the car. Five men exited the van and disappeared into a separate room, where they removed their muddy boots and outer clothes before entering the lodge.

One of the men still sitting by the roaring fireplace in the lobby fit the description of Alex Pavlovich. When J.P. spoke, the man wheeled around and lifted his hands into the air.

"Are you Alex?"

J.P. noticed the man's pronounced accent when he said, "Who are you?"

"J.P. Saucier. Hanna told me where to find you."

"I suppose you are going to kill me," Alex said.

J.P. grinned and said, "Hell, Alex, I'm a Cajun from south Louisiana. Not a Russian."

"What do you want from me?" he asked.

"Answers. I live on an island south of New Orleans and used to be a cop. Now, I train dogs.

My two business partners rescued an abused blond woman with a foreign accent. She was stripping in a Bourbon Street bar and called herself Vixen."

"Her name is Renata. How is her mental health?"

"She's suffering from traumatic amnesia. I'm trying to help her. My search led me to you. I have a bottle of Zyr in my coat."

"You must be a good policeman if you know my favorite vodka," Alex said.

"I used to be the best."

J.P. followed Alex down a series of connecting hallways. Alex's room was like Mack had described: Spartan. J.P. pulled the bottle of Zyr from his jacket and placed it on the single table in the room. Alex found two glasses and filled them with vodka.

"I'm just finishing a sixteen-hour shift. Be comfortable while I shower and change clothes."

"Thanks," J.P. said.

Alex took his glass of vodka with him into the bathroom. It was empty when he returned dressed in pajamas, slippers, and a bathrobe. J.P. got out of the chair and sat on the bed.

"You can sit in the chair," Alex said.

"If you just finished a sixteen-hour shift, you deserve it more than I do."

"Thank you. I have not had Zyr since I left Russia."

"How long has that been?" J.P. asked.

"Months. I suppose you are wondering why I deserted."

"As a former army officer, the thought crossed my mind," J.P. said.

"Our government told us the Ukrainians were Nazis, and we were fighting for the good of Mother Russia. It did not take long to see through that lie. As our casualties mounted, despair began replacing our resolve."

"I know this is painful. You don't have to tell me everything," J.P. said. "I witnessed some atrocities during my time in Afghanistan."

"Most soldiers are decent," Alex said. "Others use war to satisfy their lust for pillaging, rape, and murder."

"And Renata was a victim," J.P. said.

Alex nodded and poured himself more vodka.

"We occupied a Ukrainian town not far from Kyiv. Instead of welcoming us, the citizens threw rocks. Things grew progressively worse. Two of my men were unaccounted for one night. I went looking for them."

"You were an officer?"

Alex nodded again. "Someone informed me where they were. I went to retrieve them."

"And you found them at Renata's?"

"Renata is a beautiful woman. All the men had seen her. Two of my soldiers broke into her house. Her husband was dead when I arrived, the two men taking turns raping Renata. They held Renata's mother and daughter at gunpoint, forcing them to watch."

Alex drank more vodka and drew silent. J.P. poured another glass for himself.

"What happened?" he asked.

"I grabbed the man on top of Renata by his hair, yanking him to his feet," Alex said. "When his accomplice pointed his rifle at me, I jerked it out of his hand. Renata grabbed the rifle and opened fire. She killed both men and then handed the weapon to me. I had the rifle in my hand when soldiers burst through the door."

Alex nodded when J.P. said, "You were holding the proverbial smoking gun, and the soldiers thought you had killed your own men?"

"They dragged Renata and me from the house. They would have executed us after raping and torturing Renata."

"You're both alive. What happened?" J.P. asked.

"Artillery attack. Shells began targeting our headquarters. In the chaos, I pulled Renata out the door into the darkness. She fought me."

"She wanted to return for her mother and daughter?" J.P. said.

"We have to escape, I told her. They will torture and kill us both if we do not. I promised I would return for her mother and daughter."

"What was the name of the town?" J.P. asked.

"Bucha," Alex said.

"Do you know Renata's last name?"

"Yatsenko," Alex said. "Her mother, Iryna, and daughter Sveta."

"How did you wind up at the Mexican border?" J.P. asked.

"I posed as a Ukrainian, and we crossed the border into Poland," Alex said.

"Why didn't you just stay in Poland?"

"The Russians deal harshly with dissenters. When I learned an assassin was looking for us, I arranged to smuggle us into Mexico."

"And that's where you and Renata were separated," J.P. said.

"I crossed the border legally with Hanna, her husband, and her son. Renata disappeared in Mexico, and I did not know what had happened to her."

"She was kidnapped by sex traffickers who transported her to New Orleans. As I said, my partners rescued her. She's safe on Oyster Island."

Alex shook his head. "She is still in danger. Russian assassins do not easily give up. Someone is looking for her and may already know where she is."

"Shit!" J.P. said.

Alex slammed a full glass of vodka and began packing his clothes.

"Where are you going?" J.P. asked.

"To keep my promise."

"How do you intend to get to Ukraine? You don't even have a passport," J.P. said.

"I have something better: a U.S. Refugee Travel Document. It works the same as a passport," Alex said. "It will get me where I need to go."

"I'll take your word for it," J.P. said. "What's your plan?"

"I will book a flight into Ukraine, or at least as close as possible, and then find Renata's mother and daughter. I will get them to the Polish border. They can cross into Poland without a passport."

"You'll need help. I'm coming with you," J.P. said.

"Ukraine is a war zone. It is dangerous," Alex said.

"No more dangerous for me than it is for you, and I have a vehicle to get us to the airport in Bismarck," J.P. said. "Are you planning on returning to the States?"

"I'll stay in Poland. After the war, I'll return to Russia."

"Even if Russia wins the war?"

"An old Russian proverb says God keeps those safe who keep themselves safe."

Chapter 24

Eddie drove his Porsche 911 up the slight hill to Jack's house and parked the car. He and Basil had left the Majestic, dressed to the nines in preparation for their first court date at the St. Bernard Parish courthouse. Eddie had left his pink seersucker suit in the closet.

"Just in time for breakfast," Jack said when they walked through the door."

"We already had breakfast," Eddie said. "Isaac cooked us omelets to order."

"Did he now?" Jack said.

"Don't get bent out of shape. Isaac's a world-class cook though not half as good as you are," Eddie said.

"You're lying," Jack said. "Doesn't matter. It's saving me on groceries."

"He damn sure can't pour rum as good as you," Eddie said.

"That's a fact," Jack said.

"Where are Chief and J.P.? Sleeping late?" Eddie asked.

"J.P.'s probably in Minnesota by now."

Eddie sipped the coffee Jack had poured for him. "What's he doing in Minnesota?"

"He had a lead on Vixen's identity and flew to

North Dakota yesterday to check it out."

"So, he's on his way back?" Eddie said.

"He called and wanted me to overnight his passport and ten grand in cash to a drop box in the Minneapolis airport," Jack said. "Chief left earlier to take the cash and passport to a shipping company in Chalmette."

"What else did J.P. say?" Eddie asked.

"He wanted me to look after Lucky. Said he'd explain everything when he returned. Why are you two all dressed up?"

"Court appearance," Eddie said. "Frankie filed a lawsuit in state court."

"And?" Jack said.

"Our case is a Federal matter. Federal Court is the proper venue. The judge is hearing oral arguments to decide."

"Then maybe you'd better lay off the rum," Jack said.

"Basil passed the bar exam on his first try. He's a lawyer now. He'll do the talking."

Basil nodded when Jack said, "You nervous?"

"A little bit," Basil said.

"Is that a Model T Ford parked in front of the house?" Eddie asked.

"Exactly what it is," Jack said.

"It looks brand new. Where'd you get it?"

"It's what Chief's grandfather got for trading the island," Jack said. "We dug it out of the swamp."

"Impossible. It would have turned into a bucket of rust."

"It didn't," Jack said.

"How do you know what Chief's grandfather traded for the island?" Basil asked.

"He visited Chief the other night during the lightning storm," Jack said.

"You mean a ghost?" Basil said.

"Chief swore it was his grandfather's ghost.

None of the rest of us saw him. Funny thing, though."

"What?" Eddie said.

"Chief took us directly to the Model T the following morning. How would he have known where it was if his grandfather hadn't told him?

"That is strange," Eddie said. "You say J.P. is flying out of the country?"

"He didn't want to explain over the phone," Jack said.

Eddie glanced at Basil. "Sounds ominous. Who does he think is listening?"

"Why would anybody even care?" Basil said.

"J.P. will call in a few days to talk to you about it," Jack said.

"It is ominous if he needs a lawyer's opinion," Eddie said. "I wonder what our boy is up to."

"Guess you're going to have to wait until he calls you," Jack said.

Basil glanced at his watch. "We'd better go. Don't want to be late for our first court date."

"I'm cooking lasagna tonight," Jack said. "You're invited to eat my cooking if you aren't too good now."

"You had me at lasagna," Eddie said. "I'll be here. What time?"

"Hell, I don't know," Jack said. "Stop by on your way from the courthouse. If you go to the Majestic first, you may not return."

"No doubt I'll need a drink by then."

"Hell, Eddie. You probably need a drink right now," Jack said.

"You know me too well," Eddie said.

"You and Heather are also invited," Jack said.

"Heather's working the bar tonight," Basil said. "Eddie has bragged about your lasagna. Okay if I come alone?"

"Of course. Chief will want to hear your take on the court appearance."

Basil and Eddie were soon on their way to Chalmette, Eddie frowning as he tried to avoid the ruts and potholes in his 911.

"One of these days, the Majestic will be profitable enough to pave this road," he said.

"My cousin is the parish commissioner," Basil said. "I'll ask him if he can lay some gravel for us."

"You think he will?"

"He owes my dad lots of favors," Basil said. "He'll do it."

Basil laughed when Eddie said, "I don't want to get him into trouble. Or us."

"The voters love him, and everyone in Louisiana expects a little graft and corruption as long as it's out in the open."

"Damn, Basil. Don't ever say that around a group of lawyers."

Basil smiled again. "It's okay to be a little crooked in Louisiana. Supporters might want me to run for governor."

"You're kidding, I hope," Eddie said.

"My dad's not a crooked politician," Basil said. "If I ever run for office, I won't be either."

"You thinking about running for governor someday?" Eddie asked.

"President," Basil said.

"You have my vote," Eddie said.

The sky was light blue without a cloud in sight. Eddie had to slow the car to prevent hitting a snowy egret that flew out of the shallow water beside the road. Basil didn't seem to notice.

"Thanks for all your help with the wedding," he said.

"Don't thank me," Eddie said. "Paula's doing most of the leg work."

"She isn't paying for the biggest wedding reception ever held in St. Bernard Parish."

Eddie was almost afraid to reply. "Tell me

about it," he said.

"Paula and Jimmie got us registered at all the right places. You didn't have to pay to print our wedding invitations. I'm committed to helping you no matter what."

"It's the least I could do," Eddie said.

"Wait till you see the bill before you say that. Where are you coming up with the money to pay for the reception?"

A giant frog suddenly lodged in Eddie's throat.

"I'll manage," he said.

"You'll be the most popular person in the parish. Hell, Eddie, you could run for governor."

"You think?" Eddie said.

"This is going to help us big time in our court case," Basil said. "My dad has already called and wants to know if your invitation includes state officials and politicians."

"Why not?" Eddie said.

"Want to hear my opinion?" Basil asked.

"Of course."

"If you want to settle with Frankie, you need to marry his daughter, Josie."

"What makes you think we'll have to settle this case?"

"I don't. I was only weighing alternatives in my head if things go sour."

"Marrying Josie or anyone else isn't an alternative," Eddie said.

"I'm only trying to help," Basil said.

"Are you sensing something?" Eddie said.

"Frankie's already hammering us. He can outspend us a hundred to one."

"Probably more than that," Eddie said. "Josie wouldn't have me back even if I wanted her to."

"Paula has a few ideas."

"Does she now?" Eddie said. "What did she tell you?"

"I think she was brainstorming. She and Jimmie will be at Jack's tonight. Ask her."

A crowd had already gathered outside the courthouse as Eddie pulled into the parking lot. They entered the courtroom and found seats in the plaintive and defendant's section. At precisely nine, the clerk of court entered the courtroom.

"All rise," he said.

Everyone stood as Judge Kline, his long black robe swirling, entered the courtroom.

"Be seated." Turning to the court clerk, he said. "Who's first on the docket?"

"Southern Investments vs. Grogan La Tortue," he said.

The judge with snowy white hair glanced down at them. "Are the attorneys representing the two parties present? Please approach the bench."

Eddie, Basil, and two Southern Investments attorneys stood before the judge's bench.

"Tell me, Mr. Doles, why you feel my court isn't the proper venue for this case," the judge said.

"The transaction which is the basis of this lawsuit is invalid, Your Honor," Basil said.

"And why is that?" Judge Kline asked.

"Mr. La Tortue's grandfather didn't have the authority to sell the island."

"Because?" the judge said.

"Mr. La Tortue was an Atakapa Indian. The Atakapas would have held Aboriginal Title, also known as original Indian Title, or Indian Right of Occupancy, to the island. You can't sell something you don't have title to," Basil said. "In this case, Oyster Island would be held in Federal Trust because Louisiana never extinguished Aboriginal Title."

"The Indian Removal Act of 1830 overlooked the tribe?" the judge asked.

"That's correct, Your Honor," Basil said.

"Oyster Island is tribal land Mr. La Tortue's grandfather had no authority to sell. This is a Federal matter, and the proper venue is Federal Court."

"What's your answer to Mr. Doles's argument, Mr. Berry?"

"When the sale occurred in 1919, Grogan La Tortue wasn't born, nor was his father. Grogan La Tortue's grandfather wasn't married in 1919. When the transaction occurred, Gilbert La Tortue was truly the last of the Atakapa Indians. If the Atakapa Indians owned Oyster Island by Aboriginal Title, as Mr. Doles implies, Gilbert La Tortue was the only remaining Atakapa. He was the sole owner of the island and had all the right in the world to sell it."

"Court Clerk set a date for a hearing in ten days." Judge Kline rustled the papers on the bench in front of him. "I'll take your arguments under advisement and give my decision then."

When the judge rapped the gavel on the bench signaling the hearing was over, everyone began filing for the door. Frankie's lawyer Mr. Berry was waiting for them in the hall.

"Mr. Castellano wants to know how long you intend to persist."

"What's that supposed to mean?" Eddie asked.

"Just a reminder that you're up against overwhelming odds," Mr. Berry said.

"Please tell Mr. Castellano he's invited to Basil and Heather's wedding. And Lowell," Eddie said, using Berry's first name, "So are you."

Berry grinned and walked away without replying.

"Pompous bastard," Eddie said.

"Don't mind him," Basil said. "He's usually an ambulance chaser who got lucky when Frankie hired every lawyer in town."

Eddie gave Basil a fist bump, refraining from further conversation until they reached the parking lot.

"What do you think?" Basil asked.

"You did a wonderful job, but. . ."

"But what?" Basil said.

"Even if we successfully change the venue to Federal Court, the question of ownership will still raise its ugly head. If the court rules Gilbert La Tortue is the legitimate heir to the island, we're screwed. If he isn't, we're screwed. The only thing we'll accomplish by getting the venue changed to Federal Court is to prolong the inevitable."

"Let's at least prolong it until after the wedding," Basil said.

"A litigator is like a high-stakes gambler. You have to know when to kiss the dice and when to kiss your ass goodbye."

"I like the dice part better than my ass," Basil said. "Seriously. What'll we do?"

"There's always a way. Find a reason to contest the island sale," Eddie said.

"Fraud, maybe?"

"Maybe," Eddie said. "Do you have a copy of the Bill of Sale?"

"I do," Basil said.

"That's as good as any place to start. We'll go over it when we get back to the island. Right now, I need a drink."

"Have you forgotten about our invitation to Jack's?" Basil asked.

"Thanks for reminding me. The examination of the bill of sale will have to wait until tomorrow. As I said, I need a drink."

Chapter 25

Eddie didn't reach the island before stopping for a drink.

"Where do all the Chalmette lawyers go for happy hour?"

"Claws & Craws. I'm about as welcome there as a skunk at a garden party," Basil said. "There's a drive-through daiquiri bar on Paris Road."

"As long as I've lived in Louisiana, I've never bought a drink at a drive-through bar."

Basil grinned. "You can buy a daiquiri from a drive-through. You can't drink it while you're driving. Frankie would love to have us hauled to jail."

"I'll put the top up," Eddie said. "Let's get one."

When a woman stuck her head out the sliding glass window," Eddie said, "Two daiquiris."

"What size?" the woman asked.

"The biggest you have," Eddie said.

The smiling woman handed him two giant daiquiris in frosted cups.

"Two thirty-two ounce Mega Daiquiris, dreamy eyes. Eleven dollars and fifty cents."

Eddie winked, gave her a twenty, and said,

"Keep the change, baby."

Eddie pushed the red straw through the top of the plastic container as Basil shook his head in disbelief.

"Heather's never going to forgive me if I get put in jail," he said.

"It's broad daylight," Eddie said. "No cops are looking for drunks at this hour."

A car parked beside the road pulled out behind them as if on cue and turned on its flashing lights.

"Oh, shit!" Basil said.

Eddie stopped, placed the giant daiquiri container on the floorboard beneath his feet, and pulled out his wallet. Eddie handed him his driver's license when a parish deputy approached the window.

"I don't need your license," the deputy in khaki uniform and smoky hat said. "You. Get out of the car."

"I didn't do anything, officer," Basil said.

"What's that in your hand?" the deputy asked.

"Daiquiri," Basil said. "It's legal. The lid is still on the cup."

At this point, the deputy couldn't contain his laughter. "Did I scare you, Basil?"

"Gunner Hines, you asshole!"

Basil and the deputy named Gunner were soon hugging and laughing.

"Sally got our invitation to your wedding yesterday."

"Eddie, this is Gunner Hines, the best quarterback ever to toss the leather at Chalmette High. He's my closest friend and will be my best man."

Though he didn't show it, Eddie was relieved.

"Glad to meet you, Gunner," he said. "You must be a special person if you're Basil's best friend. He's one of the finest persons I've ever known."

"Nice to meet you, Eddie," Gunner said. "The entire town is talking about the reception you're hosting. You're a local hero, except for Heather's dad. He's pissed."

"He's invited," Eddie said.

"I'll be surprised if he and Heather's mom show up." Gunner glanced at his watch. "Got to get back to work. Watch that daiquiri, Eddie. It tastes way too good to kick over and muck up the floorboard of your beautiful car."

Basil was smiling and shaking his head when Gunner's patrol car did a one-eighty and started back toward Chalmette.

"What?" Eddie said.

Basil turned away from Eddie's stare and glanced out the window.

"Didn't say a word," he said.

Eddie's daiquiri was beginning to melt when they reached Jack's and parked the 911 safely beneath the covered parking. Everyone, including Avory and Lilly, crowded Jack's house. Odette saw them come in the door and walked over to greet them. Basil excused himself and headed for the little bar Jack had set up on the kitchen counter.

"Want this daiquiri?" Eddie said. "I hate sweet drinks and barely took a sip."

"I'll drink it," Odette said. "How did we do in court today?"

"Fought to a draw. Unfortunately, we're still in the first quarter."

"Chief has been nervous as a cat," she said.

Eddie caught a glimpse of Chief across the crowded room. He nodded, smiled, and gave him a thumbs up. The gesture seemed to satisfy the big man as he returned to playing gin with Jimmie at the plank table.

"How's it going at the Majestic?" Eddie asked.

"Meika, Heather, and Isaac are holding down the fort," Odette said. "We moved into one of the houses on the bay."

"How is it?" Eddie asked.

"I love it. We all have our own beds and bathrooms. The floors are polished hardwood, and there's expensive tile in the kitchen and bathrooms. A covered porch outside my bedroom has a hammock to lie in and view the garden. I'm in heaven, and so are my dogs."

"What about Vixen?"

"She's so traumatized she wouldn't move from her room in the hotel. Jack said J.P. is out of the country searching for her true identity."

"That's what I heard," Eddie said.

"I did some quick and dirty accounting earlier today," Odette said. "If business continues, we'll book a record month."

Odette turned away when Eddie said, "Good thing since we're hosting a parish cocktail party that will cost a small fortune. Know anything about it?"

"Paula said you gave her the okay," Odette said. "You sound upset."

"If I don't have the wedding and host the reception on Valentine's Day, Basil will quit and go home. Avory will sue me for everything I own if I have the wedding and the reception."

"You know what they say," Odette said. "Damned if you do. Damned if you don't."

"Cute," Eddie said.

"Don't take everything so personally," Odette said.

"Not everything," Eddie said. "Just my pocketbook."

"Stop fretting," Odette said. "Paula's working on a solution."

"She'd better hurry."

"Speaking of Avory, here she comes. Have fun."

"Thanks," Eddie said.

Avory's heels and little black dress would have drawn approval at a Hollywood cocktail party. She was smiling as she sipped her martini.

"You look gorgeous tonight," Eddie said. "What's the occasion?"

"Lilly and I worked all day on the script. We had to leave the Majestic, have some fun, and forget about the script before it drove us both crazy."

"Let me look at it," Eddie said.

"So, you're a screenwriter now?"

"I've read millions of legal documents. My talent is turning a good legal argument into a great one."

"A Hollywood script is far from a legal document," Avory said.

"I minored in creative writing in college. Structure is structure, no matter what you're crafting. Let me read your script. I can help."

"You can't be serious," Avory said.

"You want a free reading by a five-hundred buck an hour attorney, or not?"

"Why the hell not? You can't do any worse than Lilly and me. There's a copy in the ATV," Avory said.

"Get it for me. I'll read it now."

"In the middle of a cocktail party?" Avory said.

"I'm focused. It's one of my better traits. How long is it?"

"Ninety double-spaced pages."

"Hell, girl! I'm a speed reader. I'll tell you what's right and wrong with the script before Jack rings the dinner bell."

"If you're lying, I'm going to kill you," Avory said. "Wait here."

"Bring me a scotch on your way back," Eddie said.

"Get it yourself," Avory said. "I'm not your fucking waitress."

Eddie was laughing as he poured a tall scotch from the bar. Basil waved his arms as he talked to Jack, Chief, and Jimmie, explaining how the court appearance went. Eddie returned to the front door before they could pull him into the conversation.

"Here it is," Avory said. "I need another martini."

Eddie settled on the couch and opened the script. The room buzzed with activity, Paula and Odette helping Jack in his little kitchen and Basil had joined them.

Lilly's dress looked similar to the one Avory wore. Hers was red. She had her hand on Chief's shoulder as she watched him and Jimmie play gin rummy. Avory joined them. Jack served the shrimp étouffée buffet-style on paper plates. Odette was sitting by the fireplace, and Paula joined her.

"What did Eddie say?" she asked.

"That when Avory finds out about the Valentine's Day wedding and reception, she will come unglued."

"I can't believe she hasn't heard about it already," Paula said.

"Me either," Odette said between bites. "We need to do something. Any fresh ideas?"

"I have a jug of Cajun mood enhancer chilling in the fridge," Paula said.

"What's that?"

"It makes friends out of enemies. If I could sell it to the military, there would never be another war," Paula said. "We'll put some in Eddie's and Avory's drinks and maybe Chief and Lilly's. I haven't decided yet."

"When?"

"Don't know. I'm not sure if tonight's the right time. I brought the mood enhancer just in case."

Paula smiled when Odette said, "Is it dangerous?"

"Only if you have secrets you want to keep."

Odette and Paula finished eating and returned to the kitchen as Ben Biondo and Colin Dane entered the house."

"What on earth is that wonderful aroma?" Colin asked.

"Shrimp," Jack said. "Better have a plate."

When Jack handed them paper plates and plastic utensils, Colin said, "Your best china?"

Colin laughed when Jack said, "Where you from? London?"

"Only jesting, old chap," Colin said. "If it tastes as good as it smells, I'll eat the paper plate."

When he finished his étouffée, Ben remained in the kitchen to talk with Jack. Colin joined the rummy game. Avory's smile disappeared when Colin whispered something in her ear. Odette and Paula were watching.

"Get the jug of mood enhancer," Paula said. "It's time to use it."

Avory was fuming and on her way to the couch when Odette handed her a fresh martini. She'd finished almost the entire drink by the time she'd reached the couch. Odette followed her, giving a spiked scotch to Eddie. Paula had taken spiked drinks to Lilly and Chief. Chief almost smiled after taking a sip of the rum.

"This is the best martini I've ever tasted," Lilly said. "Does it have a secret ingredient?"

Paula nodded. "It's a secret."

"One I hope you'll share with me one day," Lilly said.

"Have you shown Lilly your Model T yet?"

Paula asked.

"Is that beautiful old car out there yours?" Lilly asked.

"It's my baby," Chief said. "Want to go for a moonlight ride?"

"I'd love to," Lilly said.

"Why don't you take Avory and Eddie along?" Paula said.

"Why not?" Lilly said. "I can't remember feeling so full of life, and I want to share it with everyone."

"Let Eddie and Avory have a moment before you join them. I'll fix a flask so you'll have something to drink on your joyride. No DUIs on Oyster Island."

Avory's frown had disappeared before she reached the couch. Her little black skirt rose over her thighs when she sat in Eddie's lap and wrapped an arm around his neck.

"I'm mad at you," she said.

"If this is how you show anger, I'm going to piss you off more often," Eddie said.

"I love the Majestic," she said. "It's so evocative and romantic."

"You saw Laurel's ghost your first night there," Eddie said. "Did anyone ever tell you her story?"

Avory kissed Eddie's cheek. "Odette showed us the little room where the mob kept her. I feel I should be mad at you," she said. "Tell me more of your ghost story."

"Laurel was the daughter of the lighthouse keepers. Mobsters killed her parents and enslaved her. She was only fifteen."

"Horrible."

"She spent the remainder of her short life as a prostitute in a ten by ten room servicing one drunk after another. She died in that room, never once leaving it."

Avory's hand went to her mouth as tears formed in the corners of her eyes.

"So despicable," she said.

"Laurel was non-verbal and never spoke a word. One of the men who used her body was a vampire. He infected her."

"It's so sad that she only knew carnal sex and never the beauty of true love," Avory said.

"Yes, she did," Eddie said.

"Tell me," Avory said.

"Paula is a traiteur," Eddie said. "A Cajun witch who can converse with the dead."

Eddie nodded when Avory said, "Are you serious?"

"The ghosts of Laurel's parents haunted the lighthouse. Jack was even afraid to go in there. Paula and Odette helped the parents cross over. Paula promised them she would help Laurel do the same."

"Vampires can't cross," Avory said. "Can they?"

"Let me tell the story," Eddie said.

"Sorry," Avory said.

"Paula and Odette visited the hotel while demons and evil spirits still occupied it. They found Laurel's bones on the carnal bed of the little room. Another skeleton was beside her on the bed."

Eddie shook his head when Avory said, "The skeleton of the rapist who killed her?"

"Laurel's lover, Christopher. Laurel and Christopher's skeletons lay wrapped in a final embrace."

"Who is Christopher, and where did he come from?" Avory asked.

"Odette and Paula learned the answer to that question when they found the bones in the little room. The ghost of Christopher appeared to them."

“What did he look like?” Avory asked.

“A young man with light brown hair and clear blue eyes, his muscular shoulders covered with tattoos. Laurel also appeared, and Christopher told Odette and Paula their story.”

Eddie nodded when Avory said, “And you’re going to tell me?”

“Christopher was a janitor who brought Laurel’s food, cleaned her room, and cared for her needs. He became her only friend.”

“Was he also a vampire?”

“You’re getting ahead of me,” Eddie said.

“Sorry.”

“The Prohibition Era occurred during the Great Depression. Christopher was sentenced to twenty years in Angola for robbing a bank during his last year of med school at Tulane.”

“I thought he was a good guy,” Avory said.

“People’s ethics sometimes bend when hungry, and their families suffer. He escaped during the great Angola prison break of 1933 and traveled to the island. The bootleggers didn’t care if he was an escaped convict. Laurel infected him.”

“Vampires are the undead,” Avory said. “They are immortal.”

“Christopher caught a client torturing Laurel and killed him. While they slept, bootleggers drove stakes through their hearts. Odette and Paula found their bones locked forever.”

“Laurel is still at the Majestic. I saw her. You know I did. Where is Christopher?”

“Ghouls and demons populated the Majestic. Paula and Odette took the couple’s bones in a pillowcase to the beach.”

“I know Odette and Paula survived because I see them across the room. I have seen no demons or ghouls in the Majestic, so they must have also banished them.”

"Thanks to Christopher, Odette, and Paula made it out of the Majestic. They took the bones to the beach, dug a shallow grave in the sand, deposited the bones, and performed a consecration ceremony."

Chief and Lilly had joined Eddie and Avory and listened to Eddie's story.

"Jack and I heard a tremendous explosion and ran to the door," Chief said. "The Majestic was engulfed in flames sending all the demons and ghouls to hell. Christopher was transported straight to heaven."

"Why didn't Laurel go with him?" Lilly said.

"She has unfinished business," Eddie said.

"What unfinished business?" Avory asked.

"A wedding ceremony to sanctify her bond with Christopher for all eternity," Eddie said.

Avory opened her mouth to reply. Before she could speak, Chief said, "Lilly and I are going for a moonlight drive in my grandfather's Model T. Want to come along?"

Chapter 26

Paula waited at Jack's front door, handing Chief a flask filled with a Cajun mood enhancer.

"Have fun," she said.

A balmy breeze blew up from the Gulf. Full moonlight had replaced the stormy weather of the past few days. Chief helped Lilly into the car and then climbed behind the wheel.

"Crank it, Eddie," he said.

The motor started on the first turn, Avory laughing as Eddie lifted her into the rumble seat and crawled beside her. Neither seemed to mind the crowded space they occupied.

"I love it," Lilly squealed as the car bounced over the ruts in the sand.

Locked in a passionate embrace, Avory and Eddie didn't mind.

"I lost my virginity in the backseat of an old Ford," Eddie said.

"Unless they were contortionists, no one has ever lost their virginity in the rumble seat of a Model T."

"We could try," Eddie said.

"Too late," Avory said. "I lost mine years ago and don't care to reenact the past."

Chief almost flipped the car when he did a sharp figure eight.

"I love this," Lilly said.

Avory tried to drink from the flask, the liquid spilling down her neck and dress when Chief attempted the tight maneuver.

"Slow this thing down," she said. "Paula's happy juice is too good to waste."

"Sure is," Eddie said. "I've never felt this good in my life."

"I've seen this movie once before," Chief said. "I think Paula spiked our booze."

"With what?" Lilly asked.

"Cajun mood enhancer," he said.

"Is it bad for you?" Lilly said.

"Not unless you don't like feeling good," Chief said. "And losing your inhibitions."

"Hell!" Lilly said. "I can do that without any help."

"Drive to the beach," Avory said. "I want to see what the Majestic looks like from there."

Chief needed no cajoling. Soon, they were speeding through the surf, laughing as saltwater splashed over the hood and windshield of the car, soaking their clothes.

"Hope you have a power washer to get the salt off your car."

"I waxed her yesterday," Chief said. "If the salt water doesn't bead off, I'll take care of it tomorrow."

A golden moon sat high overhead as Chief pointed the hood of the Model T toward the Majestic and pulled to a halt.

"My dress is wringing wet," Avory said.

"So is my favorite pinstriped suit," Eddie said.

When Avory crossed her arms and shivered, Eddie removed his damp coat and draped it around her bare arms.

"Where is your house, Chief?" Avory asked.

"He doesn't live in a house," Lilly said.

"You sleep outside?"

"In a teepee," Chief said.

"You have to be kidding me," Avory said. "Where is your teepee?"

"On top of La Tortue Mountain," he said.

"I don't see a mountain," Avory said.

"It's the highest point on the island. There's a wonderful view of the bay from my teepee."

"Take us there," Lilly said. "I've wanted to see your teepee since you first told me about it. There isn't a cloud in the sky. Tonight, you have no excuse not to show it to us."

Chief needed no further encouragement, starting up the slight incline toward the lighthouse.

"I thought the lighthouse was the highest spot on the island," Avory said.

"Not quite," Chief said.

Chief parked at the foot of La Tortue Mountain and helped Lilly out of the car. Eddie was having trouble getting Avory out of the rumble seat. A good six inches taller than Eddie, Chief held out his arms as Avory hiked her skirt and stepped over the side of the old Ford.

Light from the full moon illuminated a little trail leading up the hill.

"Is this the way?" Lilly asked.

"Yes," Chief said. "Don't get off the trail unless you want sand burrs in your pretty red dress."

"I feel so good, I don't believe I'd even care," Lilly said.

"You'd care soon as one of those burrs stuck you."

Chief grabbed Lilly's hand, helping her up the incline to his teepee."

"You don't have critters, do you?" Avory asked.

"None that will harm you. My chickens are asleep in their coop, and my cat Buttercup is probably off tomcatting."

Lilly's red skirt had hiked over her thighs as she gawked at Chief's teepee."

"I didn't realize how big a teepee is," she said.

"I'm a big man," Chief said.

"Yes, you are," she said.

"Want to look inside?" he asked.

"Yes," Avory said.

Flames arose from the fire pit when Chief threw a handful of kindling on the smoldering coals and stoked it with an iron poker. Smoke from the fire created when he added a log rose to the opening at the cross timbers of the teepee. Lilly glanced at the colorful rugs. Chief's calico cat was asleep on the pallet, and Lilly scooped her into her arms.

"Oh! What a beautiful kitty," she said.

Buttercup began to purr, not bothering to open her eyes."

"Is it comfortable?" Avory asked.

"It gets a little crowded with me, Buttercup, Coco, and Ol' Joe."

Avory's arms had crossed, goosebumps popping up on them.

"This damp dress is uncomfortable," Lilly said.

Chief tossed them each a blanket. "Wrap one of these around you. It'll warm you up."

Lilly unzipped her dress and let it slip to her ankles. Realizing Chief and Eddie were watching her every move, she grinned as she removed her panties and bra and quickly draped the multi-hued blanket around her shoulders.

"Oh, my God!" she said. "This feels like heaven."

Eddie, Chief, and Avory needed no further prompting, stripping off their clothes and covering themselves with warm blankets.

"We've already seen each other naked," Chief said. "Does anyone want to go skinny dipping?"

"No cold water for this gal," Lilly said. "This blanket feels too good.

"What about hot water?" Chief asked.

Lilly snickered. "You have a tub big enough for the four of us?"

"No tub," Chief said.

"What then?" Lilly asked.

"A magical womb that comforts the mind and heals the soul."

"Where is this place?" Avory asked.

"The top of La Tortue Mountain," Chief said.

"This isn't the highest part of your mountain?" Avory said.

"Not even close," Chief said. "Let me show you."

They followed Chief, light from the moon and stars illuminating the trail as they reached a clear, cobble-bottomed artesian pool. Lilly dipped her toe into the water.

"Is this your Magic Fountain?" she asked.

"Until a while ago, it was the most magical spot on the island," Chief said.

"This isn't what you wanted to show us?" Avory asked.

"I've experienced many epiphanies in that pool," Chief said. "There's another pool up ahead. Instead of cold, the water is hot."

"Do you have a portable hot tub you heat with a generator?" Eddie said.

Chief's steel gray hair moved when he shook his shoulders. "You'll see," he said.

The trail grew increasingly steeper. "Damn!" Eddie said. "Are you sure we're still in Louisiana?"

Chief didn't answer Eddie's question, halting instead and pointing to a mysterious light from a fog bank wafting around an unreal structure.

"What is it?" Avory asked.

The highest spot on the island lay before them. As the intensity of the light increased, they saw what looked like the top of a pyramid piercing the earth. The light emanated from an opening in the pyramid, foggy vapor gushing out behind it. Eddie approached the pyramidal structure and touched it.

"What is it?"

Eddie glanced at Chief as if he were crazy when he said, "Taste it."

"Have you lost your marbles?" Eddie said.

Chief licked his finger, rubbed it across the rocky surface, and stuck it in his mouth. Eddie, Avory, and Lilly did the same.

"It's salt," Lilly said.

"Rock salt," Chief said. "This island sits on top of a salt dome. An earthquake woke me the other night. When I investigated, I found this. The salt uplifted this part of the island and penetrated the earth at this point. And that isn't even the strangest thing."

"Where are the light and fog coming from?" Avory asked.

"I'll show you," Chief said.

When they reached the opening of the pyramid-shaped rock wall, Chief crawled into it, disappearing into the fog. He'd installed a rope ladder to make it possible to exit. His voice echoed when he spoke.

"Forget the ladder. Drop through the hole. I'll catch you," Chief said.

Chief caught Lilly when she stepped off the ledge. Avory followed. Eddie used the rope ladder. They gazed in disbelief at the large chamber hollowed in the center of the rock salt. Steam billowed up from a pool in the center of the chamber.

"I see your hot water," Lilly said.

"I measured it at one hundred degrees Fahrenheit," Chief said.

After dropping his blanket, he stepped into the steamy water and sank to his neck.

Lilly said, "What the hell!"

Avory and Eddie quickly joined them, no one speaking for what seemed like an eternity. Eddie had brought the flask and began passing it around.

"This is like a psychedelic steam room on steroids," he said. "What's in the water?"

"Salt and other minerals," Chief said. "The perfect bath for soaking away your troubles."

"I've had a catch in my neck since I came to the island," Lilly said. "It's gone."

"I know," Avory said. "This place is so strange. Where is the hot water coming from?"

"Deep in the bowels of the earth," Chief said.

Chief shook his head when Avory asked, "How does it get to the surface?"

"You'll have to ask a geologist that question," he said. "I have no idea."

"Where is the light coming from?" Lilly asked.

"Mineral fluorescence," Eddie said. "I saw an exhibit in a museum once."

"Mixed with a little magic," Chief said.

"I'm so relaxed," Avory said. "I could close my eyes and fall asleep."

"Me too," Lilly said. "Was the story about Christopher and Laurel true, or were you making it up?"

"I only told you what Odette told me. I have no reason to believe she was lying," Eddie said.

"We should incorporate it in the script," Lilly said.

"We don't have anyone to play their roles," Avory said.

"Basil and Heather," Eddie said.

"They don't look like Laurel and Christopher," Avory said.

"Don't you have a competent makeup department?" Eddie asked.

"They aren't professional actors," Avory said.

"Neither was DeNiro until he acted in his first movie," Eddie said. "Basil and Heather are young and photogenic. They're naturals. The audience will love them."

"It won't work," Avory said.

"Why not?" Eddie said.

"It would require almost a complete rewrite," Avory said. "It'll screw our ending up."

"Our ending is a piece of shit," Lilly said. "That's our problem."

"At least we have an ending," Avory said.

Avory, Lilly, and Eddie focused on Chief through the swirling steam when he said, "A wedding."

"What?" Avory asked.

"End the movie with a wedding," Chief said.

"Of course," Lilly said. "Everyone loves a wedding."

"We don't have enough cast members to pull it off," Avory said.

"How about everyone in St. Bernard Parish?" Eddie said.

"No wedding," Avory said.

"Don't bite your nose off to spite your face," Lilly said. "Ending the movie with a wedding is perfect. I can have a first draft in a couple of days."

"For one thing, we don't have enough period costumes," Avory said.

"Yes, you do," Chief said. "The storage warehouse has lots of period clothes. There's also antique gaming equipment for the casino."

"Why didn't you tell me this before now?" Avory asked.

No one answered Avory's question.

"We could pay the wedding attendees as extras. Damn, Avory!" Lilly said. "Make a real live wedding part of a movie. I don't think anyone has ever done it."

"The idea's growing on me," Avory said.

Eddie handed her the flask. "Can you say Academy Award?"

Avory grinned. "No horror movie will ever win the Academy Award for best picture."

"*The Silence of the Lambs* did," Lilly said.

"Not supernatural horror," Avory said. "Doesn't matter. I'm game. Let's do it."

An otherworldly wail interrupted their discussion of the movie. Lilly huddled into Chief's arms.

"What was that?" she said.

The giant floating head of an American Indian man appeared through the mist.

"It's my grandpa," Chief said. "He won't hurt us."

A guttural and broken voice issued from a disembodied head hovering in the steam.

"Eddie," the voice said. "Please do not let the bad men take our island."

Chapter 27

There's no easy way to get from North Dakota to Ukraine. Alex Pavlovich, J.P.'s Russian traveling companion, had known even before they started. He also knew the most challenging part of their journey still lay before them. J.P. had learned as much after a more than ten-hour flight from John F. Kennedy International Airport to Ben Gurion Airport in Tel Aviv.

J.P. waited on a bench alone for Alex to return from the ticket counter.

"Any luck?" he asked.

"We have one-way tickets to Moldova," Alex said.

"When do we leave? We've been in this terminal so long my butt's growing to this bench."

"Three hours waiting, and then another two hours in the air to Chisinau International Airport," Alex said. "Let's walk. It will relieve your stress."

"Sitting around in this place is about as exciting as watching paint dry," J.P. said.

"We'll have plenty of time for excitement."

"Thanks, Alex," J.P. said.

"For what?"

"I'd still be in Minneapolis trying to figure out what to do if it weren't for you."

"If I were a better guide, I would have taken us to an airport where we could get some Russian vodka," Alex said.

"You like rum?"

"Not particularly," Alex said. "Why do you ask?"

J.P. pulled a silver flask from his Minnesota Vikings coat and handed it to Alex.

"Try this and promise me you won't prejudge it," he said.

Alex made a face before putting the flask to his lips. When his frown disappeared, he took another sip.

"This is the best rum I have ever tasted. Maybe even better than Russian vodka. Who makes it?"

"Dominican rum bottled by Whistling Winds Distillery," J.P. said.

"How much does a bottle of this cost?" Alex asked.

"Fifteen bucks a half," J.P. said.

"Bullshit!" Alex said. "Tell me what it really costs."

"I kid you not," J.P. said. "The south Louisiana island where I live was the home of Prohibition Era bootleggers who smuggled booze from all over the world. My two business partners found a crate of Whistling Winds rum in low water. The rum was nearly a hundred years old."

"I could get ten thousand American dollars for such a bottle in Russia. I hope they did not drink it."

"They did, and I helped them. How do you know so much about the price of rum?"

"I was a liquor distributor before the army conscripted me," Alex said. "I've never tasted better rum, and trust me when I tell you I have a trained palette."

"Is that what you're going to do after the war?" J.P. asked.

"We will live, and then we will see," Alex said.

"What's that supposed to mean?"

"Who knows?" Alex said. "It is an old Russian proverb that seemed like an appropriate answer to your question."

"Did your mama give you a book of Russian proverbs when you were growing up?"

"I was born in a brothel, my mother a Russian whore. The state raised me."

"Sorry for prying," J.P. said.

"I will forgive you if you share another taste of your rum," Alex said.

J.P.'s rum was gone when he and Alex were finally on the way to Moldova. The plane was half-empty, J.P. in the window seat, Alex by the aisle.

"What's Moldova like?" J.P. asked.

"Beautiful in the summer; cold as North Dakota in the winter."

"That's what I was afraid of," J.P. said. "Have you ever been to Moldova?"

"Many times. They have vineyards and make lots of wine there."

"What do they do in the winter?" J.P. asked.

Alex smiled. "Shiver a lot."

"You were working in North Dakota. You must like cold weather."

"I have never lived in a place with little or no winter. I would love to try it once in my life."

"Move to Oyster Island," J.P. said. "I bought this coat at the airport. I don't even own a heavy coat."

"Must be nice," Alex said. "What does Renata do on the island?"

"Cleaning lady at the hotel on the bay."

"Cleaning lady?" Alex said. "You know she is

a skilled veterinary surgeon."

"She's operated on two dogs since she's been on the island. She won't admit she's a vet, even though it's apparent. I offered her a job with our canine training facility."

"We were together for many weeks, and she never once said my name," Alex said.

Alex nodded when J.P. said, "She's a broken woman with a monster case of PTSD. I sense you somehow feel responsible."

"An officer who cannot control his soldiers is as responsible for what they do as they are."

"I was an army officer in Afghanistan," J.P. said. "You can only do your best. No one expects more than that."

"Thank you," Alex said.

"For what?"

"Giving me a chance to alleviate some of my guilt."

The sun was beginning to rise when the plane started its descent. J.P. could see the snow on the ground. Snow was falling, the morning dull and bleak as they deboarded.

"How will we get into Ukraine?" J.P. asked.

"By bus," Alex said. "The borders are open. They won't even check our papers."

"How long will it take to get to Kyiv by bus?"

"Five or six hours," Alex said.

"Even if we find Vixen's mom and daughter, how will we get them out of Ukraine?"

"Vixen?" Alex said.

"Sorry. I've gotten so used to calling Renata Vixen that it's hard to change."

"No problem getting them out of Ukraine. The problem lies in getting them in to the United States. The only way I know to do it is to smuggle them through Mexico."

"I have a friend on the island who worked for the government for years. I'll call and see if he can help us."

The taxi dropped them in front of the bus station. The cab driver smiled when Alex handed him an American ten-dollar bill.

"That was cheap," Eddie said.

"Moldova is poor. You can stay in the nicest hotel for less than fifty dollars a night," Alex said.

"The place doesn't look poor," J.P. said. There are modern cars and buildings everywhere."

"Return in the spring. You'll love it," Alex said.

"Maybe when the war is over," J.P. said. "Is there an American embassy in Chisinau?"

Alex nodded, "Call your friend. Perhaps he has more influence than Renata and I had."

"Don't you think I should call after we rescue them?"

"A Russian proverb says, 'To succeed in life, you need ignorance and confidence.' I have both, and so should you. Call your friend."

Eddie was in the Majestic bar when J.P. called. "It's midnight. Are you in jail?"

"Chisinau, Moldova," J.P. said.

"Where the hell is Moldova?"

"A beautiful little country in Europe. Me and Alex are at the bus station."

"Who the hell is Alex?" Eddie asked.

"My friend and fellow accomplice. If all goes well, we'll be in Kyiv in about seven hours."

"Are you crazy?"

"We're bringing two people back to Chisinau: Vixen's mother, Iryna Kalinichenko, and her daughter, Sveta Yatsenko. I need you to work your magic so we can get them to Oyster Island without smuggling them through Mexico."

"How long do I have to perform this magic?" Eddie said.

"If all goes well, we'll return to Chisinau tomorrow."

"I'll do what I can," Eddie said. "I'm not a miracle worker."

"To succeed in life, you need ignorance and confidence," J.P. said.

"What the hell is that supposed to mean?" Eddie said.

"It means Alex and me are counting on you, ol' buddy. Have to go now. Our bus just pulled in out front."

"We cannot board yet," Alex said. "The two men sitting across from us are Russians. They were monitoring your conversation."

"So what?

"Renata is an enemy of the people. Now, the FSB knows where she is. They'll send someone to assassinate her."

"What the hell is the FSB?" J.P. asked.

"The successor to the KGB."

J.P. grabbed Alex's arm when he started toward the two men.

"Where the hell do you think you're going?" he said.

"To kill them."

"No, you're not," J.P. said. "They have already transmitted the info. It's too late."

"Then call your friend and warn him. We do not want to return Renata's mother and daughter to a corpse."

"Get on the bus, and let's get out of town. This station is probably crawling with Russian agents. You can't kill them all."

They were soon out of the rolling countryside of Moldova and into relatively flat Ukraine. Snow covered everything as they passed through bombed-out villages and cities.

"Damn!" J.P. said. "I thought the war was mostly east of Kyiv."

"The Russians terrorize all of Ukraine with missile and drone attacks. No one is exempt from the suffering," Alex said.

"Why are we going to Kyiv? You told me you met Renata and her family in Bucha."

"Not all Russians are evil. I called people I trust and tracked Renata's mother and daughter to Kyiv."

Alex nodded when J.P. said, "You know where they are?"

"Call your friend. The FSB will waste no time sending someone to assassinate Renata."

"Are you sure?" J.P. asked. "I don't want to alarm everyone on the island."

"Better that they prepare for the worst," Alex said.

Jack answered his cell phone on the second ring. "What the hell, J.P.? It's three in the morning."

"This is important," J.P. said. "I have reason to believe someone will arrive on the island shortly to kill Vixen."

"Who the hell would do that?" Jack asked.

"The FSB. The successor to the KGB. I'm not making this shit up," J.P. said.

"Where are you?" Jack asked.

"I can't tell you. Someone's probably monitoring this conversation," J.P. said.

"Are you in danger?" Jack asked.

"Probably no more than you are," J.P. said. "I have to hang up now. Watch your ass."

"Well?" Alex asked.

"A trained soldier watches what he says, and I feel like a fucking idiot. Now, I've put all of Oyster Island at risk."

"We all make mistakes," Alex said. "I should have known better. We are in a war zone now. We must return to our military training and not act like civilians."

"Dammit!" J.P. said. "I can't believe we have no more rum left."

Alex laughed. "There'll be plenty of time for rum and vodka when we leave Ukraine."

Vivid colors of reds and oranges streaked the eastern sky as they entered the city of Kyiv. It was dark when they reached the bus station. J.P. handed Alex a wad of cash when he started for the business counter. He returned from the counter with four tickets.

"We have less than two hours to find Renata's mother and daughter and then return with them before the bus departs."

A taxi dropped them off in front of a high-rise apartment complex.

"Khto tam?" a woman asked when Alex banged on the door.

"Alex," he said in English. "I have news of Renata."

The door opened a crack. An older woman peered out.

"Who is with you?" the woman asked.

"J.P. We've come to take you and Sveta to join Renata," Alex said.

"Where is Renata?" the woman demanded.

Before Alex could answer, Sveta came out of a bedroom. She ran straight to Alex and put her arms around his legs.

"Sveta, no," the woman said.

"You are the man who saved my mama," the little girl said.

"This is J.P.," Alex said. "He lives in a place far away called Louisiana. Your mother is there, waiting for you."

"It is the middle of the night," the old woman said.

"Get dressed, Iryna," Alex said. "Take no more than you can carry in a knapsack. Tomorrow, we will be in Moldova."

Iryna and Sveta were dressed in warm clothing when the sirens began blaring.

Explosions loud enough to burst eardrums began shaking the walls of the high-rise.

"Missile attack," J.P. said. "On the floor. Now!"

Alex dived atop Iryna and Sveta as the ceiling and walls began collapsing around them.

Chapter 28

Darkness had engulfed Oyster Island as Vixen returned to her room. Isaac had tried to feed her when she passed through the kitchen, insisting on giving her a muffuletta. She hadn't realized how hungry she was until the old key turned in the lock. She planned to share it with her dog Mollie, shower, and then go to bed early.

Before Vixen switched on the lights, she sensed she wasn't alone. Her senses proved correct. She grabbed her heart when she saw the man sitting on her couch with Mollie in his lap.

"Hello, Renata. We finally caught you."

Vixen's brave face belied her shaky knees. She had to grab the top of a recliner to keep from sinking onto the carpet.

"Who are you, and how did you get into my room?" she said.

"It was not hard," he said. "You can call me Snake Fingers."

Snake Fingers was short. Vixen could tell even though he was sitting. He was bald, his impassive facial features seemingly locked in a perpetual grin. His pink Bermuda shorts, a Bob Marley tee shirt, and sandals with thin black socks suggested he'd come straight from the islands. The knife in his hand flickered nervously near Mollie's neck.

"What are you doing here?" she asked.

"You know."

The man smiled when she said, "I've done nothing to you."

"Oh, but you have. You were the wife of the Russian-hating Tater who spread lies and false stories. And you killed two Russian soldiers. Now, it's your turn to suffer."

"I'll scream if you touch me."

Vixen's retort painted the man's face with an even broader smile.

"Do you know what it feels like to have your tongue cut out? You gag on your blood."

"Let Mollie go. She has done nothing to you," Vixen said.

"Mollie will die first, and you will watch me kill her. Have you ever seen an animal skinned alive?"

The man's smile grew broad when Vixen said, "You are a psychopath."

"The longer it takes your dog to die, the more time you have to live. Be thankful for small favors. You may as well sit and relax. I have many fun things planned for you though I'm in no real hurry."

"How did you find me?" Vixen asked.

"Your friends gave you away. You cannot escape the FSB. It is futile to resist. Some people enjoy the pain."

Mollie's body trembled visibly. She couldn't escape because Snake Fingers had his hand around her neck. Vixen had the muffuletta in her right hand and a bucket of solvent in her left. She'd intended to use the lye-based liquid to clean her bathroom before bed.

"Are you hungry?" she said. "There's nothing

better than a Louisiana muffuletta sandwich."

Before Snake Fingers could answer, she lobbed the sandwich to him. He reflexively let go of Mollie's neck to catch the sandwich. When he did, Vixen launched the bucket's contents at Snake Fingers' face.

Snake Fingers didn't make a sound, though his hands went to his eyes. Vixen sensed he was momentarily blinded. Grabbing Mollie off his lap, she ran out the door. Knowing Snake Fingers would follow, she ran up the hill toward Jack's house. Eddie and Basil were away from the island, and she didn't know any of the movie maintenance men.

"Do you have a gun?" she shouted as she burst through the door.

She nodded when Jack said, "Russians?"

Jack's old .45 caliber service revolver and a bandolier of bullets lay on the plank table. Grabbing the pistol, he locked and loaded it.

"How did you know?" Vixen asked.

"J.P. called and warned me," he said. "I never thought someone would arrive on the island this quickly in a million years. How many men are there?"

"Only one that I know of," she said.

"They're going to need more than that," Jack said. "How did you get away?"

"I threw a bucket of lye in his face. I should have killed him while he was blinded."

"With your bare hands? I'm calling 911."

"We'll be dead before they arrive," Vixen said. "Even if the authorities captured him, the FSB will send more assassins. Where is Chief?"

"Went to feed his chickens and cat," Jack said. "I'm calling him."

"What's up?" Chief said when he answered his cell phone.

"Russian invasion," Jack said.

"Want me to call 911?"

Vixen shook her head. "Do not call the police. We have to kill this man before he kills us. It is the only way."

Mollie squirmed in Vixen's arms. When Vixen placed the cocker on the floor, she ran to the fireplace and leaped into the oversized doggie bed with Oscar.

"Did you hear what Vixen said?" Jack asked.

"She's probably right. I'm on my way," Chief said.

"Bring your shotgun," Jack said.

Jack went to the door and opened it. The sky was clear, the night moon bright. He saw no one. Returning to the kitchen, he poured himself a mug of rum and one for Vixen. The lights went out before either of them could drink. Jack grabbed Vixen's arm, tugging it until she dropped to her knees behind the kitchen cabinet. A man's voice caused the tiny hairs on Vixen's neck to rise.

"Jack. I can see in the dark. I know where you are."

Jack pointed his pistol toward the voice and pulled the trigger. An explosion of sound rocked the room leaving behind the odor of sulfite and spent gunpowder.

"You missed, Jack," Snake Fingers said. "I must tell you, I can throw my voice." Jack and Vixen turned violently around when he said, "I'm right behind you."

Snake Fingers wasn't lying. Jack never knew it because the Russian assassin had hit his head with a pipe. Vixen was kneeling beside Jack when Snake Fingers grabbed her by the hair, yanking her off the floor.

Oscar wasn't an attack dog, though he had smelled Jack's blood and knew he was in danger. When Snake Fingers turned on the lights, Oscar attacked, biting the back of the Russian's leg just below his buttocks and refusing to let go.

Snake Fingers began beating the dog with the pipe and would have killed him if Vixen hadn't stabbed him with a kitchen knife. Snake Fingers was bleeding when he managed to nail Vixen across the face with the heavy pipe, knocking her cold and breaking her nose.

"You fucking bitch!" he said.

A pail of cold water over their heads revived Jack and Vixen. Zip ties bound their hands behind their backs, blood soaking Vixen's blouse and Jack's shirt. Snake Fingers had a bucket of solvent and poured it over Vixen's head and then rubbed her eyes to make sure they were burning.

"Be thankful you have eyes," Snake Fingers said. "I'm going to poke them out before I kill you."

"You'll never get away with this," Jack said. "The authorities will realize what happened here. You want the Americans to enter the war?"

"Murder/suicide," Snake Fingers said. "Neither of you will have a reputation left when I finish with you. Only your worst enemies will even bother coming to your funerals." The Russian used his fingers to part Jack's lips. "Nice set of teeth," he said. "I'm going to knock them out for you."

Jack closed his eyes, waiting for the steel pipe to hit him in the mouth. The first blow bloodied his lips. The second blow never came. He saw Snake Fingers struggling to pull an arrow from his neck. Chief was standing at the door, a bow in his hands. He didn't have to shoot a second arrow.

The pointed missile had pierced Snake Fingers' neck so cleanly that there was little blood. Snake Fingers was holding the arrow, unable to speak when Chief approached him.

"Too bad you have no hair," Chief said. I would scalp you before I did this."

Chief grabbed the back of the arrow and yanked it out of Snake Fingers' neck. Snake Fingers' jugular began gushing blood, his serpent's eyes growing large before he dropped dead to the floor of Jack's house.

Chief cut the zip ties binding Jack and Vixen's hands. Vixen grabbed Jack's head and began checking him out.

Jack crawled on his hands and knees to where Oscar lay.

"I'm okay," he said to Vixen. "We need to get you to a doctor and fix your nose before you bleed to death."

"Get me some toilet tissue," she said.

When Jack complied, she stuffed the tissue up her nose until the bleeding ceased.

"Now what?" Jack asked.

"Carry Oscar to the operating room." They soon had Oscar's vitals stabilized, his eyes clear, and his short tail wagging. "We are going to need x-ray equipment and many other necessities if you expect me to keep saving your dogs," she said.

Both Jack and Chief began hugging her.

When they broke away from the group embrace, Chief said. "You two need to clean this place up before someone shows up for breakfast or rum."

"You aren't going to help?" Jack said.

"I have a dead reptile to dispose of," Chief said. "It'll be spring before the gators eat him. That's all right because they like their meat a little rancid."

"I'm going with you," Jack said.

"As am I," Vixen said.

"Someone needs to set your nose," Chief said.

"I am not going to a doctor," Vixen said.

"Then I'll set it," Jack said. "I did it more than once while in the Merchant Marines. We even have anesthesia."

"Which you have no idea how to administer. No anesthesia," Vixen said. "Set it now."

Jack poured her a mug of rum and said, "This will hurt. Drink it all, and then bite down on this washcloth."

Even though giant tears rolled from her eyes, Vixen didn't scream. When he finished, Jack cleaned the blood from her face and neck, then hugged her again.

"I'm going to look like a professional boxer," she said.

"It's perfect," Jack said. "I need some rum."

"Thank you," Vixen said. "This was the second time you saved my life."

"I didn't know you could use a bow and arrow," Jack said. "Why didn't you bring your shotgun?"

"It's Grandpa's bow. It was lying on my pallet. I held the bow. Grandpa aimed the arrow."

Snake Fingers' mouth and eyes lay open, his neck splayed in a bloody death gape.

"He did a damn good job," Jack said.

"You got an old sheet?" Chief said. "I don't want to bloody up the rumble seat."

"Got something better than that," Jack said.

He went out the back door returning with an almost empty dog food sack. After he and Chief stuffed the little man's body into the bag, Jack stapled it shut.

"The bag won't be around next spring," he said.

The moon was high overhead as they drove across the sand to the back of the island. The old Model T's headlights illuminated the opening into the mangrove swamp. Chief needed no help dragging the body out of the rumble seat and carrying it to the swamp.

"Do we need to weigh it down?" Jack asked.

"Damn it!" Chief said. "That won't work. We should have thought of that before we stapled the bag."

"Open the bag and eviscerate the corpse," Vixen said. "It will sink to the bottom and not resurface." She took Chief's hunting knife from him. "I'll do it."

Vixen went to work with the knife, smiling when Jack said, "I'll never get this out of my mind. Next time I see someone filet a fish, I'll think about that crazy motherfucker's eyes staring up at me."

"Just be glad he's staring up at you and not the other way around," Chief said.

They got their feet wet when they waded into the water and pushed the body in the dog food sack away from the bank. It floated about ten feet before gurgling and sinking beneath the coffee-colored surface.

"Hope he doesn't come back and haunt us," Jack said.

"Grandpa will take care of him if he does," Chief said. "What now?"

"Give me your hands," Vixen said. "Let's swear a solemn oath that we will never again speak of what occurred tonight."

As they bowed their heads, closed their eyes, and swore the deadly act to secrecy, a wildcat stalking its prey emitted a haunting howl that echoed across the mangrove swamp.

Chapter 29

Odette, Meika, and Heather loved their new house. They'd ordered curtains online. Meika and Odette were admiring their work when the sound of Heather sobbing caught their attention. The door was ajar, and Heather's face buried in a pillow.

"What's the matter?" Odette asked.

"My wedding would be perfect, except my mom won't be here to see it, and I'll have no one to walk me down the aisle."

Heather cried harder when Meika said, "Plenty of others will see the two of you get married."

"But not Mom and Dad," Heather said.

"Have you talked to your dad lately?" Odette said.

"I left a message on his phone. He never returned my call."

Odette frowned at Meika when she said, "What an old asshole."

Odette's cell phone rang before she could say something about Meika's insensitivity. It was Avory.

"Odette," Avory said. "Where are you?"

"Isaac's covering for us for a couple of hours

so we can decorate our new house. What's up?"

"Are Meika and Heather with you?"

"Yes," Odette said.

"Lilly and I have finished the script. We need to talk to the three of you about it."

"For what reason?" Odette said.

"Meet us in the bar around six. I'll explain then."

"We'll be there," Odette said.

"Who was that?" Meika asked.

"Avory," Odette said.

"Was she on another one of her rampages?" Meika asked.

"She invited the three of us to have drinks with her in the little bar at six," Odette said.

"Because?" Meika asked.

"Don't have a clue," Odette said.

"Who's going to run the bar?" Meika said.

Odette shook her head and stared out the window. "You know as much as I do."

Eddie had used some of Avory's money to purchase a second ATV. They climbed into the new vehicle when they finished at their house. Someone was behind the bar Odette recognized. She dived headfirst over the antique wooden counter and hugged his neck.

"Bertram Picou, what in the hell are you doing here, and why are you working the bar?"

Bertram was a Cajun with dark hair, eyes, a Gallic nose, and down-on-the-bayou aphorisms peppering his vernacular. Odette climbed over the bar and hugged Lady, his beautiful collie.

"Eddie invited me down for the weekend. He didn't tell me Lilly was here, or that he was making me work for my room and board."

"Eddie told me you and Lilly were a number," Odette said.

"Yeah, and she's as nervous about me being here as a cat on a hot tin roof," Bertram said.

Odette recognized the title of the award-winning play set in New Orleans."

"Did you ever meet Tennessee Williams?" she asked.

"Way before my time," Bertram said. "Gil LaPiere, the man I bought the bar from, said Ol' Tennessee always brought his bulldog with him. Sometimes late at night, I still feel his presence at the bar drinking a Ramos Fizz and hear that bulldog's bark."

"Get out of here!" Odette said.

"I kid you not," Bertram said.

"What the hell is a Ramos Fizz?" Odette asked.

"Hell, girl, it's a blend of dry gin, heavy cream, egg white, lemon juice, lime juice, sugar, and orange flower water. I thought you knew your bartending."

"Never made one," she said. Meika and Heather sat at the bar, smiling at the interchange between Odette and Bertram. "Girls, this is Bertram Picou, the best bartender in the French Quarter. He owns Bertram's on Chartres Street."

"Ooh!" Meika said. "Susie and I were wasted in the French Quarter last summer and wandered into your bar. I've never had so much fun in my entire life."

"I never forget a pretty Cajun girl, and I remember you," Bertram said. "And who could forget your girlfriend, Susie? She's one hot, blond mama."

Meika laughed. "We broke up."

"Sorry to hear it," Bertram said. "Every man and woman in the place was trying to hit on the two of you."

"Susie and I loved every minute of it," Meika said. "J.P. Saucier has a thing for her."

"Does he now?" Bertram said.

"You know J.P.?" Heather asked.

"Since he was a kid," Bertram said. "He's a few years younger than me. A hell of a baseball player in college. Thought he was going to go pro."

"I never knew that," Heather said. "He and Susie won the St. Bernard Parish two-step contest at my dad's restaurant."

"What's your last name?" Bertram asked.

"Boudreaux," Heather said.

Heather nodded when Bertram said, "Your parents, Harvey and Carol, own Claws & Craws?"

"You know my mom and dad?" Heather asked.

"Met them after moving to New Orleans," Bertram said.

Isaac exited the kitchen and joined Bertram and Odette behind the bar.

"You girls have the night off," he said. "I'm helping Bertram."

"You know each other?" Odette said.

"Hell, baby, I know every Cajun in south Louisiana."

Bertram was grinning when he said, "Most of them, anyway."

Lilly and Avory had come downstairs and sat at a table in the back of the dark little bar. Avory's short black dress, except for the color, matched Lilly's red dress. Lilly managed to avert her attention when Bertram gave them a look.

"That's the same dresses they wore the other night when they went joyriding in Chief's Model T," Odette said. "We'd better join them."

"Take these two martinis and tell them I said hi," Bertram said.

Lilly and Avory took the cocktails from Odette. "Bertram mixes the best martinis in the world," Avory said.

"Did he say anything about me?" Lilly asked.

"Said he was going to come over here and

pinch your ass," Odette said.

Lilly's face turned bright red, visible even in the dim lighting.

"He didn't say that, did he?" Lilly said.

"Why not?" Odette said. "You're looking pretty hot in that red dress."

"Maybe I'd better return to my room," Lilly said.

"Just pulling your leg. Bertram knows you're seeing Chief. He's okay with it."

"Is he now?" Lilly said.

The conversation about Bertram and Lilly ceased when Isaac arrived at the table with drinks for Odette, Meika, and Heather. Heather fidgeted when she wound up sitting beside Avory.

"Tell us what's up," Odette said.

Heather began to cry when Avory said, "Our conversation has to do with Heather's wedding."

"Why are you crying?" Lilly asked.

"We've already sent the invitations," Heather said. "What am I supposed to do?"

Avory smiled and patted Heather's hand. "The wedding date is set. I don't want to change it."

"You don't?" Heather said.

"Not at all. There's another reason we want to talk to you about the wedding," Avory said.

"You're confusing me," Heather said.

"Me too," Odette said. "Tell us what you're getting at."

"Lilly and I have made significant changes to the movie script. Eddie told us the story of Laurel and Christopher. We've incorporated their love affair into the movie and written major parts for them. I want to cast Heather as Laurel and Basil as Christopher."

"We all know about the Majestic's resident ghost," Heather said. "I can't play her because I don't have blond hair and blue eyes. Neither does Basil."

"No problem," Avory said. "We have an excellent makeup department."

"I don't know how to act," Heather said.

"Nonsense," Avory said. "Every woman is an actress."

"Avory has hired an acting coach to work with you and Basil," Lilly said. "You'll both be perfect for the parts."

"You'll have to do some requisite nudity," Avory said.

"I can't do that," Heather said.

"Of course, you can," Avory said. "If you're going to be an actress, you must pay your dues."

"What does any of this have to do with the wedding?" Heather asked.

"The wedding between Laurel and Christopher will be one of the movie's final scenes," Avory said. "The wedding will be real, you and Basil marrying during the scene. You two will be the talk of Hollywood."

"Laurel and Christopher aren't married," Odette said.

"In the movie, they renounce their immortality because of love and desire to live as humans. We'll pay the entire wedding crowd as extras," Lilly said.

"Everyone will wear costumes of the Prohibition Era. The movie will immortalize your wedding," Avory said.

"So, the ceremony will be real?" Heather said.

"A real ceremony and a real priest. When he pronounces you man and wife, you'll be married for real," Lilly said.

"I love it," Odette said.

"I don't know," Heather said.

"Do I have a part?" Meika asked.

"Of course. You and Odette even have a few speaking lines."

"Are you serious?" Meika said.

"I couldn't be more serious," Avory said. "Well?"

"I'll have to talk to Basil about it," Heather said.

"Eddie has already spoken with him," Avory said.

"What did he say?" Heather asked.

"He will do whatever makes you happy. One more thing," Avory said.

"What?" Heather asked.

"You and Basil will have to become dues-paying members of the Screen Actors Guild."

"Will they be paid for their work?" Odette said.

"Handsomely," Avory said. "You'll begin your marriage with pockets filled with money."

Lilly and Avory grinned when Meika said, "How much money?"

Heather's eyes widened when Avory said, "They'll earn thousands, not millions. Basil and Eddie are lawyers. They'll make sure the contracts are in order. What do you think?"

"Everyone who attends the wedding will be in the movie?"

"Yes," Avory said. "And get paid as movie extras."

"How much?" Meika asked again.

"A hundred to two hundred dollars," Avory said. "Not much, though not bad either, getting paid for something they would do anyway."

"We'll do it," Heather said.

Avory hugged Heather and said, "You'll be wonderful in the role. Lilly and I have a few more loose ends to tie up. Can you have Bertram bring more martinis to my room?"

"He'll love it," Odette said. "Watch your ass, Miss Lilly."

Avory and Lilly had just left when Isaac and Paula joined the three women at the table.

Paula's grin told them she already knew about the impending movie roles. She sat beside Heather and squeezed her hand.

"I heard the news. You and Basil will soon become the most popular couple in the parish," she said.

"If only my mom and dad were here to see it," Heather said.

"Jake Locklin, the head cook at Claws & Craws, is my friend," Isaac said. "He has been there since the restaurant opened long before you were born. According to Jake, your daddy couldn't boil water and knows nothing about running a restaurant."

Heather's dark hair moved when she shook her head. "That's not what Mom says."

"Your mama is the brains of the organization. She orders the supplies, pays for the help, and hires the bands. Your daddy doesn't do much except walk around the restaurant shaking everyone's hand. He's never fired or hired a single employee."

"What difference does it make?" Heather asked.

"We have a plan," Paula said.

"We?" Heather asked.

"Your mom is here. She'll explain."

Heather turned to see her mom, Carol, standing in a dark corner of the bar.

"Mom," Heather said. "What are you doing here?"

Carol sat beside Heather and embraced her. She was an older version of her daughter, with a hint of gray in her dark hair.

"I'm here for you, baby. You okay?"

"I called Dad. He won't return my call," Heather said. "What will I do?"

"We're going to confront him," Carol said.

"When?" Heather asked.

"I brought the car. Let's go."

"I can't go now," Heather said. "I'm working."

"Go," Odette said. "We'll cover for you."

Carol refused to explain her plan as they crossed the low-water bridge and headed toward Chalmette.

"This is crazy," Heather said. "Dad has made up his mind."

"You've lost weight. Are you getting enough to eat?" Carol asked.

"I don't know what to say to him."

"I love the old hotel," Carol said. "Do you have a cozy room and warm bed?"

"Mom!" Heather said. "Haven't you heard a word I've said?"

"Your wedding will be so beautiful," Carol said.

Carol squeezed Heather's hand when she said, "If only I had someone to walk me down the aisle."

Heather's older brother Matt opened the car door when Carol parked in the Claws & Craws lot. Matt was handsome, tall, and slender, his dark hair draping over the top of his ears.

"Everyone's ready," he said. "Jake called Dad and told him we have a problem in the kitchen."

Heather hugged her brother and said, "Please tell me what's about to happen."

"You'll find out soon enough," Matt said.

"What am I supposed to do?" Heather asked.

"We stay out of sight," he said. "If this is going to work, Jake has to be the one to make it happen."

When Harvey Boudreaux entered the kitchen, he found Jake Locklin, the head cook, waiting for him. Jake looked ready for work, dressed in jeans, a tee shirt, and a greasy apron. Harvey was sipping a scotch from the tumbler in his hand.

"What's up?" he said.

"I need to take off a day," Jake said.

"You know you can take off anytime you need to," Harvey said.

"Thanks," Jake said.

"What day?" Harvey asked.

"Valentine's Day," Jake said.

"Any time except Valentine's Day," Harvey said. "It's my busiest day of the year."

"I've arranged for my cousin from St. Tammany Parish to cover for me. He's an experienced chef and will do you a good job," Jake said.

"You've never missed a Valentine's Day," Harvey said. "Why do you need to take off for this one?"

"Business," Jake said.

"What business?"

Harvey's smile disappeared when Jake said, "Heather and Basil's wedding."

"What about it?" Harvey asked.

"Heather needs someone to walk her down the aisle. Since you're unavailable, she asked me to do it."

"Did she now?" Harvey said.

"I've known Heather since she was a little girl. I taught her and Matt everything I know about the restaurant business. She grew up in this kitchen.

"What's Matt got to do with this?" Harvey asked.

"I thought you already knew about this," Jake said.

"About what?"

"Since you disowned Heather, Matt has decided to open his own restaurant."

"Now, wait just a minute," Harvey said. "First of all, I never disowned Heather. Where did you come up with that crazy idea?"

"It's what everyone in town is saying," Jake

said.

"That's a pile of horseshit," Harvey said. "My son and daughter mean the world to me. I'd never do anything to hurt either one of them."

"You kidding me?" Jake said. "You've broken Heather's heart. I don't know how you live with yourself."

Harvey doubled his fist and said, "You take that back."

"You're bigger than I am and can whip my ass. Get after it. I'm taking nothing back," Jake said.

Harvey's hands relaxed as he knelt on the floor. He was crying when he spoke.

"Forgive me, Jake. I'm a sorry son-of-a-bitch. Claws & Craws is my life. It's not more important than family. What am I going to do?"

"You could start by calling Heather," Jake said.

Heather was in another room when her cell phone rang.

"Heather, baby," Harvey said. "Please don't cut me out of your wedding."

Matt grabbed her hand before she could answer and led her and Carol into the kitchen.

Harvey stared at them when Matt said, "If you have something to say, we're here to listen."

Harvey glanced at Jake, who said, "I think you have some apologizing to do."

"I'm so sorry," Harvey said. "You're my only daughter, and I've only thought of myself. Matt, please don't open another restaurant. I'm giving you and Heather this one, effective now. Honey, I'm so sorry. Please forgive me."

"You mean it about giving Claws & Craws to Heather and Matt?" Carol asked.

"It's theirs," Harvey said.

"What are you going to do with yourself?" Carol asked.

"If she lets me, I'm walking the most wonderful daughter a man could have down the aisle at her wedding," he said. "After that, I'm taking you to Paris."

Chapter 30

Odette searched the halls and rooms of the Majestic, looking for Vixen. She found her on her knees scrubbing a bathroom floor. Mollie's tail was wagging as she tried to lick Vixen's face. Vixen jumped when Odette spoke. For the first time since she'd met Vixen, Odette realized she was smiling.

"Didn't mean to scare you," she said. "Jack asked me to give you the rest of the day off."

"For what reason?" Vixen asked.

"He didn't say."

"I have five more rooms to clean."

"I'll finish them for you," Odette said.

"You do not have to do that," Vixen said.

"You need to go now," Odette said. "Before you do, go to your room, shower, and put on some clean clothes."

"Can you tell me why?"

Odette shook her head. "Go now," she said.

Vixen was worried as she went to her room and cleaned up. Maybe the authorities had somehow found out about Snake Fingers. The thought frightened her. After showering and changing clothes, she and Mollie hurried to Jack's little house on the knoll overlooking the bay. Jack and Chief sat at the plank table, drinking rum and playing gin rummy.

"Are we in trouble?" Vixen said.

"Hell no!" Jack said.

"Then why did you call me here?" she asked.

Jack didn't answer. Instead, he poured her a mug of rum.

"You play gin rummy?" he asked.

"I need to return to the hotel," Vixen said. "I have five more rooms to clean."

"Odette is your boss. She gave you the rest of the day off. She won't like it if you disobey orders."

"Then tell me why I'm here?" she said.

"You'll find out soon enough. How's Mollie doing?"

"She has adopted me. I guess I have a dog now."

"Looks to me like she thinks she has a human."

"She refuses to leave my side," Vixen said. "She helps me scrub floors and clean toilets."

"Why don't you reconsider our job offer?" Jack said. "We need a vet, and you need a job where you don't have to work so hard," Jack said.

"I like hard work."

"But you don't know if you'll stay on the island?"

"When I came to Oyster Island, I had no memory of who I was or why I was here," Vixen said. "The encounter with the assassin made me realize much is still missing."

"You've come a long way," Jack said. "You'll soon be back to your old self."

"Something about knowing everything frightens me more than I can explain."

"J.P. says you have traumatic amnesia. It isn't easy facing bad memories, though it is the only way you'll ever return to normal."

"Maybe I do not want to know," Vixen said.

Jack's cell phone rang. He only listened, hanging up the phone without speaking. When he gave Chief a nod, the big man dropped his cards and started for the door.

"Let's go with Chief," Jack said.

Vixen followed Jack and Chief out the door. They weren't alone. Odette, Meika, Heather, Basil, Eddie, Isaac, Avory, Lilly, Paula, and Jimmie stood in a row, staring up the hill.

"What is this all about?" Vixen said.

"Not all lost memories are bad. You're about to find out," Jack said.

J.P.'s truck rounded the corner and crossed the low-water bridge, halting about a hundred feet from where Jack, Chief, and Vixen waited. When J.P. opened the passenger door, a little girl climbed into his arms. He lifted her out of the truck and sat her on the sand. When she saw Vixen, she squealed and began running toward her.

"Mama, Mama, Mama," she said.

Vixen's eyes grew large. Dropping to her knees, she lifted the little girl, twirling her in circles in the sand. Their smiles were gone, both Vixen and the little girl dissolving into tears.

"Sveta, moya dytyna, moya dytyna," she said. "My baby, my baby."

Her tail wagging, Mollie went to the little girl and licked her face.

"Is this our dog?" Sveta asked.

"Her name is Mollie," Vixen said. "She's your dog now. When did you learn to speak English?"

"J.P. and Alex taught me," Sveta said. "Alex is also teaching me Russian."

"Is he now? Where did you meet J.P. and Alex?"

"They saved Grandmother and me, took us on a bus ride, and then a trip in an airplane."

"How did they save you?"

"Alex shielded us when the ceiling fell. It broke his shoulder and arm."

"Why did the ceiling fall?" Vixen asked.

"Grandmother will tell you," Sveta said.

Sveta nodded when Vixen said, "Grandmother is with you?"

"In J.P.'s truck," Sveta said.

Vixen picked Sveta off the sand, sprang to her feet, and started walking toward the truck. J.P. opened the door, helping an older woman climb from the cab. Vixen burst into tears. Try as she might, she couldn't stop crying. With Sveta in her arms, she rushed forward to embrace her mother, Iryna. When they finally broke away from each other, Iryna whispered something into Vixen's ear.

The backdoor to J.P.'s crew cab pickup remained shut. With Sveta still in her arms, Vixen opened it. Alex Pavlovich, his shoulder in a sling and arm in a cast, sat alone in the backseat. Sveta extended her arms, demanding Alex take her.

"He is hurt and cannot carry you," Vixen said.

Alex smiled and took the little girl in his good arm. When Vixen extended her hand, he clutched it and climbed out of the truck with difficulty.

"Look, Alex. We have a dog. Her name is Mollie."

Alex knelt and let the cocker lick his face.

"You are the most beautiful dog, Mollie," he said.

Sveta had a grip around Alex's neck and wasn't about to let go. When Vixen touched his shoulder, the crowd began to applaud.

Sveta was still in Alex's one good arm when Vixen took his hand and pulled him toward the house. She stopped when they reached J.P. and Lucky. Vixen only nodded before turning away.

"We have some celebrating to do," Jack said. "Eddie donated the champagne. The gumbo's on me."

The group watching the proceedings applauded again and followed Jack into the house. Vixen, Iryna, and Sveta huddled on his couch. Oscar had recovered from his head wound, and Mollie joined him in his sizeable doggy bed. Lucky, Coco, and Ol' Joe weren't far away. Sveta fidgeted in her mother's lap.

"I want to play with Mollie and the other dogs," she said.

"I do not want you to leave me ever again," Vixen said.

"Do not be like that," Iryna said. "You have the rest of your life to hold your daughter."

Sveta was playing with the dogs when J.P., Jack, Odette, and Chief joined them. J.P. called her by her real name.

"Renata, we don't want you to return to Ukraine. We want you to reconsider going to work for our canine training facility."

"We are never returning to Ukraine. Still, I have so much to think about," Renata said.

"Work for us until you decide," J.P. said. "We won't pressure you. I promise."

"My room at the hotel will not be sufficient for the three of us," Renata said.

"We have a house for you on the bay," Chief said. "It's yours for free as long as you stay here."

"Meika, Heather, and I have one of our own," Odette said. "They are beautiful. There's even a park for walking, Mollie."

"There are no schools on the island," Renata said. "I want a fine education for Sveta."

"She's only three," J.P. said. "Not even old enough for kindergarten. You'll have plenty of time to worry about schools when she's older."

"We would have our own house?" Iryna said.

"You want to see it?" Jack said.

Iryna immediately said, "Yes."

Jack grabbed her hand. "Come on. I'll show you."

Jack and Iryna were about the same age, and she didn't protest when he pulled her to her feet.

"Do you mind if I look at the house with Jack?" she asked.

"Mollie and I want to go, Grandmother," Sveta said.

Jack scooped the little girl into his arms. "Come on," he said. "I'll let you drive."

"Mama," Sveta said. "Come with us."

Renata was shaking her head as she followed them out the door. With Jack gone, Odette and Paula began serving gumbo and champagne.

Jimmie, J.P., Alex, and Eddie were talking when Paula tapped Jimmie's shoulder.

"Can you help me move some things to the plank table?" she asked.

"You bet I can, honey babe."

Alex, J.P., and Eddie sat on the rock ledge surrounding Jack's fireplace. "Those two must be very much in love," Alex said. "At least it seems that way."

"Paula has a ring in Jimmie's nose," Eddie said. "Do you love Renata?"

Eddie's question caught Alex by surprise. "I feel responsible for her well-being," Alex said. "I do not believe it is the same as love."

"You just met Alex," J.P. said. "Don't you think your question is a bit personal?"

"Sorry," Eddie said. "Lawyers get paid big bucks to ask sensitive questions. Sometimes, it's hard to separate yourself from the courtroom."

"It is okay," Alex said. "Eddie's question is valid. Love is a commitment. So is an obligation. They do not have to be the same."

"Are you married?" Eddie asked.

Alex grinned and said, "Are you?"

"Never had the pleasure," Eddie said. Seeing his question had made Alex uncomfortable, he changed the subject. "How did you break your arm and shoulder?"

"Alex is a hero," J.P. said. "We were in Iryna's apartment during a missile attack. When the beams started falling, he threw himself on Iryna and Sveta. The falling rafter he blocked could have killed them."

"I am no hero. What I did was only a reaction to a situation," Alex said.

"You're a hero in my books," J.P. said. "You didn't have to return to Ukraine. Alex rescued Renata, took her out of Ukraine at great risk to himself, and got her to the States. They became separated at the Mexican border."

"Were you career military?" Eddie asked.

"I was conscripted and made an officer because I have a business degree from Moscow State University. I was a liquor wholesaler."

"Damn!" Eddie said. "What were you doing when J.P. found you?"

"Working the oil rigs in North Dakota," Alex said.

"You liked it?" Eddie said.

"It paid well but quickly made an old man out of me. I like the weather here," Alex said.

Odette joined them for a moment. "Bertram is running the bar alone," she said. "Meika, Heather, and I are going to relieve him."

"Who's going to mix Avory and Lilly's martinis?" Eddie asked.

"Jack has plenty of rum," she said.

"Take Alex with you and assign him a room," Eddie said.

"Thank you," Alex said.

"No problem," Eddie said. "Let's talk again tomorrow. If you're serious about staying on the island, I'll find something for you to do at the Majestic."

"You do not have to do that," Alex said.

Eddie shook Alex's hand. "I don't often have a chance to help out a hero."

"I'll go with Alex," J.P. said. "We can have a few drinks at the bar after he checks into his room."

"Avory and I will join you later," Eddie said.

Avory, Lilly, and Chief had taken seats on the couch after Jack had taken Renata, her mother, and Sveta to see the house. Avory kissed Eddie when he sat beside her. Lilly and Chief had locked arms.

"Thank heavens," Lilly said. "Food, drinks, and a handsome man to hold."

"Two handsome men," Avory said, squeezing Eddie's hand.

Basil had wandered over to the table. "I've meant to tell you something all day," he said.

"Can't it wait until tomorrow?" Eddie asked.

"I need to get back to work, and you might want to hear what I have to tell you," Basil said. "It'll only take a minute."

Eddie grudgingly let go of Avory's hand and followed Basil out the door. "I was thinking about taking the rest of the day off," he said. "What have you got?"

"Something that might win the case for us," Basil said.

"Hell, man! Why didn't you say so?"

"The deed we found in the safe," Basil said. "I pulled it out today and examined it. It's the original deed."

"So?"

"There are material differences between this deed and the one we received from Frankie's group."

Eddie had to think a moment to realize what

Basil was telling him. Basil smiled and nodded when Eddie said, "Someone altered the deed?"

"You got it," Basil said.

Eddie pumped Basil's hand. "You are the best. Take the rest of the day off."

"Yes, sir," Basil said.

Eddie sported a mile-wide grin when he rejoined Avory, Lilly, and Chief.

"Did you just win the lottery?" Chief asked.

"Maybe," Eddie said.

"Don't sit there smiling like the cat that just ate the canary," Avory said. "What did Basil tell you that's making you so happy?"

"Frankie's group altered the deed to the Majestic," Eddie said.

"What does that mean?" Chief said.

"Changes have to be agreed to by all parties to the document. Any unauthorized change invalidates the entire document. In this case, it invalidates the sale of the Majestic to Frankie's group."

"Frankie's going to be pissed," Chief said.

Eddie lifted his rum mug and said, "I'll drink to that."

Chapter 31

Valentine's Day had arrived on Oyster Island, a crowd gathering at the Majestic Hotel and Casino for Heather and Basil's wedding and the final scenes of Avory's movie. Jack, dressed in his Prohibition Era costume, found Chief sitting behind the wheel of his grandfather's Model T Ford.

"What the hell are you doing?" Jack asked. "The wedding scene is about to start. Why aren't you ready?"

"I'm skipping it," Chief said.

"You're a regular cast member and in the wedding party. You can't skip it," Jack said.

"No one will miss me," Chief said.

"You kidding me? With your height, you stick out like a sore thumb. "What the hell's the matter with you?"

"I don't feel good," Chief said.

"You've never been sick a day in your life. The entire parish has turned out for Heather and Basil's wedding. What's the matter with you?"

"Lilly," Chief said.

"What about her?" Jack asked.

"She's leaving Oyster Island. Going to New Orleans with Bertram after the final scene."

"Who told you?"

"She did," Chief said.

"I'm sorry you lost your girlfriend. We have a wedding to attend and can't be late. Get your costume on."

"I can't face her," Chief said.

"She's the one leaving you. Not the other way around."

"It's not fair," Chief said.

"Stop acting like a baby. Lilly was Bertram's girlfriend before she ever met you. How do you think he felt seeing her hanging all over you?"

"There are lots of women in New Orleans. There is no one my age on the island."

"Lilly lives in Los Angeles. You knew when you met her she wasn't staying on Oyster Island when the film ended. Get your costume on and get over it. Basil and Heather are counting on you."

Jack was sitting in the passenger seat of the Model T when Chief exited the house dressed in his period costume.

"I feel like an idiot," he said.

"Stop whining. Women worldwide will die to meet you when the film comes out."

"No one will even see me," Chief said.

"You're a member of the wedding party. You'll be in front of the camera as long as the scene takes."

"So are you, Isaac, Eddie, Jimmie, and J.P.," Chief said. "Not to mention Odette, Meika, and Paula. How am I supposed to stand out?"

"You'll be the tallest person on stage. Women will be flocking to the island to get your autograph. There wouldn't be a wedding if it weren't for you."

"You think?" Chief said.

"No maybe about it. Lilly told me how you convinced Avory to do the wedding scene."

"I had help from Grandpa, Eddie, and Paula's love potion," Chief said.

"What's in your hand?" Jack asked.

Chief stared at the object in his hand. "Grandmother's wedding ring," he said.

"What are you doing with it?" Jack asked.

"It was in my pocket."

Chief shook his head when Jack said, "You keep it in your pocket as a good luck charm?"

"The last time I saw this ring was at Grandmother's funeral. She was in the coffin, the ring on her finger."

"Then how the hell did you get it?" Jack asked.

"Don't know," Chief said.

"Worry about it later," Jack said. "Right now, we have a wedding to attend."

Chief had to park the car away from the old hotel and wade through the crowd. Officers from the Chalmette Police Department provided security, leading the way as Jack and Chief entered the Majestic.

Since there was no room for more guests, Ben Biondo's men had set up a giant T.V. screen with speakers so the people who couldn't get seats inside could watch the ceremony.

"Damn!" Chief said. "I haven't seen a crowd like this since the last Mardi Gras parade I attended on Canal Street."

"Don't trip and fall," Jack said.

Avory's set director Colin Dane had transformed the Majestic ballroom into a cathedral complete with pews, an antique pipe organ, and stained glass windows. Attendees, all decked out in Prohibition Era clothes, crowded the ballroom. With cameras ready, Avory sat in a chair on an elevated lift to better observe all the action. Security ushered Jack and Chief to a curtain behind the raised dais.

"Where you been?" J.P. asked. "We were beginning to worry."

Jack grinned and shook his head when Chief said, "Jack had to powder his nose."

Someone from the makeup department began patting Jack and Chief's faces with a powder puff as if on cue.

Jack peeked out the curtains. "Good God Almighty!" he said. "How did Avory manage to stuff so many people in here?"

"I'm telling you!" J.P. said. "There's every bit as many people outside that couldn't get in. They're pissed."

"Crews are filming the outside crowd. They'll all be in the movie. Not to mention the seafood boil everyone's invited to," Jimmie said.

"Tell me about it," Jack said. "We could smell the amazing aroma at my house. Harvey Boudreaux must have bought every shrimp, crab, and crawfish in south Louisiana."

"Did you see the dance floor he had built out there on the sand?" J.P. asked.

"How could you miss it?" Jack said. "The tent top he put over it in case of rain is bigger than the Majestic."

"Eddie's breathing a sigh of relief that someone else is paying for everything," J.P. said.

"Where is Eddie?" Jack asked.

"Holding Basil's hand," Jimmie said. "The boy is nervous as a cat in a room full of rocking chairs."

"But why?" Jack said. "After everything he's gone through, this should be a piece of cake for him."

"Guess you haven't heard the latest," Jimmie said.

"What?" Jack asked.

"Paula told me not to tell," Jimmie said.

"Tell us now unless you never want another

mug of rum or bowl of gumbo," Jack said.

"Paula will kill me," Jimmie said.

"She won't have a chance unless you tell us," J.P. said. "We'll do it for her."

"This is a surprise. Except for a single cameraman, not even the film crew knows what will happen."

"Wipe that smile off your face and tell us," Chief said.

"Basil will drop from the rafters with a full set of angel wings on his back. There'll be an explosion and puff of smoke. When the smoke dissipates, Basil's wings will be gone. They have to get it right on the first take. That's why Basil is so nervous."

"Hell, Jimmie, the rafters are forty feet above us. He's going to bust his ass," Jack said.

"There are invisible wires," Jimmie said. "Basil's biggest worry is getting tangled in the wires."

Jimmie shook his head when J.P. said, "Surely, they've rehearsed this scene."

"Nope. Basil's a natural athlete, and he's shaking in his boots," Jimmie said. "Avory wants a surprised reaction from the crowd."

"She'll damn sure get it if Basil crashes and burns," J.P. said.

Jack had no time to comment as imposing music from the antique pipe organ echoed off the walls. An altar boy appeared and led the group onto the raised dais. An old Catholic priest dressed in colorful wedding regalia entered the stage as Chief gazed over the audience.

Bertram Picou was sitting in the family pew beside Carol Boudreaux. Renata and her mother, Iryna, occupied a pew near the front of the cathedral. Sveta was in Alex's lap, one arm around his neck, the other touching her mother's shoulder.

Lilly sat beneath the chair in the boom situated high over the audience. Avory had a megaphone in her hand, looking as nervous as Jimmie said Basil was. The audience was unprepared for what happened next.

With the old priest and wedding party in place, Basil flew from the rafters and landed perfectly beside Gunner Hines, his best man. The audience shrieked when an explosion and cloud of smoke momentarily masked the raised dais.

When the smoke cleared, Basil's wings were gone. He was shirtless, his arms, broad shoulders, and massive chest covered with colorful tattoos. Golden curly locks draped his shoulders.

The crowd had little time to decompress as the Wedding March began. Every head turned, everyone craning their necks to look at Heather and her century-old vintage wedding dress, walking down the aisle arm-in-arm with her father, Harvey.

Laurel's father couldn't have walked her down the aisle, so the makeup department had transformed Harvey into the persona of a ghost. All the makeup in the world couldn't hide his mile-wide grin.

With all eyes on the bride approaching the altar, Chief gazed upward into the rafters. Above him were Laurel and Christopher, holding hands as they watched the ceremony below them unfold. Elbowing Jack, Chief cocked his head to indicate what was occurring above them. Jack glanced at the rafters, shook his head, and returned to the ceremony.

Chief suddenly realized why he had his grandmother's wedding ring. When he tossed it into the rafters, the wedding congregation stared at him as if he were crazy. If Jack or anyone else at the wedding party had looked at him, they would have seen him smiling.

Chief didn't like lengthy weddings, and Catholic weddings are the longest. He was about to collapse when he got off his knees for the third time. When an altar boy brought the old priest a final chalice of wine, he completed the wedding vows. The crowd grew silent when he pronounced Heather and Basil, Laurel and Christopher man and wife. Only Chief saw the kiss between the actual Laurel and Christopher.

Everyone cheered and applauded following Basil and Heather's first kiss as a married couple. After their wedding kiss, Laurel and Christopher floated through the ceiling and disappeared forever.

"Cut," Avory shouted. The crowd exploded with applause when she added. "That's a wrap."

The movie was in the can, and the party just beginning. As the old priest and the wedding party walked off the stage, the crowd filed outside to the giant dance floor where the Chalmette Playboys were already blasting out a Cajun classic. Heather and Harvey had the first dance. When they bowed and curtsied, the crowd parted.

Susie Larsen and John Pierre Saucier emerged from the crowd of onlookers, having the time of their lives as they danced the Cajun Two Step.

End

Book Notes

I hope you enjoyed reading *Oyster Bay Two Step* as much as I enjoyed writing it and that you liked all the eccentric characters. If you did, please consider leaving a review and reading the next book, Oyster Bay Limbo, in the series.

You may also like my *French Quarter Mystery Series* with moody private detective Wyatt Thomas, and the *Paranormal Cowboy Series* featuring Buck McDivit, my modern-day cowboy detective who likes horses, cowgirls, and Australian sheepdogs.

Thanks for being a fan. My stories would be little more than morning fog wafting across a forgotten lawn without beautiful readers like you. Thank you.

About the Author

Eric Wilder is an American author known for his gripping mystery novels set in New Orleans. He was born and raised in Louisiana, where he discovered his love for storytelling at a young age. After completing his education, Wilder spent several years in the oil and gas industry before pursuing a career as a writer.

Wilder's breakthrough came with the publication of Big Easy which introduced readers to his signature blend of suspense, action, and local color. The book was an instant success, drawing critical acclaim and a devoted following. Wilder followed up with a collection of thrillers set in the heart of New Orleans.

Wilder's writing is characterized by his deep knowledge of the city and its unique culture, as well as his skillful use of suspense and plot twists to keep readers on the edge of their seats. His books have been praised for their authenticity, vivid descriptions, and compelling characters.

Today, Eric Wilder is a respected author with a loyal fan base and a reputation for delivering topnotch thrillers that transport readers to the heart of New Orleans.

Wilder's the author of nineteen novels, several cookbooks, many short stories, and Murder Etouffee, a book that defies classification. His series features characters who often find themselves involved in the paranormal.

Eric Wilder lives in Oklahoma near historic Route 66 with his wife, Marilyn, a gorgeous pit bull named Moebius, and two remarkable cats, Buttercup and Whitey.

www.ingramcontent.com/pod-product-compliance
Lightning Source LLC
Chambersburg PA
CBHW011515240626
47154CB00010B/3044
* 9 7 8 1 9 4 6 5 7 6 1 7 0 *